CW00855212

DUE EAST, BEASTS & CAMPFIRE FEASTS

A COZY WITCH MYSTERY

ERIN JOHNSON

To all my teachers and mentors (whether I've met you in person or not).
Thank you for your encouragement, positivity and know-how.
You helped me find my way.

You're on book 7?
Thanks for reading my series!

Make sure you don't miss anything
Sign up for the Erin Johnson Writes newsletter
at
www.ErinJohnsonWrites.com

As a thank you for signing up, you'll receive
Imogen's Spellbook
a free book of illustrated recipes featured in
The Spells & Caramels Series.

1

HARD TICKET TO THE BADLANDS

I trembled as I held my arms overhead.

"Hands up or you die," the deep voice growled again from the dark shadows between the trees.

I glanced around. Annie was the last of my friends to hold her ground. I admired her grit, but.... *Come on, Annie, we don't want to die.* She slowly lifted her arms, a scowl on her face.

Iggy piped up from his lantern, which rested beside my foot. "What if you don't have hands?"

I nudged his lantern with my toe and muttered out of the corner of my mouth, "Not the time for sass, Iggy."

My friends and I stood surrounded, vulnerable with our arms in the air. All except Hank, who lay sprawled at the base of a giant tree. He didn't stir, his eyes closed.

I bit my lip as worry twisted my stomach. Horace had healed him before abandoning us—again. Thanks to my brother, the gash from the lance Hank had taken to save me had stopped bleeding. Shouldn't Hank be awake by now?

"Drop your wands."

I didn't have one, but Annie, Sam, Wiley, and Yann

dropped theirs. Our captors closed in around us, only their eyes and glowing wands visible. The ferns around us rustled as they approached, and the boughs of the trees above us shook. Wiley cleared his throat and I glanced to my right. He flashed his eyes at me and I frowned back.

What was he thinking? His eyes darted around at the glowing points of light from our attackers' wands, then back at me. I arched a brow—*what*? With his long arms still high overhead he wiggled his fingers and jerked his head at me. *Oh!* I finally got it. Since I didn't need a wand, he wanted me to work some magic? I gulped and looked around—there had to be at least two dozen of these people, based on the number of glowing wands.

Maple leaned forward and peeked at me from Wiley's other side. She grimaced and hiked her shoulders in question. Maple sang her spells, so she still had her magic, too. And maybe the others could still manage some, though I imagined it wouldn't be as strong or targeted without their wands. I gave a slight shake of my head back at Maple. I didn't know—*should* we fight back? I let out a shaky breath and tried to blow my bangs from my eyes, but the chilly, humid air had plastered them to my forehead. *Think, Imogen.*

I tried to recall some useful spells to attack with, but my mind seemed as dense and dark as the forest around us. My chest heaved and my breath came in short pants. I caught Wiley's eye. He clenched his jaw and gave me a short nod. Maple nodded at me too, her brows knitted together in worry. *Oh shoot.* We were doing this. I closed my hands into tight fists overhead and mentally readied myself.

I looked to Francis. The vampire seemed composed. I gulped. That was good. Francis was super powerful, so maybe we could pull off an escape? He hovered, as usual, a few inches above the mossy forest floor, his expression as disinterested as ever. He'd ripped up his tuxedo jacket and wound the strips around Hank to stop the bleeding, so now, between the white button-up shirt he wore and his nearly translucent skin, Francis practically glowed in the dark. His dark eyes flashed at Maple, then me.

"Now."

Magic spiraled around the vampire in a black whirlwind as I sucked in a deep breath, pulling magic from the lush forest with my swallow powers. Annie and Wiley braced, and Maple's lips parted, ready to sing her spell. But before I could even finish my breath, several small gusts of wind blew past my face and a sharp sting in my neck broke my concentration. Francis dropped to the ground and Maple cried out. I couldn't feel the connection to my magic anymore. Confused, I swallowed, then winced.

"Ow." I frowned and lifted a hand to my neck, half expecting to slap a mosquito away.

Iggy peeked out from his lantern at my feet and grimaced up at me. "Oh. You've, uh—you've got something in your—" He gestured at his own neck... or where one would've been.

I frowned, his horrified expression doing nothing to calm my rising panic. I patted around and my hand connected with something soft and fuzzy and large and attached to my neck. I shrieked and slapped at it. "Get it off me!" I high-stepped in a small circle around Iggy's lantern, shrieking. I could handle prison breaks and dead bodies and treacherous kings, but a monster bug sucking at my neck was the last straw.

"Get ahold of yourself, woman!" Iggy yelled up at me.

"Freeze!" the deep voice commanded.

"I'll handle it from here." The second voice sounded lighter, feminine.

I stopped dead and threw my hands in the air. I willed myself to stand still, even though a giant bug was stuck to my neck. But I forgot all about my personal bug nightmare when I caught sight of Francis.

He was still Francis... more or less. Two large, leathery bat wings unfolded from his sides instead of arms, and where his hands would have been were single, long fingers tipped by sharp claws. He flapped his enormous wings and blew a gust of chilly, damp air at me that sent goose bumps prickling up my arms. It looked like he'd been stopped midtransformation. He beat his wings and hovered a foot or two above Rhonda, who lay sprawled on the ground.

"Hold my legs, and I'll carry you away." Francis hovered lower, his black shiny brogues dangling in front of Rhonda's face.

She batted them away and rolled onto her back, one hand thrown dramatically over her eyes. "I've been hit. I'm poisoned." She moaned. "I'm dying. Save yourself."

I frowned—what was she talking about? As she turned her head, the feathered dart stuck in her neck became visible.

I gasped and patted at my own neck till my fingers closed around the feathers and I yanked the dart out. I winced at the sting and rubbed the tender skin where it had hit me.

"They're poisoned?" My heart pounded. Sea snakes, that would only make it flow through my veins faster!

Rhonda wailed, "I don't think they're B12 shots!"

Francis's feet touched the ground as three more darts flew through the air and embedded themselves, two in his chest and one in his forehead.

"Was that necessary?" Francis rolled his eyes and fumbled at them with his single finger on each wing, trying to pull them out. "Is it not clear that you've shut down my magic already?" He spread his leathery wings wide, the long clawed fingers curved upward as he shrugged.

"Oh darling—you've been hit as well." Rhonda blinked up at him from behind her fingers. Then she propped herself up on one elbow. "Wait—you said they shut down our magic?"

"Most annoying." Francis lifted his nose, and his nostrils flared with disdain. "And just as I was transforming." He sniffed. "Now look at me." He looked from one leathery wing to the other. "Some kind of hideous... batman."

Wiley gently plucked a feathered dart from Maple's shoulder while Annie, Yann, and Sam held ones as well. We'd all been hit... but with what?

Rhonda pushed herself up to sitting. "Oh. So they weren't poisoned darts? Huh." She was on her feet in moments, perfectly fine.

"Stop moving and be silent!" the voice from the shadows bellowed.

"I *said* I've got it," the higher voice growled.

"Eep." I froze again and pressed my lips tight together.

"Hmph. Or what?" Iggy glared. "I'm impervious to darts."

I kept my arms above my head, but shot him a flat look. Iggy's flickering orange light spilled from the lantern and lit up the winding roots, fallen leaves, and green moss that made up the forest floor. "You realize they could literally just dump a glass of water on you and you'd be out?"

Iggy scoffed. "Yeah, well, when they start shooting glasses of water at us, I'll be concerned."

I raised my brows.

Iggy's face fell. "They're not going to do that, are they?"

Well, now I felt bad. I let out a sigh and opened my mouth to try and reassure him, but was cut off when three figures dressed in head-to-toe black stepped forward. Another dropped from the tree above and landed with a soft thud. I lifted a brow. *If it looks like a ninja, and moves like a ninja....* I glanced over my shoulder and jumped when I spotted three more behind me. I dipped and scooped up Iggy's lantern, then edged closer to Hank. My friends closed ranks around him. Rhonda plucked the last dart out of Francis's forehead and tossed it aside. Maple slid closer to me, and we wordlessly found each other's hands. I gave her cold fingers a gentle squeeze.

Four people, one tall, two of medium height, and one short, stalked toward us. Their glowing wands lit up their eyes, the only parts of their faces visible under their black hoods and behind the scarves they wore across their noses and mouths. More pinpricks of light glowed all around us, the light from the wands of their comrades.

The shortest of the four strode forward, wand pointed squarely at my chest. The ninja pulled back her hood and tugged her scarf down from her face. I raised a brow, slightly surprised to find a pretty young woman standing before us. She wore her shoulder-length hair half up in a top knot and scanned our group from beneath thick, straight brows. "I am Misaki Mori, one of the head guards of Kusuri. You *will* answer my questions."

What was this about Kusuri? I frowned at Maple, puzzled. "I thought we'd gone to the Badlands?"

She nodded, a little crease between her brows. "Me too."

I glanced up to find Misaki watching our exchange with hard eyes. "Is that what you call our island? *Bad* lands?" Her tone had darkened and she shook her head. "Typical."

I lifted a brow. What was going on? *Their* island? I gasped. "Wait... do you live here?"

I gaped at Maple, whose mouth hung open. As far as I knew, everyone in the kingdoms thought the Badlands were uninhabited—aside from the monsters they'd banished here.

"Yes, we live here. Is that so hard to believe?" Misaki scowled and edged closer, her lips curled back from her teeth. "Now tell us. Where is he and what have you done with him?" She scanned our group, her intense gaze boring into each of us.

My foggy mind struggled to process. Who was she talking about?

"Answer me!" Her chest heaved and her wand glowed brighter, the light bouncing in her trembling hand.

I lifted my hands in surrender. "Uh... do you mean Horace?" I raised my brows hopefully.

Her face darkened and she pressed her lips tight together before shouting, "You know who!"

Her voice echoed around the trees, followed by screeches and the flap of many wings taking flight. She paled and grew still. We all did... listening.

I gulped, my throat tight. "We're not with Horace." I bit my lip and tilted my head from side to side. That wasn't exactly true. "Well, it's complicated. You may have seen us come *through* with him." I gestured toward the portal mirror that lay shattered on the ground. We'd barely escaped through it with our lives when Hank's dad, King Roch, set the guard on us. "But we're not really *with* him. I mean, I am his sister, but we're not part of his army."

Wiley cleared his throat and flashed his eyes at me. I frowned back, and then it clicked. Oh yeah, maybe not best to be sharing all my personal details with these strangers.

Annie planted her hands on her full hips. "You mean to tell me then, that you all"—she gestured at Misaki and who I assumed were other guards—"are *not* with Horace?"

Misaki scoffed and turned to the tall guard. "Why are we talking about this person?" She turned on us, her eyes narrowed, and spoke slowly, enunciating each word. "What have you done with Captain Kenta?"

I frowned, then glanced at my friends. Rhonda pulled her lips to the side, an arm around Francis. Though still tall, he didn't quite tower over Rhonda the way he usually did when he magically hovered. Wiley shook his head, Maple widened her eyes, and Sam shrugged and held his hands up —a gesture that would have been perfect, if only his palms were up, instead of down. I held back a grin—with his elbows bent, palms down, and his shoulders lifting up and down, he sort of looked like he was trying to fly away. I shook my head and tried to focus—right, captors interrogating us.

I turned to Misaki. "We don't know who that is. We came through the portal mirror moments before you surrounded us." I gestured at the broken glass.

She stomped forward. "You expect me to believe our captain disappears last night and you lot mysteriously show up in our forest, and that's all just a big coincidence?" She stopped just a few feet away and pointed her wand right at my chest.

I held my hands up and angled my head away from her wand. My voice came out as a squeak. "Yes?"

Her nostrils flared and she bared her teeth. She didn't look so pretty anymore—more terrifying and murderous. She opened her mouth to speak, or possibly curse me, but stopped when a grating shriek pierced the air.

Her big, dark eyes widened and she spun to look up at the tall guard who stood behind her.

His round glasses reflected the light of his wand so I couldn't see his eyes behind the spectacles. His deep voice came out calm and measured. "We need to move before the kaiju finds us." He grew quieter. "You're too close to Kenta to be objective. Let's let the council handle it."

Misaki let out a shaky breath.

"Why?" A stocky guard with broad shoulders stomped forward, his eyes narrowed at us. "Kenta goes missing, then these trash show up? What is there to decide? It's obvious. We should just take care of them now." He pounded a fist into his other palm. "Jungle justice."

Iggy sniffed. "Is that like jungle fever?"

I flashed my eyes at him, hoping he got my message. *Can it!*

The fourth guard sniffed. "Or let the kaiju do it." His voice came out raspy and hoarse, as though he didn't speak often.

Misaki shook her head. "No, Jun's right." She nodded at the tall one with the glasses. "We're taking them back to the council, per protocol."

The stocky one scoffed. "Oh, we're following protocol now?" His voice dripped with disdain. "And how are we going to explain what we were doing out here?"

Misaki stiffened. "I'll take full responsibility."

Another monstrous shriek shot through the night, louder now, closer. Shivers crept up my spine and Maple and I squeezed each other's hands tighter.

Misaki and the tall one, Jun, exchanged looks. She turned to the rest of the ninjas and barked out a few orders in another language. Dark figures dropped soundlessly from the trees around us. She turned to my friends and me, her dark eyes blazing.

"If you want to live, we march now."

The stocky one glared at us, a malice-filled twinkle in his eye. "Shouldn't we tie them up?"

Misaki pressed her lips tight together and shot us all a hard look. "The serum in those darts kills your magic."

I gasped.

Wiley lurched forward. "Who do you people think you are? You can't just—"

Jun held up a long hand. "It's temporary."

Wiley pressed his lips together, his chest heaving.

My eyes widened. "I didn't know that was possible."

Maple shook her head. "Me neither."

Wiley scoffed. "Yeah, well, you underestimated us, because you didn't know one of us was a swallow." He spun to me. "Go, Imogen, work your magic!"

I pulled my lips to the side and held up a finger. "No, I don't have magic either."

Wiley blinked. "Really? Those kinds of things don't usually work on you."

I shrugged. "Good thought, but yeah, no magic here."

Misaki let out a heavy sigh and rubbed her forehead. "The council will decide if you deserve to get your powers back." She shot an arm out and pointed to my left, through the dark foliage. "A kaiju, a monster, knows we're here and is tracking us. If you want to live, you stick close and do as I say. Understood?"

I gulped and nodded.

"Good. We move. Now." Misaki strode a few steps away.

I glanced at Hank, still out cold. "But—"

She paused and shot me a sharp look.

I gulped and waved a hand in dismissal. "You know, never mind, we'll figure it out."

Francis opened his huge wings. "I would help, but I am a bit... encumbered."

Wiley moved up beside me, and Yann squeezed my shoulder. "We can carry da prince."

I managed a small smile. "Thanks, guys."

Misaki whirled around without another word and strode off, wand in hand, calling out orders. I glanced up at the tall guard, Jun, who watched her go. I couldn't make out his expression behind his glasses and the scarf that covered half his face.

I licked my lips and summoned my bravery, hugging Iggy's warm lantern closer to me. "So...."

Jun jumped, as though he'd forgotten where he was, then looked down at me.

"So, you're not part of the Badlands Army?"

Jun held still a moment. "I'm not sure what that is." He shook himself. "Come on, we've got to go." He moved off.

I lifted a brow at Maple. "Guess that's a no, then."

"Who are these people?" She blinked at me.

I shrugged. The monster shrieked again, sending ripples of fear up my spine. "No idea. But I don't think we have any option but to go with them."

Maple waved everyone over and we gathered quickly around Hank, who still lay unconscious on the soft ground. She blinked her big blue eyes. "Is everyone okay? I mean, as okay as we can be?"

Sam whimpered, but nodded and everyone affirmed they hadn't been hurt in the skirmish at the palace.

Maple rubbed her trembling hands against her thighs. "Okay, gang, let's stick together then and be positive. We can do this!"

I shook myself. My brain was not fully functioning. I'd hardly slept the night before, too worried about the prison heist. Then we'd actually pulled off the breakout, only to be confronted and nearly killed by the king. So many secrets and tragedies had been exposed that I was honestly surprised to find myself still on my feet, conscious. I'd never been so physically, mentally, and emotionally exhausted in my life. I glanced down at Hank. I wanted to just curl up beside him and hope that when I woke up, the last twenty-four hours would turn out to have been a terrible nightmare.

I reached over and pinched Maple.

"Ow!" She jumped and rubbed her arm. "What was that for?"

"Oh, sorry." I shook my swimming head. "Just wanted to make sure I wasn't dreaming."

She frowned. "You're supposed to pinch *yourself*."

"Right. Sorry."

UPHILL BATTLE

W e marched for what felt like days, but in reality was probably just hours. I stumbled over gnarled tree roots and up rocky paths— always up. Were there no downhills on this island? Dark shadows loomed above and around us, and strange noises and shrieks dogged our footsteps. I raised my eyes to the next hill we had to climb. More tree roots laced the rocky ground.

I grunted at Iggy. "Want to bet on how many times I'll fall this time?"

Maple dragged herself up next to me, and Sam staggered up in between us. Maple raised her fist and gave it a weak shake before dropping her arm to her side. "You can do it." She managed a thin smile. "We've been through worse, right? And if we just—"

A monster screech ripped through the air. It startled me so bad, I screamed and grabbed Sam's wrist. He screamed and I yanked my arm back, but pulled a cuff of paper-thin wrist skin off Sam's arm as I did. I shook it off me and screamed again.

Misaki turned from the top of the hill and hissed down at us. "Shut it!"

I nodded frantically then turned to Sam. "What was that?"

He gulped. "I'm ssstresss ssshedding."

The kaiju on our heels was the only thing that kept me on my feet and moving. I glanced back now and then. Wiley and Yann managed to carry Hank between them, though they lagged behind with the rear guards. Francis had tried to help, but his wings were barely strong enough to fly himself along, and his legs were even weaker. I'd never considered it before, but all that floating around meant the vampire never had to use his muscles.

"Beyond barbaric." I caught him muttering to himself at one point. "Me. Walking on my feet!" He scoffed.

Rhonda shook her head in commiseration. "It's like you need a vehicle to transport you—some kind of batmobile." She winked and my jaw dropped. I always forgot Rhonda knew more of the human world than the others.

"Eh." Francis shrugged his wings. "That would be passable."

I couldn't spare him much pity though—all my concern was wrapped up with Hank, who still hadn't awoken. Maybe he needed to rest, I tried to tell myself. Maybe it was best he sleep through this arduous trek. I doubted he would've allowed anyone to carry him if he'd been awake, even if he could hardly stand. Still, my stomach clenched with worry for him.

Eventually, the sky lightened to a pale gray, and I could finally see something above me besides the dark heaviness of tangled tree branches. The oppressive claustrophobia of the snarled, teeming jungle lessened, just a bit, and the lights of a settlement came into view. Unfortunately, they glimmered at the top of a very steep mountain that towered above us. The tall guard, Jun, glanced over his shoulder, then doubled back down the path to join me. He stopped beside me and followed my gaze up.

"We're nearly to Kusuri, our town." He pointed his long arm up at the lights.

I blinked my bleary eyes. "I appreciate you being kind." I gave him a weak smile and his eyes grew round with concern. "But that is—" I sighed and hung my head. "That is one tall mountain to climb first." If I'd had the energy I would've cried. The thought of dragging myself up that mountain made me want to lie down and just let the kaiju get me. My shoulders slumped and it seemed a very real possibility that Iggy's lantern, dangling from my left hand, might yank my entire arm off, it felt so heavy.

"Here." Jun gently bumped my arm.

I glanced over at the gray ceramic thermos he held out to me.

"It's green tea, it'll give you some pep in your step." He leaned closer and lowered his voice. "Plus, there's a spell on it to give you some extra energy."

I glanced up at him, surprised that he'd go out of his way to help me. He tugged the black scarf down from his nose to reveal a handsome face with a strong jaw and sharp cheekbones. He flashed me a good-natured grin. "I always drink it on my night shifts to stay awake. It's an old family recipe. Not all of us are powerhouses like Misaki."

We both glanced up the path. I could see the petite young woman leading the way towards the town. I'd have sworn she was already halfway up the mountain.

My mouth twitched to the side—I almost managed a

smile. "Thank you." I took the thermos from him and pulled out the wide cork. Tendrils of steam curled up into the chilly, damp air. I lifted the thermos to my lips, then hesitated. I glanced back at my friends. Annie, Francis, and Rhonda trailed far behind. Wiley and Yann staggered along even further back, still carrying Hank between them. Maple and Sam continued on a little ways ahead of us. "Is there enough for my friends, too?"

Jun glanced around, then leaned in. He nodded, a little smile on his lips. "Just don't tell anyone."

I grinned and lifted the thermos to my mouth. I should probably have paused to consider if it was poisoned or cursed or something, but at that point, I was too exhausted to care. I drank a few gulps and had to stop myself from drinking more, so that there'd be enough for the others. It wasn't that it tasted so great. I ran my tongue over the roof of my mouth. In fact it tasted quite earthy, like all the green vegetables I knew I should eat, but didn't like to. *Kale, I'm looking at you.* But it left an almost sweet aftertaste and flooded me with a feeling of warmth and groundedness that I desperately needed.

I recorked it and handed the thermos back to Jun. "Thank you." I hesitated, then decided he'd been kind and I should make an effort. "I'm Imogen." I lifted the heavy lantern. "And this is Iggy." I frowned when I found him snoring peacefully inside. *Typical.*

Jun nodded and flashed me another smile. "Nice to meet you." His dark eyes landed on my sleeping flame, and he tipped his head to the side. "Both of you."

He moved off to give my friends a drink of the strong green tea, and I continued on. If Jun could be kind, maybe our captors, the Badlanders, weren't all that... well, bad. The spelled tea coursed through me and gave me renewed energy. I wiggled my chilled fingers and toes, grateful to have feeling in them again, and twisted my back from side to side, stretching. Even Iggy's lantern seemed lighter. I nodded to myself. Almost there. My eyes drifted up to the lights twinkling in the semidarkness of predawn. Wherever *there* was.

CLOSING TIME

I plunked Iggy's lantern down on the hard road paved with stones and doubled over, my hands braced against my knees. My heart pounded in my chest and as I swallowed, I crinkled my nose. My mouth tasted like blood—gross.

Tiny cuts and scratches laced up my arms and legs from hiking through the thick undergrowth, and my feet ached and burned with blisters. From toes to knees, splatters of dark mud speckled my pale legs.

When we'd made it home from the prison, I'd changed into a pair of comfy yellow shorts with a tie at the high waist and a white short-sleeved tee with a pair of leather sandals. Fine attire for hanging around the palace—not so much for a strenuous hike in a cold, dark, overgrown forest. I panted, my lungs burning, and lifted my eyes.

I didn't know how I'd managed it, though I suspected a lot of credit went to Jun's magic tea, but I'd made it nearly to the top. We'd switchbacked up this stony mountain road and as dawn broke, a striking view had expanded all around us.

I glanced to my right at the dense expanse of forest, vibrant with every shade of green and dusted with shimmering pink cherry blossoms. A valley of treetops dropped away from the road, with tall mountains rising again in the distance. I let out a heavy sigh. I might have enjoyed it under different circumstances, but it just reminded me of the wild, foreign land that surrounded me everywhere I looked. And the Badlands was an island, so beyond all the wild forest lay an ocean of water—no escape, isolated from the rest of the world. What I wouldn't have given for the warm, familiar palace bakery or the view of the sea from Hank's comfy bedroom window.

I glanced back. Yann and Wiley took slow steps up the steep road, with Annie just behind. She gripped a twisted branch in her hand that she used as a walking stick. I bit my lip, grateful again to Jun. He'd cast a spell to make Hank feel lighter, which was the only way Yann and Wiley could've managed this mountain carrying him.

Behind Annie, Rhonda staggered up the mountain carrying Francis piggyback. Beads of sweat clung to her forehead and she listed to the right. My stomach lurched as she stumbled dangerously close to the road's edge and the cliff that dropped away just beyond it. I reached out and opened my mouth to cry a warning, but Francis's giant bat wings unfolded from his sides and flapped a couple of times, pushing both of them back to the middle of the road. I blew out a puff of air in relief.

Francis, unused to using his legs for getting around, had tired quickly and resorted to flying. But he'd smacked a wing against a trunk in the forest, where the trees and vines and rocks all tangled together in a dense web, and Rhonda had carried him ever since. Granted, the thin vampire probably weighed less than Rhonda, but still—I was impressed.

I grabbed Iggy's lantern and straightened up when a few guards who'd been bringing up the rear sprinted up the road with their eyes wide and black scarves pulled down from their faces. Their soft leather shoes, with the split toe, kept their quick steps silent on the stone.

"Yaaarrrrrghhh."

I held Iggy's lantern higher so I could see him.

He finished his yawn, then blinked slowly and stretched his little flame arms. "Are we there yet?"

I rolled my eyes. While I'd been sweating and stumbling and struggling up the mountain, Iggy'd been napping.

The three guards reached Rhonda and Francis. They exchanged a few words but didn't stop. Rhonda's eyes grew wide and Francis beat his giant black wings, propelling them up the mountain faster.

I frowned. "Something's up."

One of the guards stopped dead, and the others skidded to a halt. They put their heads together in discussion, then a moment later pulled their wands out and pointed them at my friends—Rhonda, Francis, Annie, Yann, Wiley, and Hank. My stomach tightened and I glanced up the road. I could barely make out Sam and Maple, a couple of tiers above me, walking with Jun, the only guard I felt might be sympathetic to his fellows zapping us. They were too far away to call for help, and none of us had our powers. Before I could even cry out, flashes of light flew from the wands of the guards behind me. I gasped and Iggy cried, "Hey!" But suddenly, my friends sped up the trail and were upon us in moments—and then past.

"Wait—where are you guys going?"

But the group rounded the next hairpin turn and flew out of sight. My stomach sank as I realized how they'd done it—the speed spell. I *hated* the speed spell. And I'd already flown up and down one mountain thanks to it... well, technically a volcano.

A breathless guard skidded to a stop before me. His nostrils flared and he breathed hard. "The kaiju's close. We have to move—fast."

My breath caught and I looked wide-eyed at Iggy. His mouth disappeared and his eyes grew round and big. He hated it as much as I did. "Right, but like, I could probably just jog up there. No need for the speed spell, right? 'Cause like we're pretty close and I think—"

A deafening shriek sounded from below. I jumped and cowered, my shoulders around my ears. The guard and I scrambled to the edge of the road and peered down the cliffside. A startled flock of blue-gray birds flew past us, and the guard and I lurched back from the edge. But not before I caught sight of a furry brown creature the size of a bus scrabbling up the road several tiers below us. It shrieked again—an angry sound—and whipped its long tail from side to side.

I rounded on the guard. "Give us the speed spell!" Iggy and I gasped in unison.

He leveled his wand at me. A flash of light followed, and then my legs flew under me, barely touching the stone ground. My mind took a moment to catch up and when it did, I found myself nearing the first hairpin turn. I leaned hard to my left, swung Iggy in his lantern across my body, and found myself tilted nearly horizontal as my sandals skimmed the cliff's edge. I managed to make the turn, but just barely and had only a moment to recover from nearly running straight off a cliff before I had to navigate the next switchback. Up and up I went, dizzy and nauseous with fear.

"Ahhhhhhhhh!"

Iggy's screams mingled with the shrieks from the

monster below us. As fast as I ran, the monster was faster. Its shrieks grew louder and louder and raised the hair on the back of my neck, but I didn't dare glance back and risk flying to my death off the side of the mountain. I skidded around another turn, one hand scraping the ground like a speed skater. I ignored the burn in my palm and ran on. My heart lifted with hope as the road straightened.

"Imogen!" Maple cupped her hands to her mouth and called to me from the other side of the long, red wooden bridge that stretched before me. The guard who'd spelled me sprinted across it, his legs a blur. A bubbling river flowed quickly below, forming a moat around the town, which sat on the other side. I flew up the ramp to the bridge.

"Faster," Iggy squealed.

My feet thudded out a rhythm on the wooden planks. Lanterns posted in even intervals along the bridge flashed by me like telephone poles out a train window. The black stone walls that surrounded the town loomed taller and taller before me. I'd crossed the halfway point when heavier footsteps pounded on the bridge, drowning out the sound of my own. The planks beneath my feet trembled and made my legs quiver and nearly buckle. I gritted my teeth and leaned forward, urging my burning thighs to stay strong.

A screech sounded right behind me, so loud it hurt my ears. A blast of hot, moist breath licked the back of my neck and knees and enveloped me in a putrid cloud of monster breath.

"It's called dental hygiene!" Iggy shrieked.

The end of the long bridge came into sight, and just beyond it the tall gateway to the town—which they were closing! The last of the guards slid through the narrow opening. Maple and Wiley shouted at two others who appeared to be trying to close the doors.

Wait, wait, wait!

My chest burned, but I pushed on and in a blur reached the end of the bridge, flew through the gate, and slammed into my friends. Maple, Wiley, Iggy, and I lay crumpled in a heap on the hard, cold stone. I rolled over and looked up at the towering wall. Black-clad guards pointed their wands at the gate and it flew shut, a heavy wooden bar dropping into place across the iron-studded doors. A moment later the gates shuddered as the monster careened into them. An angry wail rose up over the top of the tall wall, and the gates rattled again and again. Yann helped me to my feet, and Maple and Wiley scrambled up beside me. We backed away, eyes glued to the gate while the guards held their ground, wands at the ready.

"Will it hold?" Maple breathed.

I wanted to ask the same thing, but was too busy struggling to breathe. My head swam, and my legs buckled. I dropped to the ground again, landing hard on one knee. I ignored the ache and kept my eyes glued to the thick wooden doors. Could it scale the walls? They'd looked pretty steep from the outside, but who knew what this thing was capable of? Maple dropped to a crouch beside me.

"Are you okay, Imogen?"

I could only nod. She wiped my damp forehead with her hand and then hugged me to her.

The monster shrieked again, which sent goose bumps prickling up my arms. Then a huge splash sounded on the other side of the wall, followed by silence.

I let out a shuddering breath. "Oh good." My chest heaved hard and fast. "It can swim."

Maple gave a little whimper of a laugh and I leaned my head against her shoulder.

Iggy, burning in his lantern at my other side, let out a groan. "I want to go home."

I pressed my eyes closed and sighed. *Me too*.

My little flame sniffed. "I know I said I wanted adventure, but I miss my warm, dry bakery oven right now and the—"

"Show some gratitude."

I opened my eyes and looked up.

The stocky guard stood above us, his scarf down around his neck and hood pulled back to reveal a buzzed head. "If it were up to me, we would've left you out there."

Another guard sidled up to him. "The council might still choose to kick them out." His raspy voice contrasted with his surfer look. He had full lips and bleached jaw-length hair, but his hard eyes bored into us. "If they have any sense."

Misaki stepped over and glared at the gate before turning to us. "Come on. I want to get you lot in front of the council before the whole town's up and clambering to see you."

"Gee, thanks for your concern." Iggy rolled his eyes, but Misaki only spared him a quick, hard glance before she moved up the road.

Wiley helped Maple and me to our feet. I dusted the dried mud off my legs and shorts, though it didn't help much to freshen me up, then dipped to lift Iggy. I shuffled over to Yann and Annie, who stood over Hank. They'd laid him down on a soft patch of grass beside the road. His lips moved, as did his eyes beneath their lids.

I stood over him, longing to drop down and give him a hug. But I doubted I would be able to stand back up again. "He's awake... kind of." I shot Yann a little smile.

The tall bear of a man nodded. His bushy red beard

sparkled in the pale morning light, beaded with dewdrops. "Yah. He has been talking een hees sleep a leetle beet."

I let out a weary but relieved sigh. "Good."

Wiley dragged himself over and crouched down. He slid his arms under Hank's, and Yann dipped down to grab his feet. They lifted him again, and Hank's head lolled toward me. I reached a scraped hand out and gently brushed his damp, dark hair out of his eyes.

"He'll be okay." Wiley nodded at me and I gave him a tight-lipped smile.

"I hope so."

Hank's forehead shone with sweat and a crease worried the space between his brows.

"He better." Wiley flashed me a weary grin. "He owes me and Yann that much for hauling his princely derriere up a mountain."

4

KUSURI TOWN

W e wound slowly through the main street of the town, which meandered leisurely up the mountain. More uphill... goody. The guards closed rank around us, talking in quiet but excited voices in their own tongue. I stood between Annie, with her walking stick clicking along the square stones of the road, and Sam, who shrugged and rolled his neck.

I leaned closer to him and lowered my voice. "You all right, Sam?"

He blinked at me with his big milky eyes and pushed his glasses up his nose. A thin scratch stretched across his cheek, and dark mud speckled the back of his hand. "I'm ssshedding all over again." He gulped.

My brows drew together in concern. "But you already shed a skin yesterday... er, today?" I frowned. "Recently. Is that... bad for your health?"

He rolled his shoulders and stretched his neck, clearly uncomfortable. "No. It'sss jussst." He looked left and right at the guards that surrounded us as we marched into town. "What will *they* think?"

I lifted a brow. "What do you mean?"

Sam took my wrist in both his chilled hands and his eyes welled with tears. He spoke in such a low whisper that I had to turn my ear to him to hear. "What will they think if I ssshed a ssskin and they find out I'm a ssshifter?"

"Oh." I turned to him, then looked again at our captors. My eyes landed on tall Jun, who walked in front beside Misaki. "You know, Sam, some of them have been really kind and I'm sure once we sort out this confusion, they won't see us as a threat." I spoke with more confidence than I felt. "And hey, Francis has giant bat wings right now, and they don't seem to mind."

I scrounged up the energy for what I hoped was an encouraging smile, but Sam just blinked and then hastily wiped away the tear that trickled down his dirty cheek. "But Francisss isss a vampire, and back home no one minded that. But they ssstill didn't like me."

Oh geez. He had a point there. I clicked my tongue and slid an arm around Sam's narrow shoulders. "It'll be fine, just try not to worry. Maybe you'll shed at a time when no one even notices."

He hung his head, his chin nearly touching his chest, but nodded. "I hope sssso."

We walked on in the pale morning light. A knee-high cross-hatched bamboo fence lined the road for the first stretch, with blooming cherry trees forming a canopy overhead. Delicate pink petals littered the gray stone and green moss underfoot, decorating the road like confetti. Wooden lantern posts with peaked roofs glowed among the trees trunks in the pale dawn light. Soon, we walked between two-story wooden homes and then businesses. The dark wood of the buildings and black lettering of the signs looked somber, but the twittering birds, pink blossoms, and glowing paper lanterns lent them a softness. As a backdrop to the city, more greenery and even taller mountains peeked between buildings and over black-tiled rooftops. I might have found it charming if I hadn't been bone weary and a captive in a foreign land.

As we wound our way up, my friends and I silent and the guards enjoying quiet conversations, the front door to a shop with a pot of flowers outside slid open with a cool *whisk*. The bald little old man who stepped out in slippers froze upon seeing us, a ceramic watering can in one hand. His mouth dropped open in a silent O, and then he scurried inside, sliding the door shut again. Annie and I exchanged a look.

She lifted a brow, deep bags beneath her eyes. "And so the gossip mill starts."

As though she were Rhonda making one of her infallible predictions, within moments second-story windows flew open above our heads, children pushed their way past their parents into the street, still in their pajamas, and neighbors gathered to watch our progress, speaking in expressive whispers.

"Take a picture, it'll last longer," Iggy grumbled at a group of gawkers in robes and slippers.

Annie sniffed. "Don't give them ideas."

I glanced back. Rhonda walked along, flashing smiles and waving at the gathering crowd. It almost made me smile. Back home, she and Francis were interkingdom celebrities, so she was probably used to working the crowd. Beside her, Francis bobbed along. He beat his giant wings in slow flaps, his legs dangling limply as he dragged himself along, the toes of his shoes scraping the ground. He panted, his mouth open, revealing his fangs. The exertion turned him even whiter than usual—and I hadn't thought that possible.

We passed a group of children. A little boy pointed at Francis and said something loudly before his mother hugged him tight against her, turning his face away, though he scrambled to get free. Whatever he said made Jun in front of me chuckle, though he immediately ducked his chin and tried to hide it with a cough.

I hurried forward and tapped his shoulder. "What did he say? The little boy." I angled my head toward the kid.

Jun turned around and pressed his lips tight to hide his mirth. Beside him, even the serious Misaki's eyes sparkled a little. "He, uh, he called him fudo kozo no akuma."

"Which means?" Annie plunked her walking stick down heavily on the stone road.

Jun couldn't stop his lips from curling up in a grin. "Floating clown demon."

I glanced back. He was floating, pale like a clown, and with the fangs and wings, I could see demon. *Sick burn, kid.*

"Those kids don't know anything," Iggy grumbled.

I grinned. "You're just mad you didn't think of it first."

"*You* didn't think of it first."

I lifted my brows. "*Somebody's* hangry."

"Come on." Misaki angled her head to the right, and we followed her down a narrow side street, away from all the staring townspeople. I dropped back and walked beside Sam, the road only wide enough to walk two across. I glanced back. Francis folded his wings to his sides and had to resort to using his legs. His lip curled in disdain. Dark wooden buildings stood tall beside us. I glanced up at the lightening sky to find a soft blanket of clouds hanging low overhead—looked to be a gray day. A few black crows flew past, cawing. *Cheery.* We exited the narrow alley and wound through more residential streets, no businesses or black-lettered signs in sight, just houses. They sat further apart with little gardens in front and wild spaces of green forest between them.

The stretches between houses grew longer and wilder, until Misaki led the way down a narrow, winding brick path. The path through the garden, lined with short, neat bamboo shoots, led to a wide building with a long front porch and a faded, black-tiled roof.

Blue and red birds twittered in the trees and flitted across our path as our feet scuffed up to the quiet building. I took one step up onto the wooden porch and noted the rows of shoes and slippers neatly lined up against the wall. Without speaking, Misaki, Jun, and the other guards stepped out of their muddy, split-toe shoes and added them to the lineup. Maple bit her lip, and Annie frowned at the guards' socked feet.

I lifted a finger. "Do we, uh— Should we—?" I gestured at my feet.

Misaki crossed her arms and gave me a once-over. "We remove our shoes before entering a home."

The stocky guard with the buzzed head scoffed. "Because we're not barbarians." He scowled at Wiley as he and Yann shuffled up onto the porch and gently lowered Hank to the ground. Wiley stood with a grunt and stretched his arms upward, arching his back. He stood so tall he smacked his hand against a low-hanging lantern and winced, shaking his hand.

"Yeah." A younger guard with a scarf tied around his head Rambo-style bounced over. "We're not barbarians."

Iggy's eyes narrowed and he gave the kid a slow once-over, then spoke in his driest voice, dripping with disdain. "Good one."

I shot him a look but my little flame only glared back at me. Yeah, *definitely* hangry.

The young one grinned at the stocky guy, then at the one with the raspy voice, but both ignored him. I set Iggy down and crouched to undo the buckles of my sandals. I glanced over my shoulder toward Hank. His eyes fluttered and his mouth moved, mumbling to himself. That still wasn't awake, but it was so much better than out cold. I bit my lip and willed back the tears that clouded my eyes. *He'll be okay*. But a twisting doubt made my stomach cramp. *Weeeooooo*. I glanced down at my noisy belly. Could be the hunger, too.

"Urg." It took an inhuman strength to stand back up again, but I did it. I placed my sandals against the wall next to the other pairs of shoes. My friends did the same, and I walked across the wooden porch, following a few guards who'd gone through the open door hung with two blue curtains. Misaki stepped in front of me and blocked my path. I stopped, surprised, and she lifted a dark brow at me.

"What?" I blinked at her. "I took off my shoes."

Her eyes flitted to my feet and back up again.

I glanced down. "Oh." My feet were a mess of bloody blisters, caked-on mud, and green moss stains.

"You've got a whole ecosystem going on down there." Iggy cackled.

I was too tired to come up with a retort, but it didn't matter because Iggy did it himself. "That's what she said!" He burst into wild laughter.

I winced. "Gross, Iggy."

Misaki's dark eyes widened as she stared at my magical flame. "I don't understand this one."

I shook my head. "No one does."

She pulled out her wand from where she'd tucked it in the wide black belt wound several times around her middle and pointed it at my feet. A cool ripple of air blew over my toes and when I looked down, the mud had disappeared, and my clean skin shone back at me, though the pink blisters remained.

I looked down and wiggled my toes, grateful to have clean, dry feet. "Thank you."

Misaki pressed her full lips together, forming a pout with her small mouth. "I'll have my grandma take a look at those sores."

"Your grandma?"

Misaki ducked her head. "This is my family's guesthouse." Her eyes flitted upward. "Well, more of a bathhouse now." She sobered and the heavy lines below her eyes revealed her weariness. "We don't get many guests these days."

I didn't quite understand her reaction or why they wouldn't get guests anymore, but hesitated to ask. She and Jun were acting kindly toward me and my friends, but they'd also technically arrested us so... I wasn't sure where that put us. Frenemies?

"Why are you being nice to me?" I rubbed my arm. "I thought you blamed us for your friend going missing?"

Her eyes hardened and she put on her poker face. "He's our captain. And while I still think you lot showing up can't just be coincidence..." She sighed and looked me over. "You don't seem to know your way around the wild... or to be remotely prepared for it."

I nodded. "That is one hundred percent true."

She cocked her head and glared at me. "You're not in the clear. Council still has to make up its mind, and I've got a lot of questions for you, but..." She looked almost disappointed. "I'm pretty convinced Captain Kenta could have taken you all on single-handedly and walked away without a scratch."

She let out a heavy sigh and turned away from me.

I lifted a brow. "You seem to have a pretty high opinion of this captain of yours?"

Jun, who stood nearby, looked ashen and turned his back to us, pretending not to listen.

Misaki glanced over her shoulder. "Yes. But also a low opinion of you."

I nodded. "Right, right, right." Good talk.

Feeling really pumped up by that interaction, I walked across the smooth wooden floor and knelt beside Hank. Wiley gave me a nod, and he and Yann moved away to stand beside Maple and the others. I smoothed Hank's damp, dark hair back from his forehead and bent low to whisper in his ear. "It's all going to be okay. Well, I think it is. But at least we're safe from the monsters here."

I leaned back to look at his pale face. His eyes moved below the lids, but still he didn't wake. I roughly wiped away the tear that trickled down my cheek and bent low again. I pressed my lips to his cheek and squeezed my eyes shut. "Thank you. Thank you for standing up for me. And for taking a lance for me." I blinked and more tears spilled down my cheeks, then pulled back the black strips of fabric that Francis had wound around Hank's side. I smoothed a finger lightly along the raised pink line beneath. I didn't have much medical knowledge, but the skin around it, though bruised, felt cool, and the bleeding had completely stopped.

The vampire dragged himself over, using the fingers that tipped his wings to pull himself across the porch, his legs nearly limp. The guards shot him wide-eyed looks and cleared a path for him.

I lifted my eyes. "I wish he'd wake up." I gulped. "Is it okay, you think, that he hasn't?"

Francis, despite having leathery wings instead of arms, lifted his chin and still managed to look handsome in a strange and androgynous way. "He smelled of death before your brother healed him. Now he doesn't. So I think he's doing remarkably well."

My shoulders shook with something between a sob and a chuckle and more tears trickled down my face as I looked down at Hank's worried brow. "What's he smell like now?"

Francis cleared his throat and I blinked up at him. "I'll be honest, it's difficult to tell as his scent is masked by other, more *pungent* odors."

"Oh." My eyes widened and I glanced around at the guards and my friends. "Like, some of *us*?"

Francis lowered his chin and stared down his strong nose at me, his brows lifted significantly. "Like, *one* of us."

My brows drew slightly together.

He continued to stare.

"Oh my goddess, me?" I pressed a hand to my chest, and Iggy, who I'd left in his lantern beside Maple, burst into hysterics. My friends looked down at him, then toward me.

I shook my head and shot Francis a flat look. "This coming from a man who—whose bat wings are probably crawling with mites." I scoffed.

Francis turned his head right and left, glancing at his leathery wings. He shrugged. "Possibly." He looked bored. "But no more than are in your eyelashes."

I rolled my eyes, and the vampire turned and used the fingers that tipped his wings to pull himself slowly back across the porch.

"Psh. Yeah, right. Eyelash mites. I don't have eyelash mites." He ignored me and moved off. I frowned and muttered to myself, "I don't have eyelash mites." My lip curled in disgust at the thought. "Do I?"

I was about to haul myself to my feet and chase Francis down to see if he'd been joking, when a tiny old woman with a white cat on her shoulder walked through the blue curtains that hung over the front door and joined us on the porch. The chatter hushed as she folded her hands in front of her hips and bowed. The guards returned the bow. Maple glanced back at me, a question in her eyes, and I shrugged. When in Rome…. I dipped my head in a bow, cast Hank another look, then pushed to my feet. The little old lady barely stood as tall as my shoulder, but she beamed at us, her eyes crinkled with mirth.

"Welcome!" She bowed again and laughed when the cat slid forward and had to scramble to stay on her shoulder. She reached up a strong hand with thick knuckles to pet the cat and cooed at it. "Silly Rini." She turned and walked back to the door, but paused and looked back at us. "Well, come inside. Don't you want some tea and breakfast?"

Rini, who had one blue eye and one gold, meowed, and the old lady burst into giggles again before disappearing through the curtains.

I decided I liked Misaki's grandma and her white cat—how could I not? And it was only partially due to the fact that she'd offered us food and drink. Wiley and Yann lifted up Hank again, and we all filed into the big house.

5

THE COUNCIL

isaki dispatched a few guards into town to summon the councilors. Apparently it was tradition to hold their meetings at her grandma's guesthouse.

Jiji, the little white-haired old lady, had led us through the creaky old house into a big room with windows looking out onto the front porch and the lush garden beyond. Woven mats covered the floor and I appreciated Misaki making us take off our shoes and clean our feet—I would've been embarrassed to dirty the peaceful, tidy space.

We'd sat on floor cushions at a long, low wooden table. Jiji had shuffled around, with her white cat trailing behind, and magically directed bowls of rice and clear broth to land in front of us for our breakfast. Rhonda had had to hold the bowl to Francis's mouth since his bat wings had replaced his arms.

Wiley and Yann had carried Hank upstairs to a quiet room with a mattress on the floor and left him to rest. I wanted to join him. A steady drizzle of rain fell outside, and with my stomach full of warm soup and rice, I'd struggled to keep my eyes open as the councilors trickled in, leaving their wet umbrellas and shoes on the porch.

First came a small man with glasses, then a burly guy with a shaved head. He'd come in grumbling about what could be so important to wake him up at that early hour, only to stop midsentence when he spotted us, his dark eyes growing round. A tall middle-aged woman followed, and then three older men arrived together, talking business.

Jun had helped Jiji and Misaki magically clear the table, and we'd moved across the room to sit with our backs to the windows and our eyes on the councilors who'd taken our places at the long table. They settled in on the floor, facing us, and Jiji joined the group last, slowly lowering herself to the floor at one end of the table. Her cat curled up in her lap, and the guards knelt in a row between my friends and I and the council.

Misaki rose and bowed deeply before the leaders of the town. She straightened and addressed the seven officials, including her grandmother. "Honored councilors," Misaki began. She fidgeted with the black fabric of her pants. "Let me begin by thanking you for—"

"What were you doing in the wild?" One of the businessmen, a guy I guessed to be in his sixties, interrupted her. His thick black brows slanted upward at the outer corners, giving him a constantly angry expression.

Misaki's grandma, Jiji, sat at the opposite end of the table and leaned forward to glare at him. Her white cat leapt onto the table in front of her and tucked its paws under its chest.

Misaki cleared her throat and squared her shoulders. "I —I led this group of guards into the forest to search for Captain Kenta, who, as the honored council knows, has been missing for nearly twenty-four hours now." Her voice held an edge.

The man who'd interrupted her folded his arms, draping his dark blue kimono sleeves across his middle. He gave Misaki a hard, unwavering look. "You requested permission to lead such a search group, and the council denied it." His lips curled back in a cruel smile. "You mean to say you willfully disobeyed a direct command?"

Maple and I exchanged concerned looks. Was Misaki in trouble? Even from the back of the room, I could feel the tension between her and this man.

She held very still for several long moments before bowing her head. "I beg the council's forgiveness." She straightened and spoke louder. "But Captain Kenta is the best guard we have." She swept an arm behind her toward her fellow ninjas. "Every one of these men and women volunteered to search for him."

A middle-aged woman who wore her dark hair swept up in a beautiful bun gave Misaki a kind smile. "I admire your dedication, Misaki." Her smile faded. "But you were denied permission for a reason. Unless on guard duty, no one is supposed to be out in the forest at night, you know this." She shook her head. "While we value Captain Kenta, we value each of you as well and don't wish to risk your lives for nothing."

"For nothing?" Misaki stepped closer to the kneeling council. "For nothing? Captain Kenta isn't nothing."

The middle-aged woman stiffened. "I didn't say *he* was nothing." She shook her head, her expression hardening. "But it is a fruitless mission, you must accept that. His own family has accepted that he's gone."

Misaki's shoulders heaved. "We're his family, too. And we can't just give up on him."

"You can." The angry-looking man in the blue kimono leaned across the table. "And you will. You said yourself, he went out checking monster traps *by himself, at night*." The man scoffed and threw his hands up as he looked down the line at his fellow councilors. "We all know what happened to him."

"No. We don't." Misaki lifted her palms. "That's why we went out there last night. Captain Kenta told me he was going out the night before last to check on the traps. We've been finding them sprung but empty lately, and we can't figure out how the monsters are escaping. Kenta had a suspicion, though he didn't share it with me." She glanced down. "He wouldn't let me come with him, either. He said if he was right, he wanted a chance to handle it himself. There's more going on here." She bowed deeply. "I take full responsibility for disobeying orders, but"—she swept an arm back at my friends and me—"but foreigners came to the island through a portal mirror. They're the first since Horace and his people, and that was years ago. And we find them the night after Kenta disappears? It can't just be coincidence."

"You're clawing at air here. Let me explain this to you simply—Captain Kenta was a fool and went into the forest alone at night. A monster ate him. It's tragic, but your boyfriend is dead."

Jun, who knelt in front of us, choked and clapped a hand to his chest.

Misaki's shoulders heaved. "He wasn't— We weren't— That's not—"

I lifted a brow. Huh. Was Misaki interested in this Kenta guy? It would explain her drive to find him. I swallowed against a lump in my throat. I'd do the same for Hank.

The older man sneered at Misaki. "Let it go, before you get yourself and your friends killed."

She lurched toward him. "Is that a threat, Ryuu Tanaka?"

The councilors shifted uncomfortably.

"Come now, Misaki, this is uncalled for." The middle-aged woman who sat in the center pressed her lips tightly together.

Ryuu Tanaka leaned back and glared at Jiji. "Your granddaughter has lost her sense."

Jiji lifted her round, freckled face and gave Misaki a nod. "I like a girl who holds her footing."

I did, too. Especially against someone like that jerk, Ryuu Tanaka. Not that I knew him or anything, but I disliked the way he was treating Misaki. I frowned. Though I wasn't sure I loved how she was implying we had something to do with this missing captain, either.

A thin councilman with glasses and neatly parted hair looked past the guard toward my friends and me. "I do not think we can dismiss the notion of finding Captain Kenta until we've interrogated the strangers. Despite her brusque manner, I agree with Miss Mori that it seems likely they are somehow connected to his disappearance."

The councilors' and guards' eyes all turned to us and my face flushed hot. I shifted on my cushion and attempted a friendly smile. None of the councilors returned it, not even Jiji—though that was because she was busy cooing over her cat, Rini.

"Tell us, foreigners, what have you to do with Captain Kenta?" The man in glasses looked at us expectantly.

I looked left, down the line at Yann, Annie, Sam, Wiley, and Maple. They all had bloodshot, glazed eyes. Then I glanced to my right at Rhonda beside me, and Francis, hanging upside down from the exposed wooden rafters of the ceiling. None of us seemed to be firing on all cylinders, but I knew that what we said next might determine our fate.

"Well." Iggy cleared his throat. "If no one's going to speak up, then I can—"

"No!" my friends and I all chorused.

The council looked taken aback and Iggy blinked up at me expectantly.

Well, here it went. I cleared my throat. "My name is Imogen Banks and I would like to start by thanking you all for your hospitality."

Blank faces and silence met me.

I pulled my lips to the side and jabbed my thumb over my shoulder. "Sure beats monster forest out there, am I right?" I swallowed, my throat tight.

Iggy leaned out of his lantern and gave me two thumbs up. He mouthed, "You're doing great."

I rolled my eyes at him and he snickered.

"We, um." I looked left and Annie gave me an encouraging nod. "We don't know anything about this Captain Kenta guy. Honestly. We crashed through that portal mirror and arrived here moments before Misaki and the other guards found us." I shook my head, willing them to believe us. "We honestly didn't even know there were people on the island, aside from the Badlands Army, of course."

The councilwoman in the center frowned. "The Badlands Army?"

I lifted a shoulder. "Horace's group?"

She folded her hands together. "You're not part of it?"

"No." I held up my hands and shook my head. "Absolutely not."

"Then why are you here?" Ryuu Tanaka fixed his intense gaze on me.

I looked at my friends. Should I tell the truth? At this

point, we might have an interkingdom bounty on our heads for breaking into Carclaustra and defying Hank's dad.

Rhonda spoke up. "Would you believe us if we said for a vacation?" She winked. The council shot her hard looks. "Ur." She pulled her lips wide. "Tough crowd."

"Uh!"

A gasp from the doorway drew all eyes. A skinny girl who looked about thirteen years old stood with her mouth agape, staring straight at me. She gasped again as her eyes flitted to Rhonda, then to Francis, hanging upside down from his black-socked feet.

"Get out of here, Fumi," Misaki growled.

The girl made a face at her. "This is my house, too."

My lips quirked to the side—this must be Misaki's little sister.

Fumi stepped into the big room. The peaked ceiling showed exposed rafters, and the worn old floors creaked below her socked feet. She edged closer to her grandma. "What are they doing here?"

Ryuu Tanaka gritted his teeth. "This is official business, Jiji, no place for little girls. Send her off to her chores."

Fumi scanned the line of my friends and me, and when her gaze landed on Wiley her cheeks flushed pink and she smoothed down her sleep-tousled black hair. She leaned close to her grandma. "You didn't tell me we had guests."

Jiji crinkled her eyes and chuckled. "It was a surprise to me, too. Seems we have some newcomers on the island."

Fumi bent over and stroked the white cat. It rolled over on the low table and batted at her hand with its tiny paws.

The center councilwoman cleared her throat. "Yes. And they were just telling us who they are and what they're doing here."

"Wait." The little girl straightened, her brows high up her forehead. "You don't know who they are?"

The room went quiet.

She pointed at me. "That's Imogen!"

I lifted my brows, shocked to my core to be recognized. Maple leaned forward and gaped at me.

"She's dating Prince Harry from Bijou Mer." She turned. "And that's Rhonda the Seer next to her."

Rhonda bowed, grinning.

"Black sands! That's Francis—the world's last vampire!"

My upside down friend blinked. "Nearly the last."

Misaki shook her head slightly at her little sister. "How do you know who they are?"

Fumi looked at her feet.

"Fumi?" Misaki's tone held a warning. "Have you been seeing Horace again?"

My brows hiked up with surprise.

Fumi balled her hands into fists at her sides and stomped her foot. "Not for a while. And whatever, I can do what I want."

"No," Misaki growled. "You can't."

"Yes, I can." Fumi crossed her arms. "He's nice. I just activated a mirror for him, and he brought me some newspapers. Big deal."

I frowned, utterly confused. My brother was recruiting little girls to activate mirrors for him? Why didn't he just make someone from his army do it? Unless he was trying to recruit Fumi to the BA....

"Can you get these papers for us, Fumi?" The center councilwoman asked. She folded her hands together on the table. "I'd like very much to see them."

An uncomfortable silence stretched on as Fumi's footsteps faded away up a staircase in the next room, then returned a minute later. She burst into the room with some tabloid papers in her hand. She held one up, and I saw an unflattering photograph of Hank and me on the front cover, taken at some luncheon with a duke of the Earth Kingdom. The headline read, "A Bun in the Oven for Prince Hank's Beloved Baker?"

Maple squinted to read it, then turned to me and gasped, her mouth round.

"I'm not pregnant," I scoffed, annoyed. "It was the dress, okay? It poofed out in the front."

Fumi handed the papers to her grandma, who passed them down the table. The councilors looked them over, little creases between their brows. The guy with the glasses looked from the paper to me, then back to the paper again.

Misaki's grandma looked up at me, her eyes round. "Are you the oven with a bun in it?" Her cat crawled over her back to rest on top of her head. It blinked its mismatched eyes at me.

I looked at Maple, who shrugged, then at Rhonda, who nodded. It seemed smart to just tell the truth at this point. I nodded at Jiji. "Yes." I shook my head. "I mean, no bun, but I'm the oven. I mean yes, we're the people from the paper."

The burly guy with a bald head and tanned skin folded his thick arms across his chest. He reminded me of a buff Buddha. "What are you doing here?" His eyes narrowed and he growled. "Is the prince here to set more monsters on us, like his father?"

The councilors grew still and the guards whipped their heads round to look at us.

I staggered to my feet with a grunt. "No." I licked my lips. "In fact, just the opposite. You see, well, it's complicated, but my brother"—I gestured at Fumi, the little sister—"Horace, he sort of forced us to help him break some prisoners out of

Carclaustra Prison, and Hank's dad, King Roch, found out about it and sentenced us to prison. But then Horace and one of the prisoners revealed the truth about the king dumping all the monsters here after he used them to attack other kingdoms. See, none of us knew about that, or that there were people living here besides Horace's army."

I swallowed. "And all chaos broke out and the king ordered his guard to kill us and Hank, his own son." My chest grew tight as I relived the horrible moment. "And we barely escaped here through Horace's portal mirror." I clasped my scratched and scraped-up hands together. "So please believe me, we are *definitely* not here on behalf of the king."

"So, you're criminals." Ryuu Tanaka narrowed his eyes.

Jiji clicked her tongue and leaned forward, the cat shifting to stay balanced on her head. "Did you not hear the girl? They're here seeking asylum. They'd have been killed if they'd stayed in their home kingdom." She sniffed. "Even the stone must be softer than your heart."

Ryuu Tanaka scoffed. "What does this have to do with heart? I care greatly for *our* people, to whom these wanted criminals are a threat."

The center councilwoman frowned. "How so?"

He frowned too, and gestured at us. "They have admitted to breaking criminals out of prison for Horace—how do we know they aren't spies, sent by him to infiltrate our town?"

Jiji scoffed. "Then they'd make pretty terrible spies. One's half dead, the vampire can barely walk, and they have almost no survival skills or instincts."

I nodded, grateful, but also a bit ruffled. Were we that pathetic?

"Unless that's what they want us to think." The burly bald guy stroked his chin as he glared at us.

"What do you propose then, Ryuu Tanaka?" The center councilwoman lifted her palms. "You know we can't send them back. We have no portal mirrors, and we ourselves are trapped on our island by the monster-infested waters."

The stern man flicked a hand. "Of course not. Even if we could, I'd say the less we have to do with the outside world, the better." He leveled a hard look at me. "Send them back into the forest where we found them."

My breath caught.

Misaki cast me a disconcerted look. I could practically see the wheels turning behind her dark eyes. She rubbed her fingers together at her sides, then turned back to the council. "Not before we get some answers about Captain Kenta."

Jun straightened his tall back. "I say not at all. If we leave them outside the village, they'll die. If the monsters don't get them, the Badlands Army will, or the elements, or their lack of food."

I nodded. What he said.

"Who cares?" Ryuu Tanaka lifted his palms, his wide sleeves sliding up to his elbows. "They suddenly show up on our island and we're supposed to be responsible for them? We have our own concerns here, plenty without adding these foreigners to them." He squared his shoulders. "We keep to ourselves and we take care of our own." He sniffed. "They need to take care of themselves."

The bald guy lifted his thick brows. "Tanaka's got a point."

"Really?" The center councilwoman leaned back.

The bald guy shrugged. "Best-case scenario, they stay and we're forced to care for them... and there's quite a few of them. They'll eat our food and they clearly don't know how to handle themselves in monster territory—they'll be a liability at best."

The man with the glasses cocked his head. "Now I don't know about—"

"At worst," the bald guy spoke over him, "King Roch comes down on us for harboring his criminal son and friends." He threw a thick hand our way. "And he finds new ways to torment our island."

Glasses guy shook his head. "What do you propose then, because I don't think—"

"I don't want to even hear what he proposes." Jiji drew herself taller, though she still looked tiny. "How can we talk of throwing those in need outside our walls when—"

Ryuu Tanaka slammed his hand on the table and the ceramic cups of tea rattled. "You're just too weak to do what you know needs to be done, but—"

The center councilwoman raised her hands. "This is absurd, I call for order."

The noise and arguing escalated. They weren't entirely wrong—we didn't know what we were doing. And while casting us out would certainly result in our deaths, I could see how they might think that letting us stay could worsen their own chances of surviving on this monster-infested island.

I sank back down to the ground. "This is bad," I breathed.

Ryuu Tanaka and the bald councilman shouted down the guy in glasses, while members of the guard and Misaki chimed in, the room devolving into chaos. I shook my head and my stomach sank—this wasn't going to end well for us. I could feel it.

A high-pitched yelp cut through the din and I jerked my head up as the voices quieted. I scanned the room and froze when I spotted Misaki's grandma. Jiji stood with her hands over her mouth, her dark eyes wide and twinkling. I followed her gaze to my left and leaned over to see around tall Jun. My jaw dropped.

Cat, Maple and Wiley's weird little pet, sat upright on the ground with Jiji's white cat in his lap.

I gasped. "How did he— Where did he come from?" I gaped at Maple, whose mouth hung open. She shook her head.

"Rhonda was watching him for me the day we got back from the Air Kingdom." Her eyes darted to the Seer on my other side.

Rhonda shrugged. "I'm no helicopter pet mom. I let him go where he wanted. I say, too many rules and they'll just rebel."

Maple lifted a doubtful brow.

I blinked at the little black monster, who with his leathery bat wings and rows of pointed teeth, made quite the contrast to the fluffy white cat in his lap.

Yann breathed in a loud gasp. "Oh my. I tink he may haf been riding with mee." The big man now wore the clean clothes Jiji had provided us, a simple cotton top and pants, which on Yann amounted to a belly shirt and knickers. "I tought my pocket felt a leetle beet heavy." Earlier he'd been wearing a big oilskin jacket with huge pockets. He'd offered to let me wear it during our hike through the forest, like a gentleman, but I'd eyed it and realized it probably weighed more than I did and would likely have dragged on the ground. I'd declined.

My gaze swung back to Cat. The weirdo blinked his giant, globular pug eyes, and his catlike tail whipped happily from side to side behind him. He dragged his monkey hands through the *actual* cat's soft white fur.

Iggy made a disgusted noise. "Just get it over with, Cat, don't play with your food."

Icy fear washed over me and I reached to my left and grabbed Maple's wrist. "Oh my goddess, tell me he's not going to eat that poor little kitty." I turned my head and hid my eyes against Maple's shoulder. "I can't watch."

"Imogen." Maple tapped my shoulder. "Imogen, look."

"No." I squeezed my eyes tight. "If I look up to find Cat wearing the kitty's face, I'll have nightmares for the rest of my life." Which might not be that much longer, actually.

Maple clicked her tongue. "Cat's a good boy. But no, just look."

I peeled one eye open, then turned my head. "Oh." I looked around the room, my face slack with shock. Every single councilor and all the guards bowed deeply to Cat, their foreheads pressed to the woven mat floor. The room buzzed with silence.

Cat blinked his dark eyes and flashed a sharp, toothy smile as the white cat purred and rubbed its head against his monkey paw.

"That cat has a death wish." Iggy grimaced.

I nodded in agreement.

Wiley winked at the beaming Maple. "We always knew he was the cutest."

"Yes, Wiley, yeah." Iggy narrowed his little flame eyes. "They're bowing out of reverence for your pet's cuteness."

Maple's eyes twinkled as she admired her little monster. "I think I like it here." She smiled. "These people know what's what."

6

CAT AND THE CAT

J un rose from his deep bow first. He slid his hand behind his back and fished around in the wide fabric belt he wore. He pulled out a small pad of paper and a pencil and sketched the outline of Cat holding the cat.

Rhonda, on my right, leaned forward to get a glimpse of what he was doing, then nudged my shoulder. "It's like Madonna and child." She chuckled, and Francis, still hanging upside down, cracked a smile.

The others lifted their heads, slowly, silently, and kept their eyes glued to Cat. Ryuu Tanaka glared, and I could practically see the gears turning in his head, though what he or any of the others were thinking was beyond me.

The center councilwoman breathed her words quietly, reverently. "How did you tame it?"

I looked at Maple, who shrugged. "I—well, I found him at a carnival. We think he escaped from the monster tent and I couldn't send him back there, so we kept him." She gestured between her and Wiley.

He grinned. "We call him Cat. He's our special little guy."

Iggy and I exchanged dubious looks.

My little flame sniffed. "Special's one word for it."

The councilman in glasses cleared his throat. "We live on an island filled with monsters, but of all of them, your Cat, as you call him, is the most rare, powerful, and dangerous."

Maple turned to Wiley, a huge grin on her face. "Aww." She clasped her hands together.

Jun's pencil scratched along his pad, Cat's vacant pug eyes coming to life in his drawing.

"Him?" Iggy and I said at once. Maple and Wiley's pet now gummed the white cat's head, her ears flattened wide and eyes shut tight in contentment.

Grandma Jiji chuckled. "Well, if Rini likes him, that's good enough for me."

"Are you suggesting we keep a dangerous creature among us on recommendation of your cat?" Ryuu Tanaka sneered. "The old woman's finally lost her last wits."

Misaki, still standing before the council, bristled, her shoulders hiking to her ears. "My grandmother has a point. If that creature deigns to reside among these people, surely this means something."

The bald guy sniffed and folded his thick arms. "Sure. It means they've brought yet *another* monster to our island."

The center councilwoman laced her hands together on the low table. "We've all heard tales of this creature, yet very few of us have ever seen one. Each witness's account of these encounters describes a feeling of overwhelming awe and reverence for the monster."

My eyes slid to Cat, still gumming away at the cat's now wet, clumpy fur. *Not feeling the overwhelming awe.*

"We must consider what the creature might do to us and our town if we were to cast its friends out or harm them." The councilwoman considered Cat with lips pressed tight together.

Footsteps sounded in the next room, and a young man burst in on our meeting. He stopped just inside the doorway near Misaki's little sister, Fumi. He bowed deeply before the council, his chest heaving.

"Yes, what is it?" The center councilwoman, who seemed to be in charge, blinked at the young man and shifted on her cushion. "We're in the middle of an important meeting."

The young man's eyes slid past the guards to my friends and me, still kneeling in the back. His mouth hung open as he gawked at us, and then at Cat, who continued to groom the real cat.

The councilwoman cleared her throat. "Unless this is urgent, I suggest you return later and we can—"

He wiped his hand across his sweaty brow and panted. "It is urgent." He gulped and tried to catch his breath. "My father and I were out fishing this morning." He panted again. "The cave is singing."

Every councilor sat up taller.

"I came as quickly as I could." The young man bent over, his hands on his knees.

"Go fetch a glass of water for him, will you, Fumi?" Jiji patted her granddaughter's leg, and Fumi skipped off into the next room.

The young man nodded gratefully. "Thank you."

"It's no trouble." Jiji winked. "She thinks you're cute." She leaned closer. "I read her diary."

"Grandma!" Fumi's furious voice sounded from the next room.

Misaki rounded on the council. "If the cave's singing, it

means a typhoon will hit our island in three days." She bowed deeply, then straightened again. "Please. Let us look for Captain Kenta. If he's out there hurt, alone when a storm hits.... We have to find him first."

Ryuu Tanaka's face darkened. "Not this nonsense again."

Jun's pencil paused and he grew still, then sat taller and faced the council. "You might allow us to escort those going on the coming of age quest." He gave a short bow. "We could keep them safe as they seek the kusuri herb, and search for Kenta at the same time."

Misaki shot him a grateful look, her lips pressed tight together and her dark eyes shining.

The bald guy scoffed. "Ha! Send our youngsters, including my son, into a monster-infested forest with a storm on their heels? No."

"But if we don't go now, we won't get the herb this year and we won't be able to make the elixir." Jun clutched his pencil so tightly his knuckles whitened. "There are many who need the medicine we make from the kusuri." He dropped his voice. "My mother among them."

Misaki rubbed her fingers together at her sides and gave Jun a concerned look. She turned to the council. "Jun's right. The young people can wait to prove their value to our society, but we can't wait on getting the herb... or Kenta."

The councilors looked at each other as an idea formed in my mind. I glanced left and right at my friends. "Hey. Do you guys trust me?"

Maple gulped. "What are you thinking?"

Wiley nodded.

Rhonda shot me two thumbs up.

I thought of Hank, sleeping upstairs. I hoped he'd wake soon and be strong enough for what I was about to propose.

I stood and the council turned to me with wide,

surprised eyes. I bowed, as I'd seen the others do, then straightened. Was that low enough? Any lower and I'd probably topple over on my wobbly legs. "Councilors, earlier you said that at best we would be a burden to your people." I gestured to my friends and myself. "What if we took over the quest for this herb? We could prove that we deserve to stay and—and then you'd get your elixir."

Misaki grinned. "We can escort them, show them where to find the herb, and keep an eye out for Kenta at the same time."

Ryuu Tanaka bit his cheek, his eyes narrowed and faraway as he stared at Cat.

The man with the glasses frowned. "Can you get the herb and be back within three days?"

Misaki gave a sharp nod. "Yes."

The councilwoman in the middle folded her hands, her brow creased. "I hesitate to risk so many of our guard."

Misaki shook her head. "We'll take a light force. We'll keep *them* without magic, so they'll pose no threat to us." She jerked her head at me.

I didn't like the sound of that.

Ryuu Tanaka flashed his eyes, or at least I thought he did, at the buff guard—I'd overheard Misaki call him Kai. Then the well-dressed councilman cleared his throat. "I say let them go."

The middle councilwoman lifted her thin brows. "Really?" She glanced at me, then back at Ryuu Tanaka. "So, we're in agreement then? If they pass the test and return with the herb, then they're one of us and we allow them to stay?"

I gulped.

"And if they don't…"

Ryuu Tanaka finished her thought. "They're outsiders and not our concern. We cast them out if they return empty-handed. And if they simply don't return in time...." He lifted his palms. "The storm will seal their fate."

Not a daunting task at all. I gulped. Did everyone hear that ringing in their ears?

"One more thing." Ryuu Tanaka's lips split into a wide, humorless smile. "I say, since Miss Mori has already shown such initiative, we put her in charge. The success, or more likely failure, of this mission rests squarely on her shoulders."

Misaki stiffened.

Jiji narrowed her eyes, but the center councilwoman looked at her peers. "Fine. We're all in agreement?" The others nodded, and she turned to my friends and me. "Then it is done."

7

A RUDE AWAKENING

Jiji, Misaki, and Fumi dragged rolled-up mattresses out of closets and laid them out on the floor for us. They moved about the upper story of the guesthouse, magically dusting off cotton sheets and fluffing pillows. In a short time, the room looked ready for a sleepover—we just needed popcorn and a mildly scary movie.

I took the futon nearest Hank and closed the shutters on Iggy's lantern. Everyone else settled into their beds, and Francis managed to hook his feet on the exposed wooden beams and hang upside down from the ceiling.

"I'll wake you up in four hours." Misaki gave a slight bow and padded off down the hall.

Four? I needed about twenty-four to feel rested, but I'd take what I could get.

Fumi lingered behind in the doorway to gawk at my comatose boyfriend, and Misaki doubled back and dragged her sister off by her sleeve.

I snuggled into my fluffy pillow as their voices sounded from down the hall.

"It's not polite to stare."

"Oh, so I should just glare at them like you do? Ow!"

After that, a peaceful silence settled over the room. I turned onto my side to face Hank, who lay on his back beside me. His lips moved and he grunted softly now and then. I slid my hand under his cream-colored blanket and wrapped it around his cool hand. The floor mattress felt surprisingly soft and comfortable, and even Rhonda's snoring didn't keep my lids from growing weighted. Soon enough, I drifted into a heavy sleep.

"Imogen?"

I felt like a sack of rocks. I couldn't even bear to peel my eyes open—it felt as though I'd just closed them. Could it really have been four hours already?

"Imogen."

I groaned. "Five more minutes." I flipped to my back and threw an arm across my eyes.

"Keep it down, you two," Iggy hissed.

I froze. You two? I opened my eyes and bolted upright with a gasp. It woke up Sam, who yelped, and without even a pause in her snoring, Rhonda rolled to the side, off her pillow, and chucked it at me. With her eyes closed!

I batted it away. "Hey!" Then I turned and faced Hank.

His bloodshot, swollen eyes blinked up at me. I smiled as a wave of ecstatic joy flooded over me. My skin tingled and I felt like both laughing and crying. I grabbed one of Hank's hands in both of mine. "You guys! He's awake!"

Grunts and groans were my only answers. Filtered sunlight shone in through a crack in the curtains, and Wiley pulled his pillow over his face, moaning, "Turn off the light."

But I didn't care. I only had eyes for Hank. I swallowed against the lump in my throat and leaned closer to him. I gently brushed a strand of dark hair away from his warm, clammy forehead. "How are you feeling?"

Hank let out a heavy breath, then another. His eyes fluttered and his thick brows drew together in a slight frown. "I had a bad dream." His voice came out quiet and groggy.

I pulled my lips to the side as my stomach twisted with unease. "It, uh—" I grimaced. "It may not have been a dream."

His broad chest heaved.

"But we're okay now," I added hastily. I smiled. "You're okay."

He blinked up at me and focused on my face. He paled and his eyes widened. He lurched forward, trying to push up to sitting, but gasped and clutched at his side where he'd been hit by the lance and collapsed back down on his pillow. "What's happening?" I'd never heard this note of panic in his voice before. "Where are we?"

I looked around the room, hoping someone could help me.

Francis unfolded his enormous, leathery wings and yawned. He dangled upside down a few feet away. "Oh good, you're awake."

"Ah!" Hank pressed himself down into the pillow when he caught sight of the vampire, his arms replaced by wings. Hank's wide, frantic eyes found my face.

I grasped his trembling hand again and stared him straight in the eyes. I tried to make my voice calm and soothing. "It's all right. We're in the Badlands."

Hank's jaw dropped.

I shook my head. "But it's okay. There are people who live here who've given us a place to rest."

"Which some of us are trying to do," Iggy quipped from behind his shutters.

Hank's eyes darted from side to side, his gaze far away. "The meeting my father called—the soldiers—" He gasped and gripped my hands tightly. "The lance?" His chest heaved. "That was real?"

I pressed my lips tight together and nodded. "It's okay. We made it through the portal mirror and Horace healed you."

Hank shoved down the blanket and pulled down the fresh cotton binding Jiji had wrapped around the healing wound. A pink, puckered scar about six inches long marred the skin over his ribs. He gaped at it, then up at me.

"It's all right—you're going to be just fine." I tried to sound more confident than I felt. Maple and Wiley now sat on their mattresses, watching with concerned expressions, and Sam wrung his hands.

The light faded from Hank's eyes and he grew very still. "And the prison break?"

I swallowed, my throat tight, and gave a slight nod.

A muscle jumped in his jaw as his face darkened. "And you almost running away with Horace? And—" His nostrils flared. "And lying to me about it—" His voice came out choked. "For months?"

I felt like I was going to be sick. I'd expected Hank to wake up and be as overjoyed to see me as I was to see him. But I nodded. "Yes, but I can explain—I *need* to explain—"

Hank's face closed off like a door shutting. He fell back down against the pillow and covered his face with both big hands. I was left kneeling over him, speechless. I blinked and two tears trickled down my cheeks. What had just happened?

The paper door to the hallway whisked open, but I kept

my back to it. My friends, all awake now, turned their gazes that way.

"It's time to wake— Oh." Misaki's surprised voice broke the heavy silence. "You're already up. Good. Weird vibe in here." She cleared her throat. "You have fifteen minutes to get dressed and get downstairs for some food and tea before we head out. We've given you spare guard uniforms to wear, and your boots will be outside on the porch."

Her footsteps padded away down the hall.

I swallowed and licked my lips. "Hank—we have to go on a quest and—"

He kept his hands over his face. "Fine."

I blinked away more tears. "Fine?" I let out a shaky breath. "Don't you want to talk about this, about everything and—"

He cut me off and dropped his hands from his face. "What I want is some space."

I froze. A wave of heat rushed over me and I felt slightly woozy. "Space? What does that mean?"

"I don't know." His nostrils flared. "But I can't talk to you right now."

Desperation tightened around my heart. I could feel my friends averting their eyes. This was so uncomfortable. "When can you talk?"

"I don't know, okay?" His blue eyes grew glassy and hard. "I don't know how I feel about all this, I don't know where we're at—all I know is that I need some space."

I leaned back. My heart felt like it'd plummeted to my feet. "I'll give you space." Did he hate me? Did he regret standing up to his father for me? Had I ruined his life? My lip quivered and tears poured down my face in the awkward, heavy silence.

"Uh!" Rhonda bolted upright and threw her head back.

A golden circle glowed in the center of her forehead. Hank remained still, but the rest of us turned to watch her.

"What's going on now? I can't see."

I unshuttered Iggy's lantern, and his big eyes found my face. "You okay?" he mouthed.

I shook my head and fought hard to hold back a sob.

Rhonda's shoulders slumped and she let out a heavy sigh. "Oh, man." She rubbed her temples, her fingernails painted in wild neon colors. "That one was up to interpretation." She looked at Wiley and Maple in the corner and shrugged. "Best I can say is, keep Cat off drugs."

Maple lifted a brow, her blonde hair mussed from sleeping.

Wiley grinned. "That shouldn't be hard."

Francis dropped from the ceiling and flipped midair, managing to land on his feet. He shook his wings and lifted his hooked nose. "Now seems as good a time as any." He cleared his throat as my friends and I all looked on. "I feel I must apologize, for lack of a better word, for tattling to the king."

I sniffed.

"We get it." Annie yawned and rolled her neck. "He made you do it."

Francis nodded. "I was forced to perform many unseemly tasks and keep many secrets for King Roch. But I did my best to undermine him, in my own way." He cleared his throat and turned to Hank, who still lay on his mattress. "I spent many years deceiving you. You believed me to be your bodyguard, Hank. However, your father had assigned me to be a check on your power, should you ever decide to defy him."

"Great," Hank muttered.

"However, I am thrilled to be out of King Roch's control."

"Here, here!" Rhonda winked.

"And am now attached to you, Hank." Francis bowed his head. "And I am certain that you will handle that power with restraint and goodness and—"

"I don't want to control you, Francis." Hank managed a humorless grin. "I don't want any of it. Find a way to free yourself."

"Er, well—" Francis lifted a brow, his long, black hair still impeccably slicked back.

Rhonda scrambled to her feet and skipped over to the vampire.

"Ow!" Yann yelped. "You stepped on my feet."

"Sorry!" Rhonda flashed a grin and then grabbed Francis's wing. "We can talk about this later, honey."

Hank sniffed. "No. Don't let me put a damper on what you talk about." He narrowed his eyes at Francis. "But why do you have wings?"

Wiley spoke up from the corner and Hank craned his head towards him. "They hit us with this potion that shuts down our powers."

Hank sneered. "Wow. If only my father had known about that, he wouldn't have had to hire a team of Air Kingdom magicneers to do his bidding."

I frowned. This wasn't the Hank I knew—since when was he... bitter?

Wiley's face flushed red. "I forgot about that. The king's such a horrible jellyfish of a— Ow!" He glanced at Maple, who'd pinched his arm. She jerked her head at Hank. Wiley's throat bobbed. "Oh yeah. Sorry, Hank, I forgot that was your dad I was talking about."

Hank scoffed. "Don't worry about it. He's not my dad anymore—he disowned me, remember?"

Iggy's eyes slid to mine, and he mouthed, "Awkward."

"Yeah, you know, I'm banished, an enemy of my own people." Hank coughed out a humorless laugh. "I'll probably never see my family again—"

Iggy scoffed. "Your family sucks!"

I rounded on my little flame. "Iggy!"

"No!" Hank waved it off. "It's true. I'm just the unloved son of a bloodthirsty tyrant."

Rhonda grimaced and sucked in a breath over her teeth. "Wow. This is getting dark." She dropped to a sit and stole Sam's pillow, fluffed it up, and scooted her hips on top of it. "All right, that's better." She nodded at Hank. "Continue."

Maple rose and cleared her throat. "Um—we only have about ten minutes left to get ready, so I say we all just get ready and, and—" She gulped. "And think all of this over and talk again soon."

Wiley nodded up at her from his spot on the floor. "Good plan."

The next few minutes passed in a flurry of activity. I found my neatly folded stack of ninja clothes outside in the hall and slipped into my pants and wrap-front shirt, then wrapped the wide fabric belt around myself a few times. Maple found me downstairs as I ladled some soup into my bowl.

"Are you all right?" Her big eyes widened. "That was intense."

I shrugged and willed myself to be numb. If it thought about it I'd break into tears, and we had a quest to go on.

She bit her lip and squeezed my shoulder.

After a rushed meal, Misaki gave us heavy packs to wear, loaded with sleeping bags, food, and tools. Hank managed to get around on his feet, but moved slowly, and winced when he turned too quickly. I squared my shoulders as we stood on the porch and slipped into our split-toe leather boots. I finished tying mine on, then went over to my boyfriend.

"I'll carry your pack for you." I let out a shaky breath. "I'd be happy to. I want to help."

Hank kept his hard eyes on his feet. He winced as he bent over to tie on his boots. "You've done enough."

"Don't worry." Yann appeared at Hank's side, a green backpack over each shoulder. "I'll do da carrying."

I nodded, grateful that Hank wouldn't be burdened by the heavy pack, but saddened that he'd dismissed me like that. Looking at the pack, I suddenly had an idea. I ran to the curtained doorway and pushed the fabric aside. I leaned my head in, not wanting to step inside in my boots.

"Fumi?"

Misaki's skinny little sister looked at me with wide eyes.

"Would you do me a favor? Could you please get me a pen and piece of paper?"

She skipped off and came back with what I'd asked for. I hastily penned a quick note. If Hank wouldn't talk to me, maybe I could get through to him this way.

I'm sorry. I understand why you're mad at me, and I deserve it. I messed up. But please, talk to me soon. I love you—Imogen.

I folded it up, lifted the flap on Hank's pack, and slipped it inside without Yann or Hank noticing.

I followed Yann as we snaked back through the narrow, winding streets of the town. Up ahead, Cat rode on Wiley's shoulders, waving his monkey paws at all the townspeople who'd gathered to see us off. Jun paused in front of a tea shop and bent his tall frame to kiss a middle-aged woman on the forehead. She must be his mom, the one who needed the potion.

And soon we crossed the long, wooden bridge over the moat and reentered the wild forest of the Badlands.

8

THE MARCH

My toe caught on a raised, gnarled tree root and I lurched forward. "Uh!" I threw my arms out, but a strong hand caught my shoulder and stopped my fall. I looked up, heart racing, and found Yann looking down at me.

I nodded, breathless. "Thanks."

His mouth stretched wide in a tired smile behind his unruly red beard. "Yah. Yust be careful."

He plodded on ahead of me up the narrow trail. The lush forest twined in on us from every angle. As the big man marched on, his two army-green packs bounced and shifted against his back. He carried Hank's in addition to his own. My stomach tightened at the thought of my boyfriend, and I stole a quick glance over my shoulder.

The trail wound upward at a gentle angle, and I spotted Hank toward the back of the line, down below. He shuffled forward, a gnarled walking stick clenched in his pale hand. Francis, riding Rhonda piggyback, came behind, while Wiley hiked in front of Hank, with Cat perched atop his shoulders, tufts of his hair clenched between his monkey fingers. They'd agreed to keep watch over Hank. I swallowed, my throat tight, and tears welled up in my eyes. I should just be grateful that Hank had recovered enough to walk on his own—that he was even conscious. And was it so bad that he just wanted a little space? I sniffled and plodded on. It wasn't, really, but I hated it.

I sighed and lifted a stiff leg to climb over a log that had fallen across the path. I cleared it and continued on, staring at Yann's back. I'd tried to do everything I could to show Hank I loved him and that I was there for him. I'd found him that walking stick, and I'd even offered to carry his pack. He'd ignored my offer and allowed Yann to do it instead.

I blinked some tears away, then roughly swiped my hand across my cheeks. I didn't blame him. He was hurt taking a lance for me—his girlfriend who'd been keeping things, big things, from him. He'd lost his family and his home all in one fell swoop. And now when he should be resting and recovering, he had to march through the jungle to find some herb—which, of course, I'd volunteered us to do. I didn't blame him for being upset with me, but I would've thought he'd be able to get over it enough to speak to me, at least. I sniffed. It hurt, more than my legs ached, more than I feared what our future would be after being sentenced to Carclaustra and attacked by the king... more than all that, it hurt that Hank wouldn't even let me help him when he needed it the most.

Maple jogged up to me, her pack bouncing against her back. She fell in step beside me and hooked her thumbs under the straps. I could feel her eyes on me.

I sighed. "He hates me."

"Oh." Her face fell and she sidled up closer. "He doesn't hate you. He just—" She glanced back. "He just had a lot of surprises all at once, and that's thrown him for a loop. I bet —I bet he'll come around really soon."

I shot her a watery and doubtful smile. "You're very sweet, but he'll barely even look at me." The words, once out of my mouth, made me feel heavier and older and more depressed than I could say. More tears trickled down my cheeks.

Maple slid her hand into mine and gave it a squeeze. "He loves you and once you two talk, I'm sure you'll work it out."

"I feel like I just want to lie down and sleep forever." I'd never felt so emotionally and physically exhausted in my life.

"Well," Iggy piped up from his lantern in my other hand. "If you lie down here, you will sleep forever because a monster will eat you." A sharp crack sounded in the near distance, and I froze. Goose bumps rose on my arms. Maple and I exchanged wide-eyed looks and then marched on, our footsteps silent on the soft dirt path. My flame's voice grew smaller. "See."

About half an hour later, the path finally leveled out and Maple, Iggy, and I caught up to some of the others. Misaki, Jun, Kai, the stocky guard, and his angry surfer-looking friend, Sora, stood a ways off in the woods, barely visible through the thick tangle of moss-covered tree trunks. I spotted Yann's red beard near them, and Sam beside him. I stepped off the path to join them, then hesitated. My stomach twisted with nerves at the thought of leaving the path.

"Should we wait here?" Maple's blue eyes darted toward the path behind us, where the others trailed pretty far behind.

I gulped. I didn't want to wait here alone. "Let's go see

what they're looking at." I sounded more confident than I felt.

As we approached the group through the thick under-growth, a tall bamboo cage came into view. It towered above us, twice as tall as Yann. We reached Sam first, who stood with his back to everyone, shivering.

I put a hand on his shoulder, and he jumped. "You all right, buddy?"

He pushed his glasses up his nose and scratched at the back of his neck. White flakes of skin powdered the black scarf we'd wound around his neck to hide his shedding. I looked around and found the guards busy inspecting the empty cage. I quickly dusted Sam's back off.

His bottom lip quavered.

I pulled my thin friend into a hug. "We're in this togeth-er." I leaned back to look at him and squeezed his shoulders. "Just do your best to stay calm, all right?"

He nodded, then let his head hang almost all the way to his chest.

I shot Maple a look and she pulled her lips to the side, eyes full of concern for Sam.

"Hey, buddy." I squeezed his shoulders again. "Chin up."

He gave a slight nod, then threw his head back, staring straight up at the sky. I blinked and realized what he was doing. "Not up that high."

He lowered his face and I slid my eyes to the cage. "What's everybody looking at?"

Sam gulped. "It'sss a cage for catching monssstersss." His chin quivered. "Will they put me in a cage too?"

I opened my mouth to answer, but closed it as Misaki came around the corner. Her eyes scanned every inch of the cage as she walked along it, her wand out at the ready.

"Empty. Again." She shook her head as she stomped toward us, Jun on her heels.

"Isn't that a good thing?" I lifted my palms.

She reached both hands up and tugged roughly at her top knot. "The cages are invisible until a monster wanders into one and triggers the spell that traps them inside." She dropped her arms to her sides and chewed her bottom lip. "So, if you see a cage, you want to find a monster inside it."

I frowned. "So... it escaped?"

She threw a hand at the tall, strong bamboo bars. "How? The cage isn't damaged, but the spell's broken." She threw her head back. "Grrr. It's so frustrating. This has been going on for months now. It started sporadically, but lately we're seeing it all the time."

I quirked my lips to the side. "Could something else have set off the spell? Like a strong wind?"

Misaki shot me a flat look, though her eyes blazed.

Geez. I lifted my hands. "Or not."

Jun cleared his throat and pointed a long arm to the side of the cage. "We considered the same thing when this first started, but the monster left prints. Something was definitely inside the trap."

My friends and I followed his gaze.

"Sea snakes." The hair on the back of my neck rose at the size of the track. Four long finger trenches stretched away from the hole left by the palm, to form a print that had to be at least ten feet across.

"Nope." Iggy sniffed. "Not good. I want to go home."

"You and me both, buddy."

Misaki scowled. "Our island's only like this because your people dumped all the monsters here."

"Sorry, you're right." I lifted my hands. "It's just a bit scary to be out here among that." I gestured toward the print. "Without our magic, we don't even have the ability to defend ourselves." I shot her a quick side-eye look. Had I sounded pitiful enough?

"Nice try, but you're not getting your magic back." She lifted a thick brow. "We'll protect you."

Iggy sniffed. "Excuse me if that doesn't flood me with confidence."

Misaki bristled, her face reddening, but Jun looked at her with lifted brows. She turned away with a heavy sigh. Jun looked between her and my friends and me. "We truly will do all we can to keep you safe." He glanced up and I followed his gaze. The tops of the tall cedar trees waved in a wind that didn't reach us at the base of the tangled forest. The fragrant tree boughs bobbed against a gray sky with swift-moving clouds. The light was soft and filtered, though it was still early afternoon. He glanced back at Misaki. "We'd better keep moving if we want to reach the springs before sundown."

She folded her arms tight across her chest. "Captain Kenta might have been here the other night." She bit her lip and looked down. "I wish he'd told me what he suspected. It would have given us a better sense of where to look at least. Or what might be happening. Is someone releasing the monsters?" She threw her hands up. "Who would want to? What motive could they have? Or is there a monster who can break free? Or have the creatures begun to adapt somehow?" She sighed. "I feel like I have stones for brains."

Jun cracked a grin. "Maybe just a few loose pebbles up there."

She rolled her eyes but grinned.

Kai, the stocky guard, stomped up with his friend. "Let's keep moving, we can't spend all day searching for your crush." His friend, Sora, blew his bleached blond hair out of his eyes and glared at Sam, who cringed against me.

Misaki's face reddened, while Jun looked away, his color gone.

"He's our captain." She drew herself up taller. "You should want to find him, too."

Kai shrugged his broad shoulders, his face impassive. "I'm out here looking, aren't I? Don't see him, though. Let's go."

He stomped back to the trail, and Sora followed him, though his gaze lingered on Sam. I curled my lip at Maple as soon as his back was turned and mouthed, "Creepy." She nodded.

Sam, Maple, Yann, and I fell in with Misaki and Jun. A soft carpet of leaves and moss cushioned our steps as we hiked over tangled roots back to the dirt path.

"So." I cleared my throat. "What's the deal with this herb we're after?"

"The deal?" Misaki lifted a thick brow. "The deal is we have three days to get it. Well, less now that you lot had to sleep." She sniffed.

I flashed my eyes at Maple. *Gee, sorry we're not all robots with superhuman stamina.*

Misaki nudged Jun's arm. "But if you want to know about herbs, ask Jun. He's the expert. His family owns the tea shop."

Jun grinned, a blush spreading over his cheeks. "The herb is called kusuri, and it only blooms during full moons in the spring." Jun ducked his tall frame under a low branch. "We make a powerful potion from it that restores vitality. It can bring the ill back from the brink of death, or it can give a healthy person incredible strength. Our town, Kusuri, is famous for it and named for the plant."

"Okay." I stepped over a gray rock topped with fuzzy moss. "And where are we headed to find it?"

Misaki jerked her head to the left. "North, up into the mountains at the center of the island."

Jun grinned. "There are these giant granite boulders at the very top of a mountain. The kusuri herb grows in the cracks in the stone. It's said that the kusuri, though small and delicate, had the strength to split the boulders and create those cracks. We're able to capture some of that great strength for ourselves through the potion."

Maple glanced up at Jun. "You—you mentioned your mother needs the potion?"

A muscle jumped in Jun's jaw, and Misaki turned to watch him. His throat bobbed. "Yeah. She got sick a few years ago, but thanks to the potion she's been all right. She gets tired a lot, but hey, she's still here." He pulled his lips to the side in a grin that didn't quite reach his eyes.

Misaki gave him a short nod. "We're going to get her more of it."

He looked down but nodded.

"It—it sounds kind of faraway." Maple blinked. "Are we going to make it in time?" She shot a worried glance at Jun.

Misaki lifted her chin. "It's only about a day's hike away when we're moving quickly." We rejoined Kai and Sora on the trail and glanced down the gradual slope at the rest of our party as they trickled closer. My stomach clenched when I spotted Hank trailing far behind, his eyes on the ground in front of him. "Of course, it's taking us longer than usual." She let out a heavy sigh.

Kai folded his beefy arms in front of him and sniffed. "They're not the only ones holding us up. This is the fifth cage you've insisted we detour to check."

Misaki gritted her teeth. "We have time. We're out here to look for Captain Kenta."

Kai sneered and shook his head. "I thought we were here to get the herb."

Misaki gave him a flat look. "That, too."

I lifted a finger. "And to prove we're worthy of staying in your town."

Kai and Sora glared at me while Misaki rolled her eyes. Apparently this was not their top priority.

I sidled up to Jun. "So... why does finding this herb prove we're worthy? I mean, you said a bunch of teenagers were going to do this as part of their coming of age quest, right? But couldn't you guys have sent *anyone* and gotten it already?"

"Way to really sell our value, Imogen." Iggy shook his little flaming head.

Jun grinned. "We had to delay the quest this year. It warmed up sooner than usual, and so did monster breeding season as a result."

I blinked. "Is that like shark week?" Jun frowned and I waved my hand. "Never mind."

"The monsters are dangerous anytime of the year, but during mating season it's not safe to be out at all." He shook his head. "So the quest couldn't happen, and we've already missed two full moons. This is our last chance... my mom's last chance."

I bit my lip. "I'm sorry."

He nodded. "Thanks. Usually, we escort the teenagers to do it. The idea is to teach them the values of perseverance, doing their best and working together to secure something essential to our culture—it proves they're ready to be adults." He grinned. "And in your case, that you're ready to be a part of our society."

He moved off to speak with Misaki, and Iggy and I stood apart from the others for a moment. I watched my friends hike up to us, Cat riding Wiley's shoulders, Francis holding on to Rhonda's with his bat wings, and Hank shuffling along with his eyes on the ground.

"I've never seen him like this."

Iggy scoffed. "Yeah, I don't think any of us have ever seen him with giant bat wings instead of arms."

I pressed my eyes shut tight. "I meant Hank."

"He'll get over it."

I held Iggy up to get a better look at him. "I don't know."

"He has to. His dad committed crimes against humanity, murdered Hank's mentor and only friend, killed an innocent magical creature, and *tried* to murder *him*." Iggy shrugged. "Compared to *that*, you what? Hung out with your brother without telling him?" He scoffed.

I cracked the smallest of smiles. "Somehow, I don't think it's that simple."

9

CAMPFIRE COOKING

H ours later, a misty dusk settled over the forest floor. Iggy's light reddened the shaggy sides of tall cedars, but barely cut through the chilly fog that nearly hid my own feet from me. I glanced back. The guards held their lit wands at their sides, forming twinkling pinpricks of light among the growing dark.

I spotted Misaki walking alongside Hank, and my chest burned. I stole another glance back. Hank nodded and said something to her, but I couldn't hear what. Oh, so he was speaking to *her*? I fought to tame the wild, jealous beast that flared up in my heart. I sighed, annoyed with myself. I wasn't jealous that he was talking to *her*, just that he was talking to anyone but me. Jun walked behind them, his face stony. Guess I wasn't the only jealous one.

The forest, already full of strange noises, twisting shapes, and a palpable magic, seemed to be waking up. Or maybe that was just my imagination running rampant under the stress of no sleep and tense nerves. Either way, I longed for the comfort of a campfire and a cozy blanket.

"It's official."

I held Iggy's lantern higher to get a better look at him.

He gnawed at a small branch I'd picked up from the ground for him, red embers glowing at its ends. "Cedar's my new favorite."

I grinned. "What? Not linden anymore?"

Iggy closed his eyes tight and let out a happy sigh. "Nope."

I shook my head. "I don't even know who you are anymore."

My smile dropped when Sora glanced back over his shoulder and shot me a dirty look. He turned away and stalked on, shoulder to broad shoulder with Kai. Iggy's light bounced off something shiny in Kai's pack that poked out of the oiled canvas opening in the top. I squinted to make it out, but forgot all about it when a dark figure leaped at us from behind a tree.

I shrieked and stumbled back, slamming into Sam and nearly toppling him over.

"Ha! Black sands! Did you see her face?" One of the younger guards, Reo, doubled over with laughter, one long finger pointed at me.

My nostrils flared as I fought to slow my breathing. I held on to Sam's bony shoulder to steady us both. "Good one." I gritted my teeth.

"I will murder him," Iggy grumbled.

"Got her good, huh, brother?" Reo slapped a thin hand on Sora's shoulder. The older guard shrugged it off, and Reo hastily dropped his arm to his side.

Brother, huh? Like, relatives, or did he mean it like, *bro*? I fell in behind them again, careful to leave more distance between us.

I glanced over. "Sorry I ran into you, Sam."

"It'sss okay." My shifter friend nodded, his chin disappearing into his neck.

Reo bounced along behind the older guards. He wore his black scarf tied around his head, Rambo-style. He reminded me of a puppy seeking affection with his repeated attempts to be accepted by the older guys. This made the third time today that he'd jumped out to scare us.

"We should, like, totally play a prank on them tonight, right? Like all those initiation things you guys made me do. Remember?" He skipped along behind them, straining right and left to catch their eyes.

"How does he have so much energy?" I grumbled.

"Guys. Remember? You dumped that bucket of pond moss on me? That was so slimy, good one. We should totally—"

"Enough." Sora shot him a harsh look that silenced Reo for all of five seconds before he started up again.

Thankfully, we reached our campsite soon after. We followed a thin footpath through the forest to a small clearing. The guards got to work making camp. Within minutes they'd efficiently formed a circle of stones, lit a campfire, unpacked the cooking gear, and laid out our bedrolls, thanks to their magic.

Sigh. I missed having my powers. I felt so helpless and vulnerable without them... and I was already feeling so helpless and vulnerable because of my issues with Hank. We all threw our packs into one giant pile in the center of the circle of bedrolls. I laid mine down next to Sam's and wondered how I'd find it again—they looked the same, all made of army-green oiled canvas.

Misaki lowered hers down by one strap as the heavenly smells of chicken and rice reached my nose. Some of the guards were already busy cooking over the flames. Misaki froze and frowned, then ducked down and threw open the flap of another pack. She tugged open the drawstring and drew out the hilt of a sword. Black thread wound around it, leaving diamond-shaped openings that revealed a shiny mother of pearl hilt below. I edged closer for a better look.

"What are you doing?"

Misaki jumped at Kai's harsh voice and I turned hastily away. I would've whistled to show how much I was minding my own business, but I unfortunately did not possess the skill. Kai snatched the pack from Misaki and she stiffened. I backed away, not wanting to get caught up in whatever this was.

"You're going through my things?" He glared at her, the orange light of the campfire lighting up his shoulders and the outline of his face.

She cleared her throat. "I caught sight of *that* and—and that's not government issued."

He dumped his pack on the other side of the pile, far away from her. "It's none of your business, but I decided to upgrade."

He stared her down, but she didn't flinch. "Is it a Honjo katana?"

He didn't answer.

She scoffed and planted her hands on her hips. "How could you afford that?" She shifted her weight. "Where would you even find one?"

All the other guards had frozen, now watching. Jun slid up and stood beside Misaki.

Kai's eyes grew wide and he dipped his chin like a bull about to charge. "What are you implying? That I'm not rich, like your family *used* to be?" He glared at her, his lips curled back in disgust. "You think you're so much better than us, you two and your precious Captain Kenta." He glared at Jun.

"But guys like me and Sora, we had to work hard to get into the guard, we didn't just use our connections."

Misaki drew herself up taller. "I meant how could you afford that, since I *know* what we make." She rolled her eyes. "And you know my family's not rich."

Kai shrugged. "Like I said. It's none of your business." He stomped away toward the fire, then paused and spun around. He jabbed a thick finger at Misaki. "And stay away from my stuff."

She lifted her palms in surrender and muttered, "Fine."

"You okay?" Jun looked at her, his brows drawn in concern. "I think he's just been on edge ever since... since Kenta disappeared."

She rolled her shoulder. "Yeah, well, we all have." She sniffed. "But he's acting even dumber than usual."

Jun grinned. "I wasn't sure that was possible."

She shook her head, but cracked a smile.

A couple of the guards whose names I didn't know yet set some cast-iron skillets to magically hover over the fire. They threw in oil and sliced pork chops. Yann, Annie, Maple, and I wandered closer, while the others rested on their bedrolls. I inhaled a deep breath and closed my eyes. "By the tide, that smells good."

One of the guards, a kid with a mullet, grinned. "We're making yaki udon."

I shrugged. "I'm not sure what that is, but it smells amazing." I bit my lip. "Since we're supposed to be proving our worth, can we, uh, help with anything?" I lifted my brows.

One of the other guards supervised some carrots, shallots, and garlic as the vegetables magically sliced and diced themselves, while another tossed some thick noodles onto the sizzling pork. The kid with the mullet smiled. "Nah, I think we've got it."

Yann lifted a giant finger. "We could make dessert?"

The guards in charge of dinner exchanged looks, then nodded at Yann. Mullet guy laughed. "That sounds great." He swept an arm toward the supplies they'd set out. "See if we have what you need." He pointed at the pack Kai had moved away from Misaki. "Kai's carrying the spices if you need 'em." He held a hand to the side of his mouth. "But I'd ask before you go through his pack—the guy's a little touchy."

Maple and I exchanged looks. *Yeah, just a little.*

I lifted a brow at Yann. "What are you planning to make, big guy?"

He stroked his wiry beard and squinted an eye closed, deep in thought. Then his face lit up. "I know! My grandma-ma's famous cinnamon rolls." He squealed, a funny noise from the bear of a man. "Tey're da best!" He clapped his enormous hands together. "Okay. I will try to remember... we need a pot with a lid, yeast, sugar, cinnamon." He ticked the ingredients off on his fingers.

The kid looked up from stirring the pans of noodles and pork. "We've got all of those."

"Oh." Yann winked. "And da most important—butter."

The kid grimaced and Yann's face fell. "No butter?"

"Will fat work?"

Yann tilted his head and thought about it. "Okay, chure!"

Soon the guards had helped us round up the ingredients and Yann dissolved a spoonful of yeast and sugar into a small wooden bowl of lukewarm water. The guard spelled it to activate and the surface of the water grew foamy. He then combined a big bowl of flour with the water, adding it in small increments and mixing it together with a pair of chop-sticks. After he'd mixed it all he could, he took to kneading the gooey dough with his big hands.

Maple, Annie, and I stood around and watched.

"Yann, where did you learn to bake outdoors?" Maple leaned closer, fascinated.

"My family was all lumberjacks, so we learned to yust make do with what we had." He looked up and smiled, his hands still working the dough. "Eet was how I learned to love baking."

I grinned. "I never knew that."

Mullet kid lent us his magic again and sped up the rising process. Yann improvised and used a jar of home-canned fish to roll out the dough into a long rectangle on a wooden cutting board. He mixed the fat, sugar, and cinnamon together, then crumbled the mixture over the dough.

The kid with the mullet glanced over, a line between his brows. "Cinnamon, huh?" He shrugged and shook his head.

Annie sniffed. "Does he have a problem with cinnamon?"

Yann rolled the dough lengthwise, with his fingers dancing up and down the sides to keep them even. He frowned when he'd finished. "Does anyone haf dental floss?"

The kid in charge of cooking frowned in thought. Then he grinned and fiddled with the worn hem of his shirt. He drew out one long, black silk thread and walked it over to Yann. "Will this work?"

Yann nodded his thanks and used it to slice the log into round discs about an inch thick. He then placed them inside a greased pot and the kid again sped up the rising process. Yann covered the fluffy rolls and with the help of the guards found a place for the pot to magically hover over the fire beside the pans of pork and noodles and vegetables.

The cinnamon rolls baked while we sat on the ground or rocks and ate our dinner (which was delicious) on lightweight bamboo plates. Afterwards, Yann lifted the lid and sugary, cinnamonny steam poured out. Even though my stomach was nearly bursting with the yaki udon I'd just eaten, my mouth watered for the rolls.

"Ugh." Misaki turned her head and made a face as the scent wafted over to her.

The other guards did the same, waving the steam away from their faces.

"You don't—want any?" Yann looked crushed.

Misaki drew her thick brows together. "Is it—healthy?"

Annie scoffed. "Not in the least, dear, but that's what dessert is for."

Jun coughed. "It's dessert?"

He and Misaki exchanged wide-eyed looks, then he addressed Yann. "It's just—it smells like medicine."

"Medicine?" I spit out. "Medicine?"

The kid with the mullet moved to the pans next to the fire to get seconds of dinner. He held his hand to the side of his mouth and loudly whispered to his fellow guards, "They put cinnamon in it."

Misaki crinkled her nose. "Ew, that's it."

My mouth dropped. "You guys don't like cinnamon?"

Jun shook his head. "It's not that. My family, for instance, puts it in a lot of our medicinal teas. It's good for aches and joint pain, or to aid digestion. It's strange, to us, to eat it as a treat."

Misaki folded her arms and shook her head at the pot.

"Oh." Yann hung his head, but Rhonda practically shoved me out of the way as she climbed past everyone to the pot.

She held up her empty plate to Yann. "Oh well, what a shame, more for us then."

It was true. My friends and I devoured the soft, sugary

treats, while only the kid with the mullet even tried a bite. He made a face, then spat it out. Of my friends, only Hank didn't have any. He sat apart from everyone and stared off into the trees, his back to the group.

After we'd eaten, night fell heavy on the camp. The campfire cast flickering shadows among the trees, and I huddled close to my friends. Three of the guards used a log as a bench and pulled their split-toe boots off. Misaki cast a spell over the dishes to magically clean themselves, and Jun leaned against the trunk of a tree, his sketch pad propped against his thigh and his pencil skimming over the pages. I leaned over to Maple on my left. "Bet I know who he's drawing."

I lifted my chin toward Jun, who glanced up now and then to look at Misaki, who stood over the pile of pots and plates and chopsticks beside the fire.

"Aw." Maple clicked her tongue. "So cute."

I stole a quick glance to my right. Hank had moved closer, but sat expressionless with his eyes glued to the fire.

"He's going to burn his corneas out," Iggy said in a sing-song warning.

I cleared my throat when Hank looked up and caught me staring. "I, uh—" I licked my lips, searching for something to say. "How's your side feel?"

Hank blinked, his normally bright blue eyes clouded and far away. He gave his head a small shake and glanced down at his ribs. His throat bobbed. "Better."

Okay, a response. Yes, it was one word, but it was something, right?

I opened my mouth to ask if he wanted me to grab some water for him, but before I could, he pushed to his feet with a strained grunt and moved away to stand beside Misaki and the fire. My heart sank. I leaned left and plunked my head against Maple's shoulder. She slid an arm around my shoulders and hugged me against her side. "Give him a little time."

Iggy, in his lantern at my feet, scoffed. "When we were in the Fire Kingdom and I found out Imogen was thinking of leaving with Horace, I told her what a dummy she was and *immediately* told her I'd go with." He sniffed and glared at Hank, who stood with his shoulders slumped. "At least have the decency to talk to her and tell her what a dummy she is to her face." He spun to face Maple and me and lifted his little flame arms. "Am I right?"

"Iggy." Maple lifted her brows.

I shook my head. "No. He's right. I wish Hank would just yell or tell me what a jerk I've been." I let out a weary sigh that felt as though it took all of my little remaining energy with it. "It's the silence that's killing me. Like, what's he thinking? How does he feel? Where—" I didn't even want to finish the thought. "Where does all this leave us?"

Maple hugged me tighter, but released me when Misaki stalked over. I sat up straight. All the other guards rose now, too, and dug around in their packs. What was going on?

She stopped in front of us and looked down, hands on her hips and stern as ever. "Ready to hot spring?"

My mouth fell open and I sat straighter. "There are hot springs?" Maple and I gaped at each other.

A smile broke out on Misaki's face. It made her look younger.

10

HOT SPRINGS

The hot springs were everything I'd hoped for and more. Steam curled up from the dark water and I let out my umpteenth happy sigh as I sank lower so that the hot water covered the tops of my shoulders. "This is heaven."

Maple let out a choked, "Mm-hmm," and I peeled an eye open to look at her.

"Are you crying?"

She nodded and wiped away a tear. "It just feels so good."

Maple, Misaki, and I wore our hair piled high on our heads in buns, the little tendrils around our necks wet and curling.

Annie had pulled hers back from her face with her typical headband and leaned against a rock. She lifted her toes above the surface and gave them a wiggle. "I could get used to this."

Bubbles rose to my left and then Rhonda popped her head up. She threw herself on her back and kicked about, opening her arms and legs spread eagle and giving us all quite a show, considering we were skinny dipping. I turned away and lifted a hand. Misaki just rolled her eyes. Thankfully, there were a series of small pools in the area, so the men had their own. Rhonda didn't share my sentiments.

"Are you sure we can't just cannonball into the men's pool?" she asked her in stuffed-up sounding voice. "Some of those guards looked pretty thick."

Annie nodded, her brows lifted and expression faraway. Maple and I exchanged wide-eyed looks.

"Their heads certainly are," Misaki grumbled, though she had her eyes closed and a smile playing at the corners of her mouth. She leaned against one of the thick, rough-hewn pillars that supported a small structure with a peaked roof. Water lapped at the four submerged posts that held it up and moss covered the hole-filled roof.

"So this used to be a famous spa?" Mist curled over the broken tiles on top.

Misaki nodded, her eyes still closed. "Yeah. My grandma says before the monsters came, it used to be the best on the island." She shrugged a defined, bare shoulder. "But now the only spa is on the beach, in a protected cove. It's too dangerous here."

Maple and I frowned at each other.

"Should—uh, should we be here then?" I looked around the heavy darkness that surrounded us.

Misaki shrugged. "It's as safe as anywhere we'll be. Especially since we're a small group—many more and we'd attract more attention from the creatures. We're deep in monster territory."

I nodded. "Right." The abandoned, skeletal structure suddenly gave me the creeps. So this was a *haunted* hot spring. Cool, cool, cool. I eyed the dark water that surrounded me, mist curling over the surface, and suddenly felt pretty sure that a spirit was about to surface any moment, its long black hair covering its face, to hiss at me like a cat and then make me watch a cursed VHS tape. Or something like that.

Misaki opened her eyes and waded to the edge of the pool. She climbed onto the smooth rocks, dripping water all over them, and picked her lit wand up. A spark of light flashed, and suddenly she stood dry and clothed. "I've got to pee."

"You're just leaving us here alone?" My heart rate picked up.

"Yeah, shouldn't you be guarding us?" Rhonda asked, still floating on her back. "Lazy."

Misaki shook her head. "You can take care of yourselves for two minutes, can't you?" She moved up the path without waiting for an answer.

"Hey, if you could just wait—she's gone." I turned to my friends. "Guys... I kind of have to pee, too."

Rhonda pursed her lips and blew a stream of water straight up in the air. "So go for it."

I bit my lip. "I'm kinda freaked out to go into the forest by myself though."

Maple glanced up the path Misaki had taken. "If you hurry, I bet you could catch her."

"You don't want to go?" I flashed her an exaggerated grin. "You know how we girls are always going to the restroom together."

Annie laced her hands behind her head, her lips curled up in a blissful smile. "I'm not sure you can call a monster-infested, chilly, dark forest a restroom. I'll stay right here, thank you."

I shot Maple a pleading look.

Her lips quirked to the side. "Sorry. I went before we got in." She sank lower, dipping her chin in the dark water. "And this just feels so good." She pressed her eyes shut tight and let out a happy sigh.

I looked towards the path Misaki had taken. "Should I follow her? I'm afraid to be in the forest by myself, but it's pretty weird to follow someone who's probably crouched over a hole right now, right?" I chewed at a nail. "But, like, the longer I wait the weirder it gets."

Rhonda floated past me. "You're harshing my chill, Imogen."

I bit my lip. "This is a pretty big pool, it's probably fine if I just pee in here, right, guys?" I waded a few steps toward the far end, so I'd be a ways away from my friends. "You're cool with it?"

Annie pointed toward the forest without even opening her eyes. "Go!"

I hung my head. "Fine."

I crawled out onto the slippery smooth rocks. I hugged my arms tight across my chest as steam rose from my body. The chilly air rapidly sucked away the lovely heat from the pool and sent goose bumps prickling up my arms and legs. I glared down at my friends. "Just so you know, I'm pretty sure this hot spring is haunted." I hissed the last word. "Heh. Bet you all wished you'd gotten out with me now." I hunched over, my shoulders around my ears, and shivered.

Rhonda, still floating on her back, shimmied her shoulders. "You're welcome, ghosts."

Hmph. Well, fine. I eyed my neat pile of dry, clean clothes and boots, and considered putting them on. But I figured I wouldn't be going far, and I didn't want to get them all wet, so I started up the path naked and cold. The soft moss felt slimy under my bare feet and I could barely see by the light of the campfire still burning in the distance between the tree trunks. I wished for Iggy and his light, but we'd sent him off with the boys.

"Misaki?" I called her name in a whisper and looked left and right. Maybe she'd ducked a little off the path to do her business. I hugged myself tighter, the cool air now freezing against my wet skin, and grumbled to myself as I walked up the path. "You don't need to bring towels, she said." My teeth chattered. "I'll dry you off with my magic, she said." I'd have dried myself off if Misaki hadn't taken our magic with her people's special potion.

I stopped dead when movement up ahead caught my eye. A shadow passed in front of the campfire and my stomach froze. I moved closer and relaxed when I realized it was Misaki. I opened my mouth to call her name, but hesitated when I saw what she was up to.

She crouched in front of an open pack and dug through it, tossing the contents out onto the ground. From the way her eyes darted around, I got the feeling it wasn't hers. Was she looking at Kai's sword? I crept closer and peered around a tree trunk. She held up a folded piece of cream paper. Her eyes quickly scanned it, then she set it aside. I gasped. That was my letter—she was rummaging around in Hank's pack. But why? She thrust her arm in and searched some more.

Snap! Misaki froze and looked to my left, toward the sound of the cracking branch. Some leaves rustled on the far side of the clearing we'd made camp in, and Misaki leapt to her feet in an instant. She replaced the pack's contents, including my note, then tugged the pack closed, and sprinted toward me. I froze, my heart pounding in my chest. Did I step out from behind the tree and pretend I hadn't seen her? Or stay hidden and return to the pool, claiming to have just used the bathroom? My fear of being alone in the forest decided for me.

I stepped out from behind the mossy trunk and tried to act casual. You know—just a nice, naked stroll in the forest at night. "Hey, there you are."

Misaki jogged up to me, breathless, and shot a quick glance behind her. "Did you follow me?"

I nodded, my teeth chattering.

"Why aren't you wearing clothes?" She looked me up and down, then frowned. "I'm not interested."

I frowned. "H-hey, I-I'm not either." Then why did it sting a little? "W-wait. B-because you're not into g-girls, or you're n-not into th-this?" I gestured at myself. "I m-mean y-you could do worse, I-I'm just s-saying." My teeth clicked together.

She walked past me and I followed. "What are you doing then?"

"I need to pee and I d-didn't want to go by myself." I trotted along behind her, bouncing to try and get warm. "I don't w-want to wander into a patch of p-poison ivy, or a monster spider nest, or s-something."

She let out a heavy sigh and stopped. She pointed to our left. "Go there. I'll wait."

"T-thanks." I gulped. "Do you have any toilet paper?"

She shot me a look and I moved off the path through the soft carpet of leaves and moss. I crouched behind a tree trunk. "Can you hum or something?"

She scoffed. "Are you a toddler?"

She kept quiet and stage fright took over. I shifted and willed myself to go, my thighs burning from holding the deep squat. Crickets chirped and an owl hooted, but the soft sounds of the forest didn't provide enough cover to make me feel comfortable.

BLEEEAAHHHH. A loud, terrifying animal noise echoed through the forest and my heart jumped in my chest. I gulped. Well, that did the trick—scared it right out of me.

"Hurry!" Misaki hissed from the path. "We have to go—now!"

11

MONSTER ON THE MOVE

Misaki and I raced back to the hot springs pool and rounded up my girlfriends. Misaki spelled us dry and clothed in an instant, and with my heart thumping in my chest, we ran back to the campsite to find the men already breaking it down. Floating packs whizzed by my head, pots and pans stacked themselves, and sleeping bags magically rolled themselves up. We spotted our guys, and Maple rushed into Wiley's arms. He hugged her tight against him.

I longed to rush into Hank's arms and have him embrace me. But he stood quiet, walking stick in hand, and kept his gaze down. It nearly knocked the air out of me. Francis climbed onto Rhonda's back, hooking his single bat fingers over her shoulders, and Yann helped Annie into her pack.

Wiley gently nudged me with his elbow. "What's going on?"

I gulped, my throat tight. It took some effort to tear my eyes from Hank and bring myself back to the present, even with all the frenzy.

I shook myself. "I'm not sure. Did you hear that noise?"

Sam stepped forward and handed me Iggy's lantern. "The sssprings helped me ssshed sssome sssskin without anyone noticccing." He handed me Iggy's lantern and I mustered a grin.

"That's great, Sam."

He moved off, his arms limp at his sides, and looked for his pack among the pile.

Wiley leaned close and spoke to Maple and me in a lowered voice. "Yeah, no one noticed, unless you count me finding his face skin floating on the surface." He shuddered. "It was the stuff of nightmares."

"Nightmares."

I frowned and lifted Iggy's lantern. He stared off into the distance, eyes glazed and mouth slack. "You okay, buddy? Did you have an all right time with the guys?"

He blinked, eyes still unfocused. "I've seen too much."

I frowned at Wiley, who chuckled. "Turns out Iggy has a very prim sense of modesty."

I grinned. "Oh." I smiled at my little flame. "You scarred for life now?"

He blinked, still staring off. "I suppose I had to grow up someday."

Jun strode up to us. He shifted the full pack on his back, and the pots and pans inside clanked together. "Come on, guys, we've got to move. There's a monster nearby."

Yann hefted up Hank's pack and I glanced at Misaki. Should I tell Hank she'd been rummaging through his things? I bit my lip as she pointed and sent a few guards running off, then whirled and gave orders to Kai and Reo—his Rambo scarf on. The younger guard's eyes darted from Misaki to Kai, his eyes wide and mouth slack with fear. I gulped. There'd be time to figure out the pack thing later—for now we just had to get out of here and survive.

I slung my heavy pack onto my aching back. The straps dug into the tops of my shoulders. Maple stood behind me and strapped my bedroll to it. "Guess we don't get to rest here for the night." She let out a heavy sigh and turned her back to me so I could attach her bedroll to her pack for her.

Rhonda slid her arms under Francis's thighs and bounced, hiking him higher on her back. His giant wings wrapped around her like a cloak. "You can rest when you're dead." She tipped her head from side to side. "Unless you're one of those hot springs ghosts you mentioned." Her dark eyes sparkled with mirth. "I think we showed them enough to keep them *very* excited for a while."

I grinned. Weirdo.

RAAAHHHHH! A bleating scream cut through the night and icy fear washed over me. The hairs on my neck pricked.

Jun grew grim. "The giga deer are drawn by smells." Jun nodded. "They generally don't bother us, but they've attacked a handful of times and this one seems to be getting closer. If it's hungry and desperate, it may go for our food."

He held his wand over our group and a light flashed from the end of it. "That spell should help mask your scents with that of moss and leaves and dirt."

"So Imogen just smells like herself then?"

I shot my grinning flame a flat look. "I see you've recovered."

Misaki stomped over. "We're ready, let's go."

Misaki, Jun, and a couple other guards led the way, my friends and I following single file. Reo, Sora, Kai, and another guard brought up the rear. I watched Annie's back, the mottled shadows of the low-hanging tree branches flickering over her shoulders. No one spoke, and even the small sounds of the forest, the cricket chirps and frog ribbits, had gone silent. We kept on, ears pricked for another monster scream, but none came. Maybe we'd outdistanced it.

After a few minutes of quiet hiking, the trees thinned and we skirted the edge of a small, rocky clearing. I nearly slammed into Annie's back when she stopped suddenly, frozen. I followed her wide-eyed gaze to my left, toward the clearing, and my stomach clenched tight with fear. I could feel Yann stop dead behind me.

A giant deer, as tall as the trees, picked its way into the open space. Moonlight illuminated the two black, spiraling horns that shot upwards from its head, sharp and deadly. Its black cloven hooves clanked against the rocky ground, and white spots speckled its brown hide. Its huge ears flicked right and left, and its black, wet nostrils flared.

I held my breath. It looked to its right, in the direction we'd come from. My chest heaved with shallow breaths. The giant deer picked its way over the rocks and moved away from us. I let out a shaky breath and part of the tightness in my chest relaxed.

Then the wind changed. The leaves rustled in the trees overhead, the wet tendrils of hair at the back of my neck grew chilly, and the grass that sprouted between the rocks of the clearing waved. The giga deer froze and jerked its head up. Its nostrils flared rapidly as it smelled the wind, and it swiveled its head in our direction. Big dark eyes stared right at us, as though the deer could see us through the trees. I stayed rooted in place with fear.

The deer opened its mouth and bleated. I winced and jerked my hands up to cover my ears, the sound deafening. In an instant, it bounded across the clearing and broke through the tree line. Shouts sounded and wands glowed in the darkness. The deer crashed through the brush, straight to Hank, and bit down on his back.

12

GIGA DEER

I screamed and dashed through the dark forest. Iggy's lantern swung wildly in my hand and my pack slammed against my back. I ignored the branches scratching my arms and the pain in my ankle as I stumbled over a rock.

"Hank!" I stretched an arm out, desperate to have my powers back. I felt helpless without them. Helpless as the giant deer bore down on him.

The deer reared its head, thrashing its sharp spiraling horns into the branches of the trees. My heart stopped as I spotted Hank dangling from the pack in the deer's mouth at a height that neared the tops of the tallest cedars. Misaki, Jun, and the other guards crashed past me, wands ready in one hand, their drawn swords in the other. One of the guards fired a spell at the deer. It ducked its head at the last minute and the ball of light flew past.

Misaki shot the guard a stern look. "You could've hit him."

Annie appeared beside me and squeezed my shoulder. "C'mon, dear!"

I nodded and we ran on, closer, until I had to crane my neck to look up at the creature. Balls of light flew through the dark and Misaki shouted orders. I gasped as the deer veered towards Annie and me. I grabbed her by the straps of her pack and yanked her to the side. We fell over a gnarled tree root as the deer's hard black hoof stomped down in the spot we'd just stood.

Annie panted. "We'd have been crushed, flat as pancakes."

I scrambled to my feet and helped her up. My stomach twisted as I gazed down at the shallow crater the hoof had left behind. A shout rang out, and I looked up through the tangled branches. Hank fumbled with the clasp at his chest as the deer tossed him about. Guards dove out of the way of its horns as the deer dipped its head and shook again, like a dog with a toy. I saw my chance.

I threw off my pack, handed Iggy to Annie, and sprinted over to the guards. I held my palm out to Misaki. "Give me a knife."

She frowned and turned away from me, but I gripped her wrist and stared her down. She considered me, narrowed her eyes, and then in a swift movement, reached into her waistband. She pressed the black handle of a short knife into my hand. Misaki kept a wary eye on me, wand raised, but I turned away from her and eyed Hank.

I gulped in a breath and steeled myself. This was probably a terrible idea, but it was the only one I had. I ran forward, straight toward the monster. The deer swept its head to one side, and I dove on my stomach. I landed hard on the rocky ground. "Oof!" Horns flew over me with a whoosh of air that raised goose bumps on the back of my neck. I army-crawled forward over leaves and tree roots, and rose to crouch right below Hank. The deer hung its head low, and shook it from side to side, dangling Hank just a few feet off the ground. He glanced at me, his face pale and the whites of his eyes showing. "I can't undo it." He grunted as the deer shook him again, then paused. It snorted, blasting me with its hot breath. At this angle I could see that the metal clasp at Hank's chest had been crushed and wouldn't open.

I gripped the canvas strap at his chest and gritted my teeth. I prayed the deer would hold still for another moment. I brought up the knife sideways, under the canvas strap, then twisted it and pulled toward myself. I sawed with all my might and the strap snapped. Hank dropped heavy on top of me, knocking the knife from my hand. He wrapped his thick arms around me and braced his entire body, shielding me from the giga deer and its dangerous horns. I peeled an eye open and looked over his shoulder. The giant creature towered over us. Hank's pack looked tiny in its mouth.

Balls of light flew through the air and burst against the creature's head. It cried out and dropped the pack, which plummeted to the ground. The deer dipped its head to retrieve it, its horns aimed right for Hank and me. More glowing spells struck the deer on the nose and the creature screamed. I covered my ears and cowered under Hank as more balls of light crashed into the monster's head. The whites showed all around its big eyes and it startled.

I grabbed Hank's shoulder and he rolled to the side and pushed to sitting as I scrambled onto my elbows. The giant deer abandoned the pack and crashed away through the forest. It bounded across the clearing and disappeared on the other side among rustling trees.

I glanced over at Hank, my chest heaving. His throat bobbed as he watched after the deer for another moment, then he swung his gaze towards me. My chest welled with a rush of emotions, not least of which was happiness that he was looking at me, actually seeing me. His eyes grew glassy and he leaned toward me, his lips parting to speak. But the moment ended when a guard cried out.

We both turned toward the sound. A couple of the guards were bent over something. I squinted to see better through the tree trunks and the dark shadows of the night. More guards sprinted that way.

Hank rose with a grunt, then reached out to me. My spirits soared as I wrapped my fingers around his warm, strong hand. He pulled me to my feet and just as quickly let go—and with that, my spirits fell again. I trailed a few steps behind him as we made our way over to the others. He glanced back. "Thank you—for saving me."

I grinned and opened my mouth to respond, but Hank cut me off.

"You didn't have to do that."

I stopped dead, dumbstruck, then jogged over rocks and branches to come up beside him. "Hold up—what now?"

He didn't look up, but his throat bobbed. "I dove in front of that lance back in Bijou Mer." A muscle jumped in his jaw as we hiked toward the guards, who'd circled up around something on the ground. "And you saved me tonight. So we're even now, okay?" He glanced up at me, his eyes clouded. "You don't owe me anything."

I opened my mouth but it took me several flabbergasted moments to find the words. "Owe you?" I scoffed. "Owe you? I saved you because I love you. What are you even—"

Hank stopped and paled. I turned, frowning, to see what he was staring at and gasped. Someone lay sprawled face-down on the ground, surrounded by the guards.

"It's Sora." Jun, who'd been crouching near the commotion, rose. The moonlight highlighted his sharp cheekbones and stricken expression. He turned towards Reo, who skidded to a stop and dropped down beside the blond guard. Jun shook his head. "The deer struck him as it bounded away." His throat bobbed. "Your brother's dead."

13

BIG BROTHER

W e all gathered around Sora's body. Reo sobbed beside his brother, his forehead pressed to Sora's lifeless back. While my brief interactions with Sora hadn't been pleasant—mostly he just glared at me— my heart sank for Reo and all the guards. That could've been any of us.

Kai had been close with Sora as well. The stocky guard moved behind Reo and put a hand on the young guard's shoulder. Reo shrugged it off and threw himself over the body, sobbing harder. I lifted my brows, surprised. I didn't need to know Reo well to know that he'd really looked up to Kai, his big brother's friend. I bit my lip. This was obviously hitting him hard.

Misaki gave Reo a few minutes. She paced back and forth, muttering to herself. She glanced over, her eyes red, and eyed Cat in Maple's arms.

"We should've set your Cat on it. Maybe Sora would still be alive."

Maple's jaw dropped and she hugged her furry pet

tighter to her chest. "This little guy against that huge thing?" She scoffed and shook her head.

My friends all hugged Hank in turn, and he responded with nods and quiet words. He and I returned to our stony distance.

I stood aside, my eyes full of tears, and a mix of anger and sadness burning in my chest. Did he really think I'd saved him out of obligation? It was ridiculous! After all we'd been through, he didn't know that I loved him? Or did he know, and he was just punishing me? It wasn't as if I expected him almost dying to just erase all that had happened back in Bijou Mer. But I hoped he'd realize that he'd almost died, we both had, and that in the big scheme of things, our love was more important than keeping up the silent treatment. Why didn't he get that?

A twig snapped and I looked up. I'd moved a little ways away from the group and stood partially hidden from view among the trees. I leaned forward and looked toward the rocky clearing. Misaki crept through the open space. She glanced right, then left. *Hmm.* She might just be on edge watching for monsters... but then again, she'd had this look when she dug through Hank's pack. I moved closer to the tree line to get a better view. I spotted Hank's torn, lumpy pack. It lay on its side on a mossy rock, and Misaki headed straight for it. My spidey sense tingled with suspicion.

I stepped out of the tree line and strode quickly forward in an attempt to head her off. "Oh, hey, Misaki." I tried for nonchalant tone.

Her head jerked toward me and she opened her eyes wide. "Imogen." She remained tense as I jogged up to her, hopping from stone to stone.

"You found Hank's pack, huh?" I tried for a casual tone.

She nodded and we walked toward it together. "I

thought it was odd the way the giga deer went right for him —his pack, specifically."

I frowned. "That's a good point." I bit my lip. Had she spelled his pack or something when I caught her rummaging through it? Had she set a monster on Hank and was now trying to cover it up? I looked to my left. The others stood among the trees, within sight. Surely she wouldn't do anything to me in front of them... would she?

We reached the pack and Misaki dropped to a crouch beside it. She pushed with both arms to roll it over. The chest strap hung open in two pieces, broken where I'd cut it to free Hank. She waved her wand over the gashes in the canvas fabric and the pack suddenly looked as good as new. Misaki then yanked the drawstring open. My folded letter tumbled out the top, along with a big bunch of strange, dark purple leaves and branches. She sucked in a breath and jerked her chin up to stare at me wide-eyed.

I frowned. "What is it?"

She grabbed Hank's pack and a big handful of the leaves, and shot to her feet. "We have to get rid of it."

I narrowed my eyes. I bet that's exactly what she wanted to do—to hide the evidence. I jumped up and snatched a handful of the waxy leaves from her. "No. I think we should show the others." Before she could react, I leapt away to the next rock and sprinted toward my friends as fast as my aching, burning legs would allow.

"Imogen!" Misaki let out a frustrated growl behind me. Her footsteps sounded behind me on the stones.

My heart thumped in my chest as I neared the rest of our group. "Guys!"

Reo continued to sob beside his brother, though someone had placed a blanket over Sora's body. But everyone else looked my way.

"Keep your voice down," Kai hissed.

I jogged to a stop and Misaki skidded up beside me a moment later. Breathless, I held up the purple leaves. "We found this inside Hank's pack."

Jun's eyes widened.

"Isss it a sssnack?" Sam blinked at me, his glasses glinting in the moonlight.

I nodded. "Yeah, probably not." I jerked my head toward Misaki at my side. "She seemed to think it mattered though."

Jun swept up to us and addressed Misaki. "Is it attrahunt?"

She gave a terse nod, and held up the bunch she still had in her hand. Jun lowered his wand at the leaves we held in our hands, and a moment later the plants sizzled to charcoal and crumbled away.

I jumped back, my mouth open. "Hey!" Black powder covered my palms.

Jun shook his head. "That herb is a favorite of not only giga deer, but many different types of monsters. They can smell it, from miles away even." Jun frowned, his thick brows low over his eyes. "It's banned in the town. The older generation even cleared it from the forest around town."

I frowned. "Then where'd it come from? And how did it end up in Hank's pack?"

All eyes swiveled to Hank. He leaned against his walking stick and didn't even raise his eyes. "The herb wasn't mine."

Iggy clicked his tongue. "Let me guess. You were holding it for a friend?"

Rhonda cleared her throat and all eyes turned to her. She held a finger up, her neon green nail practically glowing in the dark. "So, we *shouldn't* be picking random plants?"

Misaki frowned. "Is that a real question?"

Rhonda dug her hands in her pants pockets and pulled out two big handfuls of gray mushrooms. "So, for instance, this is bad?"

Jun stepped over and peered at the 'shrooms in her upturned palms. "They're not going to attract monsters, but I don't know why you'd carry them around." He shrugged. "They're not edible."

Rhonda jumped back and threw them to the ground. "They're poisonous?"

Jun grinned. "Nah. But they're hallucinatory."

Rhonda frowned. "Oh."

The guard turned away to face Misaki, and Rhonda took the opportunity to duck down and pop a mushroom into her mouth.

"Rhonda!" I hissed.

"Three secong ruge," she muttered around her mouthful.

"Spit it out." I flashed my eyes at her.

She shook her head, cheeks bulging.

Iggy whined. "I want one."

I shook my head at my little flame. "No, you don't." *Way to be a bad influence, Rhonda.*

Misaki lifted a thick brow at Hank. "You didn't pick the attrahunt? You're sure?"

His eyes flicked to her face for a quick moment. "I'm sure."

I gulped, an eerie feeling creeping up the back of my neck.

Misaki let out a shaky breath and looked slowly around at the other seven guards and my friends. "Someone, one of *us*, planted it then."

I scoffed. "*Someone*, huh?" I shoved my hand onto my hip. This sea witch had some nerve—suggesting *someone* planted it, when it was *her* who'd tried to get my boyfriend killed.

She frowned at me. "What do you mean?"

I rolled my eyes. "Oh, okay, yeah, play innocent." I leaned closer and bared my teeth. "I saw you." I turned to Maple, Rhonda and Annie. "When I followed her out of the hot springs to—" I glanced at all the guards. "To take care of some personal business, I found her back at the campsite rummaging through Hank's pack."

Annie darted her eyes to Misaki. "Are you sure it was Hank's? They all look the same and we had them piled together."

I nodded, my cheeks burning. Hank kept his eyes on the ground, but I was very aware that he stood nearby and that he was listening. "I left a note for Hank in his pack and it tumbled out when Misaki opened it."

Hank looked at me, surprised. A gasp cut through the thick silence. Reo looked up from his brother's body, his face filled with pain. Then he hung his head again and sobbed over the body.

Kai stood behind him, a deep frown on his face. "So, Misaki, you planted the herb to attract a monster and kill Hank?" He shook his head. "But it was my friend who paid the price." His lip curled in a venomous sneer.

The color drained from Misaki's face as all eyes swung to her. "Of course I didn't plant that herb." Her nostrils flared with her heavy breathing, and she clenched her hands into fists at her sides.

"Then why were you going through his things?" I lifted my brows.

Misaki sighed. "Fine. Yes, I looked through Hank's pack." Her eyes shifted to me. "I saw Imogen slip him a note earlier and I thought it might contain information about Captain Kenta or what you lot are actually doing here."

I sighed. "We told you why we're here."

She lifted her palms. "Well, I don't trust you."

Jun frowned. "Did the note have information?"

She shook her head and glanced at me. My chest tightened—would she reveal the extent of our relationship issues?

"No." She licked her lips. "So I kept looking, but I didn't find anything."

Jun looked down and nodded. The tension in my neck relaxed a little. I was grateful that Misaki didn't tell everyone what I'd written to Hank.

She let out a quiet breath. "So yes, I went through the pack, but I didn't plant that herb." She pressed her lips tight together. "Which means someone else here did, after I'd gone through it."

Kai folded his thick arms and scowled at her. "Sure, *if* we believe that *you* didn't do it. And we're just what, supposed to take your word on that?"

She glared at him.

"He did wander off into the woods, right before the deer screamed." Iggy widened his eyes. "Just saying."

Kai glared at my flame. "Yeah, with Reo. Nature called. Besides, your vampire had gone off, and Ben and Sora, too."

Iggy rolled his eyes, but nodded, begrudgingly.

Guess that warm water had done a number on some bladders.

"Look." I lifted my palms, not entirely sure I believed Misaki, or Kai, but willing to consider other possibilities. "Maybe it wasn't any of us." I shrugged. "I mean, Horace and his Badlands Army are running around loose on the island somewhere, right? Maybe they're messing with us."

Misaki shook her head. "You perhaps know your brother better than we do, but neither he nor his sizable army have ever interfered in our affairs."

"Hm." Annie shrugged. "He *has* tried to kill Hank before."

I nodded.

"But." She frowned. "He saved Hank's life right before he slithered off. Why would he save him just to turn around and kill him?"

I sighed. Yeah, that didn't make much sense.

Misaki straightened. "Whatever happened, we can't linger here. The giga deer may be back. We'll march till daybreak, and sleep in the morning."

A strangled cry made me jump. Reo clutched the blanket that covered his brother's body. "I'm not leaving him."

Misaki looked strained, her eyes tight. "I'm sorry, Reo. But we have to. We'll send up a flare so that our people can recover his body, and we'll spell him hidden from animals and monsters."

Reo let out a choked sob and allowed Kai to drag him to his feet and away from Sora. After the body had been hidden and a magical white flare hung in the sky above to mark the spot, we moved on. I felt even heavier and more exhausted than before, but I pushed my sluggish mind to go over the facts.

"Iggy, someone tried to kill Hank by planting the herb in his pack. They knew a monster would attack."

Iggy's lantern swung gently in my hand as I walked along. "Hm. Maybe Rhonda did it, wild on mushrooms."

I didn't deign to respond. None of my friends had done it, I was sure of that, which left the guards. Misaki easily could be lying, though part of me wanted to believe her, because I'd actually started to like her. I'd been watching her most of the time, and I didn't see her put any of that plant in Hank's pack, but she might have done it before I found her. I clomped along the trail behind Annie, my heavy pack bouncing on my shoulders. Misaki and Jun led the way up ahead. I liked Jun too, but he was clearly into Misaki.

"Maybe Jun got jealous of Hank and Misaki talking and he did it to take Hank out of the picture." I knew I'd felt a little pang myself. Plus, he knew all about herbs and would likely have been able to get ahold of this banned, rare plant.

"No offense." Iggy leaned out of the lantern and peeked up at me. "I know they say love is blind, which is what I'm assuming is going on here. But Jun would have had to feel real threatened and—have you looked at your boyfriend recently?"

I frowned. "Hank's handsome."

"Normal Hank, yeah. He's dreamy." Iggy flashed his eyes at me. "But he's all limpy and scruffy and mopey right now."

I quirked my lips to the side. I hated to admit it, but Iggy did kind of have a point.

I glanced behind me. Kai walked with an arm around Reo, practically dragging the devastated young man along. I wasn't a big fan of Kai's. He seemed most capable of doing something so cruel. And then there was that mysterious sword he had. "What about Kai?"

Iggy waited a beat. "He is a jerk, but he doesn't seem the brightest. Would he know about rare herbs?"

I shrugged. "It's probably dangerous enough that the guards would be briefed on it."

And then there was Reo. He just seemed so goofy and innocent—I couldn't see him murdering anyone. And I

hadn't gotten to know the other guards well enough to spec-
ulate about them, but I intended to change that.

I glanced back again. The white flare hung low in the
sky marking Sora's body. I gulped. Hopefully, that'd be the
only one we needed to send up. My stomach twisted with
worry. With monsters all around us and a murderer in our
midst, I didn't feel too confident about that.

14

SKETCHY

The small patches of sky visible through the treetops lightened to the bright gray of a rainy morning. We stopped to make camp between the trees, and this time everyone dumped their packs next to their own bedrolls instead of in a center pile like we had before. Nobody was to be trusted. Misaki and a couple other guards wandered off with fishing poles to catch our breakfast. I unrolled my sleeping bag over a cushy mat of fallen leaves. *Nothing like fish first thing in the morning.* The soft bubbling of a stream sounded nearby—they couldn't be going far.

Jun pulled out his sketchbook and Kai spoke in quiet tones to the devastated Reo. The kid with the mullet, who I'd learned was named Ben, magically lit a fire and then got to unpacking the cookware.

I waved my friends over and we gathered in a tight circle. I glanced around as we put our heads together. "One of them tried to murder Hank. We need to figure out who before they strike again."

My boyfriend scoffed, his eyes on the ground. "Why bother?"

My chest flushed hot. "Excuse me?"

He shrugged. "My own father tried to kill me. There seems to be quite a queue of people ready and willing to take me out."

I gaped at him. Was he serious? He didn't care that someone had it in for him?

Maple cleared her throat and gave Wiley a little nudge. He jumped and licked his lips. "We, uh, we all know how modest Hank is, but I think we can safely say no one wants any more murder, so I'm with Imogen. We should figure this out."

I nodded. "I'm going to talk to some of them, see if I can suss anything out." I looked at Hank, hoping he'd at least acknowledge me, but he kept his eyes down.

Maple looked between Hank and me, a little crease between her brows. She sucked in a breath and drew herself up taller. "You know..." She gulped. "Hank."

Wiley and I exchanged wide-eyed looks. Despite all my boyfriend's pleas to call him Hank, Maple had always insisted on calling him Prince Harry. This was wild.

Maple continued. "We're all your friends, too. And regardless of—of the circumstances, I think it's sad that you're not talking to us. That must've been hard with your father."

Wiley grimaced. "Ugh, he's the worst." He startled. "No offense, Hank. Sorry."

Hank looked up. "None taken."

Maple ducked her head. "Oh goddess, I hope I haven't crossed a line." She shook her head. "Oh, Maple, you fool, you've gone too far."

She curtsied, then backed away a step, and then bowed.

Hank pinched the bridge of his nose. "I'm not a prince anymore, you don't have to bow to me." He sneered. "My own father tried to kill me."

I lifted a finger. "Actually, he tried to kill *me* and you saved me." I lifted my brows. "Thank you—again."

Hank stood unshaven and partly hunched over, clutching his side. He waved it off.

Iggy scoffed. "By the tide, you are not pulling off this pouty hobo look."

A smile twitched at the corner of my mouth, and Maple continued to bow and curtsy, backing away to the other side of camp.

Wiley scratched the back of his neck. "I'm gonna go—" He thumbed toward Maple. "Check on that."

Annie chuckled. "Good idea."

Hank sighed and moved over to his bedroll without another word.

I balled my hands into fists and gritted my teeth. "Good talk."

Annie squeezed my shoulder. "He's just really down, dear. He used to be like this a lot more before you came around." She gave me a thin smile. "It's not your fault."

Maple and Wiley returned. Maple fanned herself. "I can't believe I said that to a prince!"

Oh, Maple.

Rhonda nodded, and Francis slid down from her shoulders to stand on his own. She stood up straighter and turned to me. "Is something going on between you guys?"

I sniffed. "He's not speaking to me. He hasn't been since he got here."

She nodded. "Oh, right, because of the whole seeing Horace and keeping that and the prison break from him."

She folded her arms and cocked a brow. "Which you all kept from me too, by the way."

I let out a heavy sigh. "Rhonda, I'm sorry. I really am. We didn't want you and Amelia to get hurt."

Sam whimpered. "Poor Amelia. Do you think ssshe'sss okay?" He wrung his hands together and more skin flakes dusted his shoulders. The stress was making the poor guy lose his skin at a rapid rate.

Yann nodded. "Oh yah, Sam. Amelia ees a wery tough wooman." He clapped Sam on the back with his enormous hand and sent the thin shifter lurching forward. Yann steadied him. "Sorry."

Maple bit her lip and looked between Wiley and me with big round eyes. "And my family... do you think the king will go after them and punish them because of me?" She plunked her head into her hands and let out a choked sob.

Annie folded her arms around Maple. "They'll be all right, dear. We just have to take care of ourselves so we can see all our people back home again." A crease formed between her brows. "But I do wonder what's happening out there in the world."

I nodded. "I'm sorry I dragged you all into this." And I was. More than I could express. "I feel so guilty."

Maple lifted her red, wet face, and Wiley hugged an arm around her shoulders. "No, Imogen." She shook her head. "Horace got us into this and to be honest...." She sighed. "I hope this doesn't sound crazy, but I appreciate what he did."

My mouth fell open. "You do?"

"Well, if he hadn't, the truth never would have come out." Her lips quirked to the side.

I looked around the circle and my friends nodded their agreement.

"Plus." Rhonda's dark eyes twinkled. "We get to see the

Badlands." She lifted her arms and gestured at the twisting greenery and curling mist that surrounded us. "I've been almost everywhere in my hundreds of years, but I'd always wanted to see this place."

I supposed, under different circumstances, I might have found the lush, magical island charming. If it weren't for the monsters, murder, and very real possibility of being kicked out of the town and left to fend for ourselves. Oh, and my brother and his army roaming around somewhere.

I grimaced at Maple, and she forced a smile. "It is beautiful... in a creepy way."

"Like Rhonda." Iggy cackled, but the Seer just smiled and nodded. Of course. She *would* take that as a compliment.

Annie folded her hands in front of her hips. "We just have to trust that everything back home will work itself out. In the meantime, we have to stay alive."

I nodded. "Right. Which starts with not getting murdered."

Francis lifted his nose. "That would be preferred. Though I must say, being dead has its perks."

I frowned. "We'll have to take your word for it."

Rhonda patted his little wing finger. "No, no, honey cakes, you're *un*dead."

"Right, well, wish me luck—I'll let you guys know what I find out." My friends nodded and moved off to sleep or take care of personal business. I cast one more look toward Hank. He lay on his bedroll, a scarf over his face.

Annoyed, I surveyed the guards and decided to start with Ben. I joined him by the campfire where he crouched, unpacking cutting boards, knives, and pots and pans. I dropped down to sit on my heels beside him.

"Hey."

He looked up and blinked in surprise. Ben had a like-able look to him. He wore his black hair short on top, long in the back—maybe in the Badlands mullets hadn't gone out of fashion. Maybe that's what being cut off from the rest of the world did to you. But he shot me an easy smile, his eyes crinkling in the corners. "Hey, yourself!"

He pulled a cast iron wok out of his pack and my eyes widened. He caught my expression and laughed. "We spell it to weigh less."

I grinned. "Thank goodness." Then I frowned. "Hey, my pack weighs a ton, can we get some of that spell?"

Ben shook his head. "Nah, sorry. Part of the whole prove-yourself quest—it's tradition."

"Ah." I watched him lay out more dishes. "Can I help with anything?"

He looked around and shrugged. "Nah. I've got it, I think. Thanks."

"Sure." I nodded, unsure how to start. I decided to just jump right in. "So... that other guard, Reo... that was his brother who was killed?"

Ben glanced toward Reo, who slumped against the base of a tree, tears streaming down his cheeks. "Yeah." He shook his head. "Reo pretty much worshipped his older brother—even though he was mean to him." He cracked a half-hearted grin.

I lifted my brows. "Mean? Like, there was rivalry between them?"

Ben shook his head. "Nah. More like just normal brother stuff. All us younger guys totally look up to Kai and Sora, they're—well, they were, like the coolest. Reo always wanted to do what Sora did, and course Sora was way too cool for Reo, so he never let him. I think Reo thought becoming a guard, like them, would change things."

"Did it?"

Ben shook his head. "Reo was always the little brother. It pretty much stayed that way."

I poked at the soft dirt with my finger and got some under my short nail. "Why do you guys look up to them so much?" They seemed pretty harsh to me.

"Oh, man." Ben set a frying pan on top of a pot with a clank. "They're like the first guys from our part of town to make it into the guard. It's always just been the rich families' kids who got in, but Kai and Sora showed us that even if we're sons of fishermen, or laundresses like Kai, we can be guards, too." He nodded. "It's pretty cool."

I nodded. "Yeah. That is." I looked up. Kai still stood beside Reo, towering over him. He looked angry, as tough as ever, but maybe his presence was comforting to Reo. I wouldn't have enjoyed it, but maybe Reo felt differently. I blinked and looked around the camp. Huh—where had Jun gone?

I rose to my feet, my burning thighs nearly giving out from under me. "Let me know if you change your mind and I can help."

Ben nodded and I moved over toward the boulder Jun had been sitting on. I looked around, trying to act nonchalant. Should I start whistling? Would that help my act? His sketchbook lay on the rock, pencils nearby—totally unattended. Maybe I could just sneak a little look. I wasn't sure what I expected—a detailed murder plan, sketches of dead bodies? But I hoped for something that might give me a clue as to whether he planted the herb.

With one more look around the camp, I flipped the open book right side up and found a drawing of a plant with purple leaves—the attrahunt! I lifted my brows. My investigation of Jun was off to a pretty good start. I bit my lip and flipped through the book. The pages contained lots of sketches of plants, a variety of monsters of all shapes and sizes, and a whole lot of Misaki—her face, her hands, her smile.

"See anything good?"

"Ah!" I jumped and the book tumbled from my hands. I stooped to lift it, and Jun, who now stood in front of me, did as well. I handed him the notepad, but it'd landed on a drawing of a yellow berry and bent the page. I grimaced as he smoothed the page down with his wand. "I'm so sorry."

He held it up with a tight smile. "Good as new."

"No." I shook my head, inwardly cringing at the awkwardness. "I mean, I'm sorry about snooping."

He shrugged. "It's all right. A little embarrassing maybe."

I frowned as I caught a hint of pink on his cheeks. "Embarrassing?" I pressed a hand to my chest. "I'm the one who should be embarrassed—and I am."

He turned and leaned against the big rock he'd been sitting on earlier. I stood there a moment, wanting to flee and hide in a cocoon of my own uncomfortableness. But, I wanted answers about who'd tried to hurt Hank, and Jun might have them. I took a deep breath and moved a little closer. "They were good, your drawings. Have you always been an artist?"

Jun cracked a grin. "I've always liked to draw, ever since I was a little kid, but I'm not sure that qualifies me as an artist. My family owns a tea house and it kept me busy while they were working." His dark eyes twinkled. "As I got older, I'd draw labels for all the teas, and I illustrated our menu." He shrugged. "It's always been fun, but it doesn't pay the bills, so here I am, a guard."

I pointed at his sketchpad. The drawing of the berries

lay open on top. "Are those all plants and monsters that you've seen out here?"

He nodded. "Yeah. One of the best things about being a guard is getting to explore the island. I like to catalog all the unique plants and creatures I've seen." The pink flush on his cheeks darkened. "And I suppose you know what else I like to draw, too."

Misaki! My stomach twisted and I brushed my bangs out of my eyes. "I mean— I may have— I saw a few—" *Real smooth, Imogen.*

Jun chuckled and lowered his voice. "It's all right. If anyone had to see those drawings of her, I'm glad it was you."

I lifted my brows. "Really?"

He nodded. "Yeah." He let out a sigh and stared at his booted feet. "You, of anyone here, knows how it is when the person you love just doesn't feel that way about you."

I gaped at him. "What?"

He looked up, eyes wide, and lifted a palm. "I'm sorry if that sounded presumptuous. It's just—well, I couldn't help but notice that you reach out to Hank and he doesn't seem to reciprocate."

I felt as though a bucket of ice water had been dumped on my head. I took a step back.

Jun's face fell. "Hey, I'm really sorry. Who am I to say anything? I've only known you two for what, a day? I'm probably totally off, and that comment was way out of bounds."

I shook my head. "No. You're right. That's how we've been acting, but that's not us—not the real us." I squared my shoulders. "Excuse me."

I spun and marched across the campsite before Jun could say another word. I couldn't take it anymore. If a total stranger thought Hank wasn't into me, no wonder I was feeling that way. I couldn't take the silent treatment anymore. I needed to know what was going on. I reached my friends and Hank, who sat on his bedroll.

"Hi, Imogen—oh." Maple's smile dropped from her face.

I barely registered it, my eyes on Hank. "I need to talk to you."

He glanced up at me for a brief moment, then back down. He gave a slight nod.

"Oh, you know, I just remembered this... uh... super cool rock I saw, faraway from here." Wiley thumbed over his shoulder, his eyes wide and full of meaning.

Annie blew out a big puff of air. "Well, a cool rock? I've *got* to see this."

"Take me with you," Iggy pleaded, and Wiley stooped to lift him in his lantern.

"I'd like to sssee what'ssss hiding under the rock."

"Sure, buddy, whatever you want." Wiley ushered Sam away, and Yann joined him.

Maple squeezed my shoulder and gave me an encouraging look before moving off with the others.

Rhonda folded her arms, a big grin on her face. "I wish I had popcorn. This is going to be good." But Francis hooked a wing around her shoulders and guided her off with the others, though she grumbled until she was out of earshot. Which left me suddenly all alone with Hank, who still stared at the ground.

I let out a heavy sigh and bit my lip. "Hank, you might be able to pretend I don't exist, but I can't. I'm always aware of you, where you're at, if you've smiled today, how much you're using your walking stick." I swiped my bangs from my eyes with a trembling hand.

"This silent treatment thing is killing me, so can you just

tell me what I can do to make this right? I'm sorry—I'm deeply sorry that I didn't tell you about meeting with Horace sooner. And I'll keep apologizing, if that's what it takes to make you understand, but I never wanted to hurt you."

I dragged the backs of my hands across my cheeks and wiped away the tears that had trickled from my eyes. Still Hank didn't even look up, and frustration burned in my chest. I dropped down to a crouch in front of him. He sat with his knees bent up and his long arms wrapped around them. I shook my head. "All my friends understood when I told them. They didn't just cut me out."

He lifted his face to mine finally. His normally bright blue eyes looked dull and bloodshot, and dark stubble covered his jaw. "I'm not cutting you out." He dropped his eyes again and shook his head. "I just... I don't know how to process all of this." He rubbed his wrist. "It's a lot." His nostrils flared and he looked up at me, hurt in his eyes. "And you know, it's been what? A day since I found out? A day since my father tried to kill me and you and your brother exposed him to be a murderer? You've known about Horace for months. You lied." Tears welled in his eyes. "You lied to my face about that, for months, and just because I need some time to process, more than a day, I'm the bad guy?" He shook his head and pushed to his feet.

I frowned up at him. "I never said you're the bad guy."

But he was already on his feet. "I'm not ready to talk about this." He stalked off into the tree line.

"Urg!" I gritted my teeth and dragged my fingers through my hair. I dropped from my crouch to sit on the ground and leaned my forehead against my knees. Tears streamed down my hot face as a mix of sadness and anger spiraled in my chest.

How had we gotten here? Hank and I had always been so happy together, so in love. And now that we were finally free to really be together without interference from his family or anything else, we were barely speaking. Maybe Jun was right. Maybe Hank just didn't feel the way about me that I felt about him. Or maybe I was rushing him and he just needed time. But how much? And couldn't he see that our days might be numbered? One member of our party was already dead, and Hank had been the target. Shouldn't that have been a wake-up call to prioritize what was really important in life? Unless I just wasn't the priority anymore.

I let out a heavy sigh. Whatever Sam had found under that rock, which I was pretty sure Wiley had made up, that's what I felt like. Like rock scum. Not even the kind that sits on *top* of a rock. I was *bottom*-of-a-rock scum.

The skies opened up and a heavy shower fell on the camp. The rain matted my hair to the back of my neck, and still, I didn't move. The guards ran around, some sheltering the fire, others our bedrolls. I didn't have the energy to care. I lifted my face and blinked up at the gray sky poking through the treetops. The branches overhead shook in the heavy rain. I dropped my forehead against my knees again and let the cold drops trickle under my collar and down my back.

15

MISAKI

"Hey!"

The sound startled me from my deep moping. *Deep.* I lifted my chin, and rain streamed down my forehead.

Misaki and the guards she'd gone off with jogged into the campsite at the same time that all my friends reemerged from the trees. No sign of Hank, though. Misaki had a black hood pulled over her top knot, which formed a little peak on top of her head. She scanned the group, then shouted at Kai, "You were supposed to cast the umbrella spell!"

"I've been busy." Kai jerked his head at the dejected Reo at his feet.

Jun tucked his sketchbook into his waterproof pack, then jogged over to Misaki. "Let's do it."

She gave a curt nod, and they lifted their wands. Light flashed from the ends and suddenly a protective bubble formed around us, visible only because the rain streamed down it like it was a windshield. I roughly wiped my face with the back of my cold, wet sleeve and pushed to my feet. Our whole group converged on the meager campfire. Ben crouched over it, using his wand to coax the deluged flames back to life.

I slid up beside Maple, who handed me Iggy in his lantern. "So. How was that amazing rock Wiley wanted to show you?" I shot her a dry look.

Maple grinned. "Sam was pretty disappointed there wasn't an actual rock."

I glanced at my shifter friend, who used his shirt to wipe his glasses dry.

Maple looked around, a little crease forming between her brows. "Where's Hank?"

I shrugged. "He stomped off a second ago. I'm sure he's nearby." I willed myself to ignore that unsettled worry about him in my stomach. He shouldn't be wandering in the woods alone in monster territory with a murderer among us. I sighed. But he'd made it pretty clear he didn't want to speak to me. He probably wouldn't appreciate hearing my concerns, either.

Maple winced. "It didn't go so well, then?"

I leaned my head against her shoulder. "It was bad. He told me he needed more time to process it."

Maple leaned her head against mine. "Well, you don't know what he's going to decide, right? We shouldn't assume it's going to be bad."

I sighed, deeply weary. "That's the thing. I think deep down, even though I was nervous to tell him, I assumed he'd understand why I needed to meet my brother and why I'd kept it from him." I groaned. "But now, I truly don't know how he's going to feel. He might be done with me." Tears welled in my eyes. "Just that being a real option, that he might not love me anymore, is—" My throat grew tight and I squeezed my eyes shut, unable to talk.

"Oh." Maple clicked her tongue. "Oh, don't think that. He loves you. I'm sure."

I wasn't. And it was the worst feeling, ever.

"Where's the fish?"

I looked up and blinked to clear the tears from my blurry eyes. Kai stood across the fire from me, the orange flames lighting his face from below and casting stark shadows at his jaw and cheekbones. Though it was midmorning, the thick cloud cover made it seem more like dusk. Rain pelted the magical bubble overhead.

Misaki licked her lips. "I wanted to check the traps by the bog first."

Kai let out a disgusted sigh and folded his arms across his chest. "You haven't even been fishing? What are we supposed to eat?"

Misaki glared at him. "Relax." She turned to Ben. "The fire looks great—if you and Jun start on the rice and veggies, I'll be back soon with some fish."

Jun nodded. "Sure. Did you find anything in the trap?"

She shook her head. "Empty. Sprung, just like the others. This is more escaped monsters than we've ever seen before."

She and Jun exchanged worried glances.

"Well I know *I'm* feeling super safe," Iggy scoffed.

"The rude flame is right." Kai nodded.

Iggy's mouth dropped. "I'm not rude. I just tell it like it is."

Kai ignored him. "I'm starving, so if you're gonna go fish, like you *said* you would, now's the time."

Misaki lowered her thick dark brows. "Fine."

She turned to go, but Jun reached out. "Wait. You shouldn't go alone."

She hesitated, and on an impulse, I grabbed Maple's arm and pulled her forward. "We'll go with you."

Maple turned to me, eyes wide. "We will?"

At that moment, Hank, soaking wet, shuffled into the protective bubble. He looked up and gave Francis a short nod before dragging himself over to his bedroll. The part of me that'd been worried about him relaxed. A split second later a new knot of anxiety tightened in my stomach over having to stay in this confined area with him.

I nodded at Maple. "Yep. We're going."

She frowned.

"Please?"

She blew out a little puff of air. "Okay."

Misaki frowned. "Do you even know anything about fishing?"

"Why, they call me Scales McGee." I dragged Maple over to her as she and Wiley exchanged worried looks.

Misaki's frown deepened.

"Like, fish scales? Scales McGee?" I shook my head. "We can help."

The little ninja girl looked me up and down. "Fine."

Reo, eyes red and swollen from crying, stumbled up to our group. All eyes turned to him and a silence fell. He gulped, shot Kai a side-eyed look, then let out a shaky breath. He opened his mouth. "Guys—I have to—to say something about my brother." He trembled, visibly, and tears streamed down his cheeks. "I—"

Kai moved to his side in an instant and put an arm around Reo's shoulders. He pulled him tight against his side. "Hey, little buddy. You don't need to do this now."

Reo gasped and devolved into sobs.

Kai looked around at us. "He's still real shaken up."

Misaki shook her head, her face pinched. "Well of

course he's shaken up, his brother just died a few hours ago."

Kai dipped his head and spoke into Reo's ear. "Come on, let's go have a chat, just you and me." The burly guard guided Reo away, and we all stood in silence for a couple of moments as we watched them.

Misaki let out a heavy sigh, then addressed the group. "We'll be back soon." She started off, and Maple and I followed.

Rhonda waved goodbye with a big smile on her face, like we were taking a cruise to the Bahamas.

Maple and I pulled our hoods over our heads and I closed the glass on Iggy's lantern before we stepped out of the protective bubble. Rain tapped against my hood and little splatters of water landed on the tip of my nose. Iggy's light guided our way along a deer path through the tall, thick trees and undergrowth.

The rain fell heavy, reaching us even through the thick canopy of greenery overhead. I *did* want to get away from Hank for a bit, but I had a bigger motive than that for going fishing with Misaki—I needed to figure out if she might want Hank dead.

So far, Reo seemed unlikely to be capable of murder. Every single other guard seemed more hardened than him. Ben had been friendly, and didn't raise my suspicions. I stepped over a tall root that burst from the ground and twined to thigh height. I turned and offered Maple a hand over, then followed Misaki on into the misty forest.

Jun had been pretty cool about the fact that I'd been snooping in his sketchbook, but maybe he'd made that comment about Hank to throw me off. He clearly knew a thing or two about herbs, between growing up in his family's tea shop and all the plants he'd drawn during his forays as a guard. And he seemed pretty obsessed with Misaki. He might have been jealous of her speaking with Hank and planted that herb in his pack. My stomach clenched up as a new thought hit me. Could he have something to do with their Captain Kenta's disappearance? The others had teased Misaki that she had a crush on the captain. Maybe Jun had grown jealous of her feelings for Kenta and decided to take him out of the picture! I glanced back at Maple and made a mental note to run that theory by her later.

I returned to my line of thought and cast through my memory. I couldn't think up any specific reason Kai might want Hank dead, but the guy seemed thuggish and gave me bad vibes. I scrunched up my nose. Then again, if he wanted to kill Hank, he might be the kind to challenge him to a duel or something, take him on in broad daylight, versus try to lure a monster to him. Which pretty much just left Misaki. And I planned to use this little fishing expedition to get some answers out of her.

As we hiked on, just a little further, a rushing stream that paralleled our path came into view through the misty trees. The tapping of raindrops mixed with the soft rush of the stream, and we cut to the right to stand at the water's edge. Misaki set her pack down at the top of the bank and pulled out a bamboo pole broken down into three pieces. She fitted them together, added the line, and fixed a worm on the end of the hook. She turned to Maple and me. "You ladies ready to help?"

"Yeah, of course." I licked my lips. "How would that go, again?"

She rolled her eyes, but couldn't completely hide the smile that played at the corners of her mouth. She dug around in her pack, then handed me a small net and bucket and Maple a box of worms.

I frowned and leaned over her bag. "How does that all fit in there? You have a *Mary Poppins* thing going on?"

Maple and Misaki both shot me quizzical looks.

I shook my head. "Never mind. Human thing."

I set Iggy's lantern under a rock overhang so he'd stay dry, then the three of us picked our way down the slippery, muddy slope to the rushing stream below.

"I'll supervise," Iggy called down to me.

"Great. So helpful." I winked at my little flame.

Misaki waded out through the wild waters and perched on a wide, flat rock in the middle. "When I catch one, you grab it with the net." She pointed at me. "Then throw it in the bucket with some water till I'm ready to gut it."

I wrinkled my nose and Misaki frowned. "You've never fished, have you?"

I shook my head, and she rolled her eyes. "You want to eat, don't you?"

I nodded.

"Okay, then get tough." She turned to Maple. "And you'll hand me more tackle."

Maple whimpered. "But the poor worm."

Misaki's nostrils flared and she gave us flat looks. "They're already dead. Can you two handle this?"

"Psh." I waved a hand. "We've got it."

Maple turned to me, her eyes wide. "We do?"

I winced. "Maybe? Come on, we've got to get her to spill to see if she really did plant that herb, okay?"

"You ladies ready?"

Maple and I jumped and turned to Misaki. "Yep," we said as one.

She raised her brows, but turned to the river and cast her line. As we prepared to wait, I racked my mind for the best way to start our conversation.

"A minute ago, you said 'human thing.'" Misaki shot me a quick glance. I stood on a smooth river rock within reach of her, my toes freezing from the water running over them and soaking through my leather-soled boots. "Have you been to human lands?"

Well, sweet. She started the talking for me. I nodded. "Yeah. Actually, I was raised by humans."

Misaki jerked her head up to look at me, wide-eyed.

I smiled. "I know. I didn't even know I was magical until less than a year ago."

She turned to Maple, who stood on a rock behind her. "You, too?"

"Oh no." My friend shook her head and sent rain flying from her hood. "I'm from Bijou Mer."

"The Water Kingdom," Misaki breathed.

Maple and I exchanged looks. "You know about Bijou Mer?"

Misaki nodded, her eyes on her line in the water. She slowly reeled it in, gathering the line in her hand. "Yeah, we learn all about the magical kingdoms." Her throat bobbed. "I love it here, this is my home, but—" She sighed. "But I've always wanted to see what else is out there. We can't, you know. Our island is surrounded my monsters, so we can't leave by water or by air." She huffed. "And your infuriating brother won't share his portal mirrors with us."

I grinned and held up a palm. "Hey. I find him infuriating, too."

Misaki looked sideways at Maple. "Could you tell me about it—Bijou Mer?"

My friend gave a shy smile. "Of course. It's a lovely village. It winds up a mountain, with the palace on top, and my family has a bakery there, down this narrow little back alley, but all the locals know how to find us. At night, the tide rises and the mermaids come out, and every summer as kids my brothers and sisters and I would go to the Summer Sea Carnival and come home sick from cotton candy clouds and—" Maple's face crumpled and she devolved into sobs. Misaki looked up, startled.

"Maple." I stretched an arm out but couldn't quite reach her, not without toppling into the fast-moving water below us.

She sniffled. "I'm sorry. It's just, thinking about home got me thinking about my family, and if the king's going after them, and if they're in danger, all because of me." She burst into tears again.

"I'm giving you a hug from afar." I reached both arms out and Maple gave me a sad smile, though tears still streamed down her face.

"Thanks."

Misaki glued her eyes to her fishing line. She reeled in the hook without a fish, then cast it into the water again.

I sighed. "Maple, I'm sure your family's safe. I am. Amelia's there, and Hank's brother Cas is a pretty decent guy, and Urs Volker. They'll stand up to the king." I shrugged. "Plus, who knows where my brother is. He could be there, too."

She whimpered. "Horace threatened to kill my family, too, if I didn't break into Carclaustra." Her chin quavered. "Everyone's trying to kill my family and it's all my fault."

I shook my head. "No one's trying to kill your family." I deeply hoped that was true. "And in any case"—a heavy weight settled on my chest—"it's *my* fault. All of this is. Horace is my brother, and the king and he only know of you because you're *my* friend."

We stood in heavy silence, the damp cold eating through layers of clothing down to my bones.

Misaki let out a groan. "I hate to say it, but I know how you two feel."

I glanced up. "You do?"

She wound the line up in her hand, her eyes on the rushing water as raindrops beaded down her hood. "I'm trying to keep everyone safe, but Sora *died*—under my watch." She shook her head. "It's horrible. And it never would've happened if Captain Kenta was here." She bit her full bottom lip. "Before he disappeared, he told me he thought I'd make a great leader someday." She scoffed. "Some leader I've made. I can't even keep my people alive. Which is why we need to find Kenta, but what if I'm just getting everyone killed trying to find him?" She groaned.

I lifted a brow. "So that's why you want to find him so badly? Because he's a good leader? No *other* feelings for him?" I raised my brows.

Misaki shot me a flat look. "Not you, too. He's my captain, that's all."

A muscle jumped in her jaw and I had a feeling that was all I was going to get on that subject. I wasn't sure if I believed her or not. I licked my lips. "For what it's worth, I think you're doing a great job."

She sighed and let out a half-hearted, "Thanks."

"Really." I lifted my brows. "You're decisive, and—and brave, and you know what you're doing."

Misaki kept her eyes on the water. She was tough to read.

I tried for a little girl talk. "So... no interest in any of the guys, then? How about Kai? He's pretty beefy, and Ben was telling me everybody looks up to him."

Misaki snorted. "The *young* guys look up to him, because they think he's big and tough." She shook her head.

"You disagree?" I cocked a brow.

"He wants prestige and flashiness, but the truth is it's a tough job. And the pay isn't the true reward, it's keeping our people safe." She shrugged. "Besides, the pay isn't much. He has to be lying about that new sword of his. There's no way it's a real Honjo katana, but he wants everyone to think he's so rich and cool." She shook her head. "Captain Kenta could've had a Honjo, if he wanted one. His family's wealthy enough, but he uses his government-issued sword because he always leads by example."

I bit my lip. "So you're not into Kai... what about Jun?"

She jumped and looked my way. "Why? Did he say something?" She didn't wait for an answer. "The girls in town are always fawning all over him, wearing their finest kimonos for visits to his family's tea house." She sniffed. "Please, like we don't all know what you're up to." She sighed. "But they do look pretty. Meanwhile, I'm over here covered in mud and river water, battling monsters and typhoons." She blinked at the water.

I hesitated, debating if I should tell about Jun's drawings of her. She jumped and her line pulled taut. "We've got one."

We spent the next half hour or so busy reeling in a total of nine fish. Afterward, Maple and I turned our backs and let Misaki do the gutting on the riverbank. I held Iggy close, and Maple and I sucked up his warmth.

"I can't look. Iggy, is it bad?"

I held the lantern up and my little flame looked over my shoulder at Misaki and the fish. When I lowered him, he'd turned green. "Gruesome."

I quirked my lips to the side. "We know Misaki's handy with a knife and plenty tough enough to kill—but would she go after Hank?"

Maple shrugged. "Maybe not him personally, but maybe

she has a vendetta against his dad, the king." She frowned. "She seems so nice though."

I grinned at her. "You think everyone's nice."

She folded her arms and lifted her chin. "Well, most people are."

Iggy shook his little flame head. "Oh, pure, innocent little Maple. I'm surprised your mom lets you go outside by yourself."

She rolled her eyes.

"Done."

"Gah!" Iggy startled and Maple and I jumped as Misaki appeared right behind us.

"And for the record," she lifted a thick, straight brow, "if I wanted to kill someone, you'd know it. Because they'd be dead." She walked on, a line of gutted fish strung over her shoulder. "Come on. And while we're at it...." She turned to face us. "I shouldn't have been talking like I was. Forget everything I said."

I held up my palms. "Hey, I thought we were kind of bonding."

"I guess I do find you guys easy to open up to." She shrugged. "It's probably because you seem so helpless and pathetic and nonthreatening."

I folded my arms. "This is seeming like less of a compliment."

She grinned. "See? So sensitive." She spun around. "Let's go eat."

As we walked back, another thought occurred to me that I hadn't even considered. What if Sora had planted the herb in Hank's pack, and then been accidentally killed? Maybe none of the guards remained a threat to us, and I could relax a little.

We'd nearly reached our site, the comforting smells of

rice and roasted vegetables and campfire wafting through the clean, rainy air. My stomach rumbled. "Sea snakes, that smells good."

A cry rang out.

Maple and I exchanged wide-eyed looks, then followed Misaki and ran the last leg of the path back to camp.

16

THE JADE FISH NECKLACE

I burst into the protective bubble with Iggy in hand. The rain ceased to beat against our hoods and shoulders in an instant. Jun looked up from where he knelt over a backpack, and Wiley and the rest of our friends rushed to meet Maple and me. Even Hank stood and moved over, slower than the rest.

"What is it?" Misaki threw back her hood and looked around. "We heard a shout."

Jun rose to his feet, his face pale. "Ben and I were cooking and I needed some grated ginger." His throat bobbed. "Kai's carrying the spices, and I called for him, but he and Reo must be out of earshot."

Misaki frowned and looked between Jun, Ben, and the other guards, whose names I hadn't learned yet. "Why did they leave? Where are they?"

Ben stood from the pot he'd been stirring over the fire and shrugged. "Kai said they went to go talk. That Reo was having a hard time and needed some privacy to mourn."

Jun looked pained as he held up a clenched fist. "I went to Kai's pack to look for the spices and found this." He turned his hand over and opened his white fingers. A jade fish lay in his hand, attached to a black leather string.

Misaki gasped and pressed a hand to her mouth. The whites shone all around her eyes and she looked from the necklace to Jun, then back to the necklace.

The color drained from Ben's face. "That's Captain Kenta's necklace." He blinked. "Why would Kai have it?"

Misaki jabbed a gloved finger at the necklace. "Captain told me his grandfather gave that to him. It's been in his family for generations. He never took it off."

Jun watched Misaki intently, as if gauging her reaction. "I agree, it looks bad, but we don't know what it means."

Misaki balled her hands into fists at her sides. She set her jaw, and her whole body trembled. "Oh. I think we do." She shoved the line of fish at Ben and threw off her pack. She bent over, pulled her sword from the bag, and drew the blade from its sheath. "I'm off to have a word with Kai."

"Wait!" Jun stepped in front of her.

Iggy grunted. "Someone's got a death wish."

I nodded my agreement. With that murderous look in her eyes and a sword in her hand, I would think twice about getting in Misaki's way.

"Someone want to explain what's going on?" Rhonda planted her hands on her hips. "I mean, I usually know way ahead of time." She touched the spot on her forehead that glowed when she received a vision. "So I have a harder time than most when I'm out of the loop." She turned to my friends and me and winked.

Oh, Rhonda.

Misaki side-stepped, but Jun blocked her way again. Her chest heaved, eyes fixed on Jun. "Get out of my way."

He winced as though she'd slapped him, but stayed his ground. "Wait. We need to discuss this."

"Hold on." I stepped forward. Apparently I had a death wish, too.

Misaki shot me a murderous look, her face a splotchy mix of white and red. Her chest heaved and her nostrils flared.

"Hear me out." I held up my palms. "Let me spy on them. I'll see if I can overhear anything about the necklace or Kenta. Maybe he'll confess."

Misaki's lip curled back in a sneer. "They'll hear you coming a mile off. I'm going." She flashed her eyes at Jun. "I'll listen in on them, okay, before I act."

I cocked my head. "You can get close enough to hear what they're saying through the rain?"

She bared her teeth at me. "I'll use an amplifying spell."

Jun shook his head. "It'll amplify the rain, too."

She pressed her lips tight together. "But you can do it, because?" She lifted a brow at me.

I straightened my spine. "Because I'm a swallow. And I can turn into a bird, for instance, and hover on a branch above them."

Misaki scoffed. "There it is. You think I'm an idiot? If we give you back your powers, what's to keep you from escaping?"

I lifted my arms wide. "Escape? To where? The monster-infested forest? No thank you." I pointed at myself. "You remember me and the fish, right? You called me pathetic."

"And rightly so." Iggy nodded his agreement.

"Thanks so much, buddy."

Iggy nodded. "I got you."

I shook my head but turned back to the fuming Misaki.

She glared at me. "You'd attack us."

"Again, what would that accomplish?" I raised my brows at her. "Look, I promise I don't have an ulterior motive. I want to know who planted that herb in Hank's pack more than anyone, and it might be connected to that necklace. Plus, let's say we attacked you. Even if we could find our way back to the town and manage not to get eaten by monsters, your people wouldn't let us back in without you."

Jun cleared his throat. "You know, there's another possibility. Sora may have been the one who planted the herb." He shrugged. "This may all be a nonissue at this point."

Misaki shook her head. "What about Captain's necklace then?" She blew a heavy sigh out her nose and resheathed her sword. "Fine." She fished around in her pocket, then held her hand out. A small vial of red liquid rested in her gloved palm. She shoved the little glass bottle at me. "Drink this."

I reached a hand out, but hesitated.

"Go on, drink it. We don't know how much longer they'll be out there."

I grabbed the vial.

"Hold on." Hank shuffled forward. "What's in that? How do we know it's safe?"

Oh, so now you care if I'm safe. I ignored him and pulled out the tiny cork.

"It's the antidote to the darts we hit you with earlier." Jun nodded. "It'll give her back her powers."

I tipped the liquid down my throat and it burned as it went down. I licked my lips. "Spicy."

Hank shook his head at me, the bags dark under his eyes. "That could have been anything."

I shrugged. "There have been a thousand moments I might have been killed in this forest, and *now* you're concerned." I was being a brat, I knew it, but I couldn't understand him.

Hank's face darkened. "Right. That's right. You don't care

if you're risking your own life, so why should I have anything to say about it? Join your murderous brother atop a volcano, break into the most dangerous prison in the kingdoms." He flipped a hand. "Why should that be a concern for your boyfriend?"

I opened my mouth to speak, but closed it again. I didn't even know where to start. My chest and throat burned hot with anger... and also the potion. I squared my shoulders and turned away from Hank to face Misaki. "I'm going. I'll be back soon."

"Be safe." Maple squeezed my hand.

Letting my anger spur me on, I pulled sharply from the power of the falling rain and in a whoosh of magic, transformed into one of the orange-faced sparrows I'd spotted so often among the branches. I hovered midair, beating my wings without having to even think of them, like breathing. I looked down at Misaki's upturned face, her mouth round in wonder. Jun nodded at me, turned, and pointed. "They went off that way."

I dove forward and flew hard through the trees.

17

A LITTLE BIRD TOLD ME

I swooped under a branch, swerved left around a mossy tree trunk, then spread my feathers and arced over a pile of gray granite boulders. If I didn't have a beak, I would've smiled. Whether it was a moth or a bird, I loved transforming into flying creatures. Was it as fun for Sam when he became a snake?

I scanned the trees for Reo and Kai and kept my earholes pricked. A strange sound brought me up short and I gripped a slender, leafy branch with my clawed feet and tucked my wings at my sides. I gave them a little shake to throw off the raindrops. Then I listened.

The rain rushed around me. Small animals and insects rustled in the treetops and scuttled along the rough bark of the trunks. And under it all came the sound of human voices. I puffed up my chest, crouched, and then leapt into the open air. It was an exhilarating rush. I'd never been skydiving, but it had to be similar. And then, as I fell, I opened my wings and flew toward the voices.

Glowing balls of light came into view—wands! I swooped closer and landed on a bare branch right above

Reo and Kai. They'd certainly wandered deep into the forest —what did they need such privacy to discuss?

I hunkered low and held my wings close to my sides for warmth. I turned my head slightly to hear better.

Reo moaned and buried his face in his palms. "I have to tell them. I can't live with this—it's killing me."

I froze. That didn't sound good.

Kai paced, back and forth, back and forth, clearly agitated. He shook his head as he stomped around. "Get yourself together." He cast a disdainful glance at Reo's back. "A monster killed Sora."

Reo lifted his face from his palms, his complexion red and swollen. Tears poured from his puffy eyes. "It was just supposed to be a prank. A stupid prank." He moaned again.

What was *this* now? I gripped the branch tighter in my bird claws and leaned further out into the open air to catch every word.

"We all make mistakes. You need to let it go." Kai stalked over and grabbed Reo by the shoulders. He gave him a rough shake.

"How?" Reo wailed. He hung his head and his shoulders shook with his sobs. "I killed my brother! I *killed* him!"

OMG. If I had eyebrows, they'd have jumped all the way to my hairline. I gasped—only, it came out a kind of squawk.

Reo and Kai looked up at me in an instant. And there I was, a little bird leaning way out from my branch, ear turned toward them, right above their heads. Not suspicious at all.

I froze and as Kai frowned and narrowed his eyes, I feared he was looking right through me. *Sea snakes! Act like a bird, Imogen.* Only, in my panic and surprise, I couldn't quite remember how. I righted myself and toddled around on the branch, flapping my wings and randomly pecking at the air and the branch. That was what birds did, right?

"What is this?" Kai muttered.

I could feel his eyes on me. In a last-ditch effort to appear more birdlike, I attempted to make a bird noise. What did birds sound like again? My panicked brain latched on to something, I opened my beak, and— "Quack!"

I looked down at Kai's darkening face.

Nope. That was wrong. I leapt from my branch and winged as fast as I could back to camp, my tiny heart thundering in my feathered chest. I'd heard Reo's confession. I had to tell my friends! I swerved and dove and pushed myself faster and faster until I crashed through the protective bubble, pulled magical power from the rain again, and transformed back to my regular human self midair. I tumbled to the ground, somersaulted past the fire, and slammed to a stop, spread eagle on my back.

Maple's face appeared over me, Iggy's lantern dangling from her hand. "Are you okay?"

Iggy's eyes twinkled. "You need to work on sticking your landing."

Yann and Wiley reached down and took my hands. They hauled me to my feet and Maple dusted the leaves off my back. Misaki and Jun rushed over, along with the other guards and my friends. I locked eyes with Hank for the briefest of moments. His glassy eyes looked me over and his face relaxed, as though he was relieved.

"Well?" Misaki raised her brows at me, impatient.

I opened my mouth to speak, when Kai crashed through the tree line and skidded to a stop inside the magical bubble. Misaki frowned as she looked between us. "What's going on?"

I backed up as Kai stomped straight for me. I pointed a

trembling finger at him and shouted, "Reo confessed to killing his brother!"

Kai stopped in his tracks and everyone seemed to hold their breath.

Misaki's throat bobbed and she turned to face Kai. "Is this true?"

Kai pressed his lips tight together and his chest heaved. He shot me a dirty look, then addressed Misaki. "Yes."

Maple gasped and Ben's jaw dropped. Misaki swayed on her feet. "And you kept this a secret?"

Kai blew out a heavy breath. "Reo came to me, distraught, right after it happened." He licked his lips. "He—he said he'd tried to pull a prank on Misaki. He thought he was tucking stink weed into her pack."

I frowned. "It wasn't her pack, though."

Kai shook his head. "Apparently, Reo saw Misaki digging around in Hank's pack and assumed it was hers."

Misaki shook her head. "But stink weed looks nothing like attrahunt."

Kai shrugged. "He's not the brightest, what can I say?" He scoffed. "Look, the kid came to me horrified. He said he'd done it to be one of us. He thought pranking Misaki would impress his big brother. Instead, it got Sora killed. The poor idiot was so upset, I tried to tell him it wasn't his fault but...." Kai trailed off and shook his head.

Jun stepped forward. "How do you explain this?" He held up Captain Kenta's jade fish necklace.

Kai eyes blazed and his face turned white. "You went through my pack?" His voice was deadly quiet.

Misaki stepped between beefy Kai and tall Jun. "He needed the spices and you'd wandered off. Explain this." Even though he towered above her, she puffed up her chest and stared Kai down. I had to admire her bravery.

Kai took a couple of heaving breaths and looked down. "Look. You got me." His voice came out flat. "I've been working security for Ryuu Tanaka's estate."

Misaki staggered a step back. "That's completely against guard rules. We can't be objective and just if we're being paid by private parties."

Kai shrugged, his eyes still on the ground at his feet. "I know. But my family's dirt poor and he pays well... really well."

Misaki lowered her brows. "Honjo sword well?"

"Yeah, whatever." Kai sighed. "Anyway, I don't know how, but Kenta figured it out and confronted me a couple nights ago when I was on my night shift." He rubbed the back of his buzzed head with one thick hand. "Things got heated and we, uh—we got into it a little. I think I gave him a black eye."

Misaki dug her nails into her palms, her face dark.

"Anyway, he said he was disappointed in me. That'd we talk later, and he stalked off. Said something about checking the traps." Kai's eyes flicked to Misaki's face, then back down again. "After he left, I saw his necklace on the ground. It must've come off during our scuffle. I knew how important it was to him and I started feeling bad about the whole thing, so I grabbed it to give it to him when I saw him next. But that's the last time I saw him. He disappeared that night."

Misaki's eyes blazed. "I'm not sure I believe you."

Kai shrugged and stared her in the eyes. "Well, it's the truth."

Their chests heaved.

"My money's on Misaki for the stare-off," Iggy whispered.

Kai stalked forward towards Jun and thrust out his palm.

"Give it back." A muscle jumped in his jaw and he lowered his eyes. "Please. I want to be the one to give it to Captain Kenta when we find him."

Jun's eyes flashed to the seething Misaki, then to Kai, who stood with his head hung. He sighed, then handed the necklace over to Kai. "We can sort this later, but where *is* Reo?"

Kai's throat bobbed. "I took off after her." He jerked his shaved head in my direction. "He said he'd be right behind me."

Misaki and Jun exchanged looks.

Misaki bounced on her toes. "Reo's alone in the woods?"

Kai nodded.

"Let's go find him." She sprinted off, and the rest of us rushed off behind her.

18

A CONFESSION

We crashed through the wet, soggy forest. Rain tumbled down on our heads and hoods. I pushed a branch aside to pass and it sprang back, pelting me with water up the backs of my legs. We hadn't even paused to leave someone behind and tend the camp, just all rushed off to check on Reo. What would it be like for him when he realized we all knew? I frowned as I ran on, my booted feet squishing down into the mud and matted leaves below. He'd seemed tortured, so maybe it would be a relief?

Misaki, Kai and Jun stopped up ahead and froze. I shot a quizzical look at Maple and urged my aching legs forward. I hadn't slept in ages, but the transformation to a bird and the flight back had given me a rush of adrenaline.

I stepped to Jun's side, and Maple and Wiley, with Cat on his shoulders, skidded to a stop beside me. I gasped at the sight and turned to warn Maple, but too late. She covered her mouth and hid her face against Wiley's wet chest. He hugged her tight and used one hand to shield Cat's pug eyes. I, almost against my will, turned to get a second look.

Reo sat propped against the trunk of a tree, his head slumped to his chest and a sword through his stomach. I pressed a trembling hand to my mouth. Jun stepped forward, slowly, cautiously. A quill lay on the ground next to Reo's right hand, which gripped a rolled-up piece of parchment. Jun carefully slid the paper from his hand, then retreated to join the rest of us. He unrolled the parchment and Misaki read over his shoulder.

Kai spoke in a flat, heavy voice. "He said he couldn't take the guilt of accidentally killing Sora...he must've killed himself."

My stomach turned. How horrible.

Misaki dipped her head. "His poor mother—losing two sons the same day?"

Kai dragged a hand across his mouth. "I shouldn't have left him alone."

So that was that, then. Reo had never meant to target Hank. He'd been pranking Misaki to fit in with Kai and Sora, but had accidentally lured the giga deer that killed his brother. And he couldn't take the guilt. I looked down at the dark muddy ground. My heart felt heavy with sadness for the poor kid.

Misaki let out a shaky breath. The branches of the trees whipped and bowed in the strong winds. She glanced up. "The storm's gathering. We only have until the end of day tomorrow, at most, to get the herb and get back to town."

Well, moving right along then. I raised my brows. I knew she was tough, but I couldn't tell if she was stamping down on her feelings to keep the group going, or if she truly could handle this kind of tragedy so easily.

She stared at the ground, deep bags below her eyes. "I'll spell his body hidden. Ben, you send up a marker like Sora's so we can collect him later."

Ben swiped a tear from his cheek and nodded, unable to look at his deceased friend.

Misaki turned to Jun, Kai, and the other two guards. "Get everyone fed. We'll rest for a few hours and see if we can get the herb before night falls."

Jun lifted a brow. "That's risky, climbing to the mountaintop. What if we don't get down before it's dark?"

Misaki sighed and glanced up at the shaking treetops. "I'm afraid if we wait till tomorrow, the winds will be too strong to be in the open."

Jun nodded. "True."

"So no oversleeping." Misaki cleared her throat. "Let's go."

She and Ben lingered beside Reo's body as the rest of us turned back towards camp. I walked along behind Jun and frowned as I noticed him rubbing his fingers together. Red liquid stained the border of his fingernails and he rubbed it off onto his black pants. I squinted in the dim, misty light. Had it been paint? My stomach twisted. Or maybe blood? This whole situation had me on edge.

19

THE PEAK

I awoke to Jun packing up the pots and pans. He moved carefully, but a little clank and bang here and there startled me awake. I blinked and scrubbed at my blurry eyes. I stretched and winced. Every muscle in my body felt stiff and achy—even muscles I didn't know I had hurt. I rolled to my right side and poked Maple. She frowned and peeled one eye open.

"What?" Her voice came out hoarse.

I wanted to sleep for about three more days, and my face felt cold outside my warm and snuggly down sleeping bag. I would've stayed put, nice and cozy, but nature called.

"I have to pee. Do you?"

She grunted. "No. I'm asleep." Her lips barely moved.

I snaked my hand out of my sleeping bag again and poked her. She winced and moaned. "Come on. Please? I don't want to go by myself."

By gigantic effort, Maple dragged herself out of her bedroll and tugged on her boots and jacket. Jun and Misaki moved about, breaking down camp, their swords already strapped to their hips. Lumpy blankets and sleeping rolls littered the ground, where everyone else still slept. I pulled Maple's hood up over her head and lifted Iggy's lantern. "Ready?"

She stifled an enormous yawn with the back of her hand and nodded, her eyes half-closed. I threw an arm around her shoulders and hugged her. "Have I told you lately what a good friend you are?"

She sniffed.

We wandered not too far from camp, took care of business, and then headed back. We'd nearly reached the border of camp, coming in from a slightly different angle, when Maple gasped. She pointed a pale finger through the misty rain at the bare foot that protruded from a tangle of roots.

I jumped and covered my mouth, stifling a little squeal. "What is it? Who is it?" I held Iggy's lantern higher and we edged closer, Maple hanging on to my arm.

"Oh my goddess, it's Sam." I let out a squeaky whimper and Maple and I climbed over the roots. "I'd know those overgrown toenails anywhere."

She sniffed as she combed through the roots, trying to find a way to get to our friend. "He always says snakes don't have nails." Her voice rose with her panic. "So he forgets to cut them."

Iggy snorted. "What's Imogen's excuse then?"

A muffled cry came from inside the tangle of wet, gnarled roots. "Help!"

"Sam!" I peered down through a gap in the roots. Sam's milky blue eyes blinked up at me. "Sam, what's happening?"

"I fell asssleep and now—now I'm trapped!" The whites shone all around his eyes.

"We'll get help!" Maple turned to me wide-eyed. "They'll

hear if we call out." She cupped her hands to her mouth and called towards camp. "Help!"

The roots moved below my hands and closed the opening over Sam's eyes.

"No!" I banged at them. Misaki had earlier forced me to drink the potion that took my powers away, leaving me helpless—again! The roots writhed and wrapped Sam up in a cocoon.

I leapt back and scanned all around. The opening at his feet looked just big enough to allow him to get out—if he acted fast.

"Sam! Change! There's an opening at your feet." My heart thundered in my chest and Maple bit her nails.

"Hold me up!" Iggy pointed at Sam's disappearing foot.

It took me a moment to process, but then I got his meaning. I opened the glass lantern door wider and crouched beside the writhing roots. Iggy crawled to the opening and stretched out, touching the roots. Steam rose from the wet plant and then a high-pitched whine sounded and the roots lurched away from my flame, widening the hole at Sam's feet.

"Now, Sam!" Maple shouted.

I hoped for a small green snake to slither out. If Rhonda had received a vision, despite losing her powers, maybe Sam could still transform, since his nature was shifter. Instead, a wet, naked Sam slid through the opening and landed in the mud at our feet. I looked from him to the cocoon the roots had formed. The pale, translucent shape of Sam's body showed through the gaps—he'd shed his skin. The roots tightened and with a sickening crunch, smashed Sam's shed skin to bits, including the shell of the foot that'd been sticking out.

I gagged.

Misaki jogged up. "What's wrong? I heard a cry?"

Sam scrambled to his feet and hid behind Maple and me, who stood shoulder to shoulder. Misaki frowned at the wet, naked Sam, then at Maple and me. She then glanced at the tree. Her lips quirked to the side. "Listen, I don't want to know what kind of weird stuff you guys are into."

I lifted a palm. "It's not what you—"

She cut me off. "Don't want to know. At all. But that—" She jerked her chin at the tree. "That's a monster tree. You can tell by the teeth."

Oh yeah. It did have sharp teeth in the hollows of the trunk. *Horrifying.*

"So I suggest, whatever freaky stuff you're doing—do it far away from that. It's carnivorous."

I gulped.

She turned to go and Maple and I lingered a moment. I gave Sam my jacket and we made our way back to camp.

"What happened?"

Sam shrugged. "I lay down to take a nap, and when I woke up—there I wasss. The rootsss must have dragged me off." He blinked his milky eyes from Maple to me as rain soaked my bun into a heavy mess and blurred my vision. "Thank you for sssaving me." He looked down. "You too, Iggy."

My flame nodded. "I'm glad you didn't turn into tree food."

We stepped into the warm, dry magical bubble. The others moved about, getting dressed for our afternoon expedition to retrieve the herb and rolling up their beds. Hank frowned when he spotted me, his face drawn with concern. He pressed his lips tight and dipped his chin, back to work packing his bag.

Rhonda sauntered over and looked the pantless Sam

up and down. Luckily, the jacket was long enough to cover all the important parts—barely.

"I like the new look, Sam." She winked. "Rawr!"

Iggy scoffed. "Pervert."

Rhonda leaned closer and looked at Sam's face. "And your skin looks amazing."

"Thanksss," Sam said from under the hood.

Maple and I leaned closer to look. Sam's skin glowed dewy and smooth.

"Snakes. It does." I nodded.

"It's like you got a facial, Sam." Maple smiled.

"I kind of wish I could shed now." I grinned, but Sam paled.

"Ssshh." He held a finger to his lips, but with the pad of it touching his mouth.

So close, Sam.

"I don't want them to know I'm a ssshifter, remember?"

I nodded. "Got it. We won't breath another word of it."

Sam blinked his pale eyes at me.

"But we should probably get you into some pants."

WE BROKE DOWN CAMP, strapped on our boots, and suited up in a fresh change of our black ninja outfits. We marched through the gloomy gray afternoon toward the mountain that loomed up ahead. I blinked up at it, wincing when rain fell in my eye. Wooly gray clouds obscured the peak. I glanced behind us. Barely visible through the treetops, a glowing white orb hovered midair, marking the spot where Reo's body lay. I gulped and faced the narrow, muddy trail ahead. We were on a dangerous trek, and no one was guaranteed to survive it, but I was determined to get my friends and myself back safely.

We marched on to the base of the mountain, then climbed the slippery, narrow path that wound steeply up its rocky slope.

I groaned as I staggered upward. I had to lean way forward and my thighs and calves burned.

"You think this is bad?" Wiley said from behind me, a smile in his voice. His breath came out in short pants. "We still have to get back down."

I moaned. "I think I'll just slide." I struggled to take a breath, the air thin.

"It's not so bad." Rhonda cruised past me, her arms pumping and feet stepping quickly. All she needed was a pink tracksuit to join a morning power walking group. I frowned as she passed me. Then again, the little old ladies probably didn't have a vampire hovering over them. Francis's feet were tucked under Rhonda's armpits and he flapped his gigantic wings as she hiked so that her feet barely touched the ground.

"Cheater," I grumbled.

Finally the path leveled off as we reached the summit. As we'd climbed, the trees had thinned, and now only thick green ground cover blanketed the ground, broken up by gray boulders. The mountaintop lay out before us, craggy and narrow. White, misty clouds drifted across the beautiful, rugged landscape and as they blew to the side, they revealed towering monoliths in the near distance.

Misaki turned to face us. Stray strands of hair whipped across her face. She pointed to the monoliths and shouted to be heard over the wind. "That's where the kusuri grows. Once we're out in the middle, we'll be open to attack from air monsters and anything else. There's no cover."

"And *we* have no magic. This is filling me with confidence." Wiley plastered on a giant grin and Misaki rolled her eyes.

"We're here to protect you. Just be alert."

Wiley saluted her, then hugged an arm around Maple. "We got this. It's almost over."

Blonde hair blew across Maple's face. She pulled it back under her hood and nodded. "I hope so." She lifted the flap to Wiley's pack and Cat popped his always disturbing little face out. She scratched behind his bat ears and he let out a high-pitched groan. His bulging pug eyes closed tight with happiness.

"Hang in there, little sweetie. Just a little further." Maple tucked the flap over him again and we set off across the mountaintop.

The narrow trail only allowed us to walk single file, and was marked by wide, flat stepping stones. The grasses and herbs around us grew to thigh height and thrashed as the wind picked up. The rain came down in buckets, sideways. I glanced back at Wiley and hiked my brows up.

"This is crazy!"

"What?"

I shook my head. "Never mind!" I'd shouted, and he stood only a few paces behind me, but the wind blew so strongly we could barely hear each other. I marched on, Iggy in hand. My foot hit the next wet, muddy rock and slid to the side. My stomach lurched and I threw my arms up to catch myself. I found my footing and let out a shaky breath. To my right, the slope dropped steeply away. Another wrong step like that one and I could find myself falling off the mountainside. I gulped and continued on carefully.

We'd reached about halfway to the monoliths, I guessed, when a thick cloud blew over us. I could barely see my own hands stretched out in front of me. Iggy's flames formed a little bubble of light around us, bouncing off the mist. Goose bumps prickled my arms and legs as the temperature dropped. I glanced back. I couldn't see Wiley, who'd been right behind me, much less the rest of my friends and Hank back there.

He'd left his walking stick at the base of the mountain, telling Francis he felt well enough to go without it. I'd wanted to caution him to bring it, just in case, but I'd pressed my lips tight and held my tongue. He wasn't talking to me, which meant he definitely didn't want my advice. Still, I hoped he was doing all right in this rough terrain.

A deep, grating rumble sounded from somewhere nearby. I froze. "What was that?"

"Thunder?" Iggy squeaked.

It sounded loud enough to be, but though the rains and winds buffeted us around, I'd yet to see any lightning. I took a few more steps and the white cloud around us thinned until I could make out Rhonda and Francis. The deep, scraping noise sounded again and I stopped cold, as did my friends ahead of me.

The cloud drifted away and unveiled a giant rock structure just to the left of our path. The column of stacked boulders loomed above us, stories high. My stomach tightened.

"I don't think that was there before." The cold wind sent raindrops stinging against my face and knuckles. I held Iggy's lantern aloft and squinted into the dim light of the overcast afternoon. A horizontal crack stretched across the top rock.

The stone split, revealing a tooth-filled mouth. The rock creature hissed. Iggy and I screamed.

20

ROCK SNAKE

Misaki and Jun, up ahead, raised their wands and fired spells at the now moving rock column. Glowing orbs of light flew through the air and collided with the stone, to no effect. The wind whipped harder around us. The top rock twisted with a loud grating noise and a forked tongue made of pebbles snaked from the mouth and tasted the air. The head jerked and turned to look straight at Iggy and me. My stomach twisted. I had no powers, no way to defend myself—none of us did.

I cupped my free hand to my mouth and shouted. "Misaki! Give us the antidote!"

Her face turned my way for a brief moment, but she went back to firing spells at the rock creature. A couple of guards burst through the thin mist and shoved past me, wands aloft. They joined the attack, hurling magic at the monster. Rain poured over the creature's gray body, turning the smooth rocks black and mirrorlike. Another deep rumble sounded and the creature uncoiled, lowering its head to the ground. It slithered through the thrashing grasses, nearly disappearing despite its size.

My jaw dropped. "It's a rock snake."

"Rock snake! I call it as a band name!"

I rolled my eyes at Iggy. "Great. But what do we do?"

A clacking noise sounded to my left, the sound of stones banging together. The snake was on the move.

Misaki dashed up to Rhonda and Francis, paused a moment, and then ran up to me and Iggy.

"Here." She pushed a familiar vial of red liquid at me. "Drink it."

I popped off the cork and tipped the spicy liquid down my throat. She moved to run further down the line, but I reached a hand out. "Wait."

She paused, her eyes wide. "What?"

"You're giving us our powers back?" I lifted a brow.

Misaki gave a curt nod. "You'll need them. This thing is strong and it's lethal."

"What's effective against it?"

She snorted. "Nothing. We usually just run from it, it's not that fast. But we're trapped out in the open. We need all the help we can get."

She ran off to give the rest of my friends their magic back. I took a deep breath. It felt good to have my power again. Without it, I felt I'd lost one of my senses. Now I could feel the power coursing through the wind and the rain and the slow rock monster that moved nearby in the grasses.

A faint cry reached me over the howling winds and pounding rain. The rock snake coiled up and lifted its boulder of a head high, its sightless face fixed on Rhonda. The crack that marked its mouth split wider to reveal a moss-covered maw and jagged stone teeth. The guards fired at it and spells ricocheted off its hard body, but it ignored them and tensed up, ready to strike my seer friend. Francis transformed fully into a bat and flapped around its head.

Annoyed, the rock snake snapped at him, and my stomach clenched with fear. Francis managed to stay just out of reach, but I feared for him. I closed my eyes and sought the creature in my mind. I found it, heavy and solid and old. I took a deep inhale and as I pulled in the chilly, damp air, I pulled too from the monster. It wasn't easy, just a little trickle came, but I sipped at it, more and more, hoping to weaken it.

Clacking and grating noises made me open my eyes.

"Imogen." Iggy's voice rose at the end. "What did you do?"

The snake turned away from Rhonda and Francis and the guards who still pelted it with spells and focused on me. Its tongue tasted the air.

"Eep." I froze and dropped the connection between us. But not soon enough. Slowly, the snake slithered over, surprisingly graceful for an enormous creature made of rocks. My breath came in frightened gasps.

Misaki appeared next to me, along with Maple and Wiley, their wands at the ready, except for Maple who sang her spells.

"I could barely pull from it." I blinked at Maple.

The color drained from her wet face. Then her eyes lit up. "I have an idea."

As the snake approached, Misaki and Wiley fired at it. It didn't even appear to notice, just kept coming closer and closer. Hank jogged up to us, holding the spot on his ribs where he'd been lanced. The wind blew his hood back and rain trickled down his handsome face. Grrr. Even when I was mad at him, I found him handsome.

He held his big palms up, closed his eyes, and fired a spell at the monster. Ice covered the boulders that made up its segmented body. Maple glanced up from fidgeting with

Wiley's pack, then went back to work opening the draw-string top. The creature literally froze for a moment. Then cracks appeared in the ice, and the spell shattered. The monster came for us, moving again, even faster than before.

"Ha!" Maple's white fingers pulled open the pack and Cat sprang out. "Sic 'em, boy!"

I raised my brows at her.

She shrugged. "They said he was the most powerful creature on the island. Maybe he can stop it." She turned to her little pet and frowned as Cat scampered toward the giant snake. "Not too close! Be careful! Oh." She bit her nails.

Cat bounded up to the creature and stared at it. The eyeless snake paused and hissed. They stayed that way, very still, for several long moments in a standoff. The guards and my friends stopped their barrage of spells to watch.

"What's he doing?" I barely dared to breathe the words, afraid to break whatever trance the snake was in.

Maple shrugged, but Misaki glanced over. "Your Cat, as you call him, has the power of mind control."

"Ha!" Iggy burst out with a humorless laugh. "Oh good. It gets better."

But Maple and Wiley exchanged impressed glances.

Wiley nodded like a proud father. "I always knew our little guy was special."

Misaki frowned. "Though it usually works when you stare into the creature's eyes... this rock snake has none."

The rock snake shook its stone head, and dropped its jaw. It hissed, bits of moss and pebbles flying from its mouth

"I don't think it worked." I backed away.

The snake opened its mouth wide, moss and greenery dripping from its jaws. Cat whimpered and bounded back to us, his ears pressed down flat. He scampered up Maple's leg and into her arms.

"You did your best." Maple nuzzled the wet, shaggy creature, who petted her face with a weird little monkey hand.

"Pets shouldn't pet you back." Iggy shook his flame head. "I'm just saying."

"Bigger problems." I shrieked as the snake coiled and struck. I dove to the right with Misaki, as Maple, Wiley, and Hank scattered left. The snake slammed into the ground where we'd been, splitting the rocks that marked the path with a loud *POP*!

Now the snake swung its head right and left. It'd split our group into two, cutting me, Francis, Rhonda, and all the guards off from the way back. Francis spun back into man form, his toes hovering above the ground again.

I frowned. "What works against rocks?"

"Paper?" Iggy burst into giggles.

I shook my head at him. I didn't even have words.

A shout made me spin around. Rain stung my cheeks as the wind howled and shrubs thrashed around us. The snake lifted its head, focused sightlessly straight at Hank who stood with arms wide, protecting Sam. My heart tightened. Despite all that had been going on between us lately, I couldn't deny it. Hank was an amazing man, and I loved him. And I was about to watch a monster strike him down.

I opened my mouth and screamed, "No!" But the wind carried my voice away so that even I barely heard myself. Francis transformed into a bat in a whirl of black magic, but the winds immediately threw him to the ground, and Rhonda dove to his side. I looked away from them, back to the snake. Spells hit it, to no avail.

It opened its mouth, body tensed.

"No!" I wailed.

And suddenly Sam was gone. I squinted, struggling to see through the rain and misty clouds. Then I spotted him. A small green snake slithered around Hank's booted feet, straight towards the rock snake. "What is Sam doing?" My heart stopped.

The little green snake that was Sam slithered in spiraling circles. He stopped and his pink tongue flicked out, tasting the air. Then he coiled himself up in a little ball, closed his eyes, and stayed still a moment. The rock snake cocked its head and tasted the air, apparently fascinated.

I frowned. Was he flirting?

Sam uncoiled himself and slithered in winding patterns up to the rock monster. He got closer and closer and I held my breath, hoping with all I had that Sam knew what he was doing. Sam reached the base of one of the boulders and nuzzled his face against it.

GRRRRIICCCKKK. The rock snake shifted and lowered its head, right next to Sam. Sam rubbed his face against the monster's, and the creature let out a deep grunt.

My jaw dropped. "I think it's smiling."

As Sam and the rock snake cuddled, Hank, Wiley, Maple, Cat, Yann, and Annie snuck by and joined us. We all moved further up the path, then looked back, huddled against the side of a towering boulder that partly shielded us from the wind and rain. After a moment, the rock snake slithered back to the spot it'd been, its rocks clacking and scraping. It coiled up among some smaller boulders and settled its head on its tail. Sam, the little green snake, slithered up the path until he stopped right before us. In a breeze of magic, he transformed back to his human form. Rain plastered his thin hair to his scalp and blurred his glasses. He slumped his shoulders and hung his head.

"Now you know."

My friends and I exchanged confused looks, then pounced on him. We wrapped him up in the middle of a group hug.

"Sam, you were amazing." I hugged him tight, my arms around his middle.

"You saved us, Sam." Maple kissed his cheek and a rosy blush spread across his pale, wet face.

Wiley ruffled his hair, Hank squeezed his shoulder, and Yann grabbed him in a big bear hug that lifted Sam off his feet. When he plunked Sam back down, we all spun to face the stunned guards.

Misaki blinked. "This whole time? You're a shifter?"

Sam sniffed and nodded, then dropped his chin to his chest.

She stepped forward. "How'd you know that would work?"

Sam looked up slightly. "Ssshe had her eggsss nearby in her nessst." Sam pointed at the circle of boulders that surrounded the now peaceful rock snake. "I thought ssshe mussst jussst be protecting them. Maybe ssshe'd feel more friendly towardsss me, becaussse I'd look like a baby sssnake."

My heart ached.

Maple clasped her hands together under her chin and her eyes shone. "Awwww."

Misaki stared at him another moment, then her face broke out into a huge smile. She threw her head back to the gray stormy skies and laughed. She pressed her gloved hand to her chest. "That is possibly both the bravest and cutest thing I've ever heard."

Sam jerked his head up and blinked at her. Misaki grinned at him. "Well done, Sam."

His chin quavered. "Y-you don't care that I'm a ssshifter?"

Jun came up beside her, grinning. "You have the powers of a wizard and an animal? That's pretty badass."

Tears trickled down Sam's face, mingling with the raindrops. "B-but I wasss ssso afraid. You hate the monssstersss. I thought you'd hate me."

Misaki and Jun exchanged looks. Misaki's face softened and she stepped closer, taking Sam's hands. "We don't hate the monsters." The wind whipped stray tendrils of black hair across her face. "We find the king who set them on us pretty evil, but not the monsters themselves." She shrugged. "They're just animals." She grinned and jerked her head toward the rock snake. "Like your mama snake over there. You're a special person. Don't feel bad about who you are."

"Touching." Kai raised his brows. "Should we get on with it?"

Misaki sighed and gave Sam a little nod, then turned and moved to the front of the line again. I squeezed Sam's hand and he beamed, his nonexistent chin held high. "Ssshe called me a ssspecial persssson."

"You are, Sam." I smiled at him. Or at least that's the expression I was going for. My face was numb from the wet and cold.

Misaki turned back and called over her shoulder, "Let's go get that herb!"

Rhonda strolled past, arm in arm with the floating Francis (who now had arms again). "Yes, let's get that herb." She winked. "It's 4:20 somewhere."

21

THE KUSURI HERB

I hefted my pack higher up my shoulders and marched on, single file, behind Francis, whose toes trailed above the slippery stone markers. I leaned forward into the wind and staggered right and left as I fought to place one foot in front of the other.

Dangling from my hand in his lantern, Iggy pointed forward. "Mush!"

"I'll mush you," I grumbled.

"Ew. Not interested."

I rolled my eyes, surprised he'd even heard me over the howling winds. "I said mush, not 'smush.' We're not in the mermaid kingdom. Get your mind out of the gutter."

Iggy cackled.

Nerves on edge, I glanced right and left, peering through the pale gray mist that drifted across the mountaintop. Monsters could be lurking anywhere, ready to strike or swoop down on us from the skies.

Up ahead, Cat perched on Wiley's tall shoulders. The little creature looked around with a toothy grin and scratched behind Wiley's ear. I shook my head. Maybe the

Badlanders were confused. So far, Cat didn't seem all that powerful to me.

With ears pricked and shoulders tensed, we finally reached the base of the stone monoliths. The grouping of tall boulders shot out of the mountain at odd angles, some piled on top of each other and looking for all the world like that stone snake.

I narrowed my eyes. "Did that one move?"

Misaki pulled us all into a huddle. "The kusuri has black flowers and pointed leaves." We bent our heads together to hear her. The wind whipped across our backs and rain pelted our hoods. I held on to Rhonda and Sam at my sides to keep from being blown over. "Pick as much of it as you can. We can only linger a few minutes." She glanced up at the darkening, cloudy sky. "We've got *maybe* an hour of light left to get back down the mountain and find shelter. Go!"

The guards turned and bent low to hike the steep slopes up to the rocks themselves.

"No hands in the middle cheer?" I grinned. My friends just shook their heads at me.

"Why do you love that so much?" Iggy shook his little flame head.

I shrugged. "You have to admit, it's kinda fun." I shuddered. The temperature had dropped and I felt colder standing still than I had while hiking.

"If you say so," Rhonda muttered as she wandered off.

I took a deep breath and started up the slope. We had to go off trail here, and the heavy rains had softened the ground to slick mud. I grasped at the tangled ground cover with my free hand as I climbed.

I headed for a tall rock, black and shiny in the rain, with a vertical crack running through it. Misaki had mentioned before that the herb was said to be so strong it could split rock—maybe some of the plant grew in the opening of this one. I'd nearly reached it when the muddy ground gave way under my foot. I fell hard on my stomach and slid down the steep slope, feet first toward the path and the cliff's edge just beyond it.

I gasped for breath as my brain fought to make sense of the topsy-turvy world. A strong hand closed around my own. With a slight jolt to my shoulder, I jerked to a stop and hung still, panting.

I looked up and found Hank standing over me. A muscle jumped in his jaw as he stared at me with those bright blue eyes. His hand tightened around my own and he turned more fully to face me, testing his footing. Then he reached down, grabbed me under my other arm, and hauled me upright. I stood chest to chest with Hank as the rain buffeted us from all sides. Rain poured down our hoods and faces.

Hank looked me up and down, his eyes tight with worry. "Be careful."

I nodded. "Thanks for grabbing me."

A smile tugged at the corner of Hank's mouth. "May I?" He gestured at my mud-smeared front. Black soil and bits of plants covered me and even Iggy couldn't see out the glass of his lantern, it was so covered in mud.

I cleared my tight throat and managed a smile. "Sure."

Hanks stretched his palms open and my skin tingled with the effects of magic. I guess Misaki and the others had decided to let us keep our powers for now. Either that, or they'd forgotten to take them back, and I wasn't about to remind them. I found myself, and Iggy's lantern, suddenly free of mud. "Thanks."

Hank nodded.

And... it got awkward. I lowered my eyes to his chest. There was so much that needed to be said, but I didn't really want to say any of it. I just wanted things to go back to normal between us.

"Imogen."

I jerked my head up.

Rain trickled down his pale face and big, red nose. *He must be cold.* Tears welled in his eyes. "I know that we need to—"

CRACK!

In a blinding flash of light, a bolt of lightning struck the boulder I'd been climbing toward and split it in two. Hank threw an arm over my shoulder and pulled me to the ground with him. We lay flat—and once again, I was covered in mud.

My chest heaved and I could feel the electricity in the air through the raised hairs on the back of my neck and arms. A split second later a booming clap of thunder sounded, like someone had pounded a timpani right next to my head. I cowered lower to the ground as it reverberated through my chest.

"Imogen."

I turned my face to Hank. Mud spattered his cheeks and the tip of his nose. "We've got to find cover."

I nodded. He took my free hand and helped me to my feet. My legs wobbled below me. I glanced toward the sizzling black ground by the boulder. If I hadn't slipped, that's probably where I would've been standing when the lightning struck. My stomach twisted, and I thought I might be sick.

Hank stepped down the slope, skidding and slipping as he went, but he managed to help steady me as I picked my way down behind him. Hopefully some of the others had managed to grab some kusuri herb.

I found Maple, Wiley, and Sam waiting back on the

stone-lined path. Maple spotted my hand linked in Hank's and her blonde brows jumped. She gave me a wide-eyed look and I pressed my lips together and shrugged. I had no idea what was going on, but getting out of this lightning storm was first priority. I'd figure out my relationship issues later.

"We've got to get off this mountain and into tree cover." Hank and I leaned close to the others so they could hear him over the wind.

Wiley nodded and held up a handful of stalks with black flowers and pointed leaves. "We got some."

Maple held up some more. "Me, too."

More blossoms burst from Sam's pockets.

"Good." I shrugged. "I don't know how much they need, but hopefully this will do it." I frowned and looked around. "Where's everyone else?"

Despite the raging storm and worry tugging at my gut, I couldn't help but be very aware that Hank hadn't let go of my hand and continued to hold it tight. I tamped down a smile as happy tingles floated through me. I knew nothing was fixed yet, but I had a little hope again.

Rhonda and Francis half-skipped down the slope next, with Francis easing Rhonda's way by floating her off the ground with him whenever she might have stumbled. Then Annie and Yann joined us from around a hill. Annie sniffed at the steep slope as Rhonda and Francis careened to the bottom.

"Hmph. We went for the low-hanging fruit." Annie nodded at Yann, who held up an enormous armful of the herb. "There's some growing just beside the path up there."

I grinned. "Nice job."

Misaki, Jun, and the rest of the guards rejoined us next,

some from around the hill, others down the mountainside. Kai trailed behind, his wand held at his side.

Misaki reached us first. "Everyone get some?" She looked around, out of breath.

"For the most part." Annie pointed at Yann's enormous bundle of it.

Misaki raised her brows. "Impressive."

Iggy turned to Hank and me. "Slackers."

Jun came up next, taller still than Hank or Wiley. He looked around at everyone's collection of kusuri. "Good work. We've got plenty."

Misaki turned back the way we'd come. "Let's go."

Hank and I, still hand in hand, turned to follow, our friends right behind us. We'd barely gone ten steps when the hairs on my neck rose, the air buzzed with electricity, and a blinding flash of hot bright light blinded me. The booming thunder sounded immediately and I cowered down. I blinked and tried to clear the afterimage of Misaki's boots that floated around my field of vision, the last thing I'd seen before the lightning strike.

"Run!"

More thunder came, or at least it sounded like thunder. Hank dragged me forward and I stumbled, trying to keep up. I finally blinked my eyes clear and looked back over my shoulder. My breath caught.

A black mark scorched the hillside above where we'd been standing. Another bolt zigzagged down from the sky and struck close to where the first had. It hit one of the giant stone monoliths and split it, sending the halves tumbling down the hillside. I caught sight of Kai, standing on the path, wand raised, just before the boulders slammed to a stop, cutting him off from the rest of us. More lightning and more rocks followed, burying the path in an avalanche and tumbling over the cliffside.

Misaki spun around and held her wand to her throat. "Kai!" Her voice was amplified loud enough to be heard over the deafening thunder and tumult from the falling rocks.

"I'm okay," came the amplified response. "Go back to town. I'll find another way down and follow back."

Between the rocks blocking the path and the lightning striking the hillside, there was no way he could come this way and survive it.

Misaki set her jaw. "Good luck!" She lowered her wand and addressed us. Everyone else had managed to follow her unharmed. "We need to get down, and quick, but be careful. The path is slippery." She winced as another bolt of lightning struck the hillside between Kai and the rest of us. She muttered to Jun. "This much lightning is unusual for a typhoon."

He nodded. "It's happened before, though."

Misaki gave each of us a serious look. "Carefully, now. Let's go."

"Wait!"

I turned around. Maple's blue eyes looked huge on her face and she clasped her hands together under her chin. "We can't find Cat."

Wiley had spun his backpack around to hang from his front. He dug through it, handing bunches of black flowers to Maple, then shook his head. "He must've jumped out when we were picking kusuri."

We all turned to look at the hillside. The storms still raged all around, though the lightning seemed to have paused. A pile of rocks covered the slope and completely blocked the path below.

"He could be trapped." Maple sobbed and Wiley hugged her tight to his side.

My stomach twisted, and Iggy and I exchanged worried looks. Neither of us was a big fan of the little creature, but still, I didn't want him hurt. And even more than that, I didn't want Maple to be so sad. I left Hank's side and rubbed my friend's shoulder.

"Hey. They said he's the most powerful monster on the whole island. He'll be okay, right?" I turned to Misaki and raised my brows, hoping she'd jump in and make Maple feel better.

Misaki sighed. "He has mind control powers. I doubt that's going to help in an avalanche."

My face fell and I leveled her with a flat look.

She frowned and then realized what she'd done with a little jerk. "Oh, uh. I mean, yeah. He'll—he'll be, you know, okay."

I shook my head. So unconvincing.

Maple's shoulders shook as she sobbed against Wiley's side. "Poor little g-guy. H-he's probably s-so scared and alone."

Francis drifted over. "I might be able to assist. I'll fly back and see if—"

Rhonda shook her head, which sent her braids flying. "Nope. You'll break your wings in this wind, not to mention the lightning." She slid her arms around his thin middle and cooed up at him. "I know Maple's worried about her little creature, but I'm worried about mine, too."

They were so weird. But Rhonda had a point. Though that gave me an idea, one I wasn't all that excited about.

I held up my free hand. "Look, you all know I'm not the hugest Cat fan, and this"—I gestured at the lightning storm avalanche pile—"is frankly terrifying, but if you want me to risk my life and see if this very independent wild animal is okay, I could change into a little animal." I glanced at Rhonda and Francis. "Nonflying, of course, and see if I can squeeze through the cracks of the precarious rock pile to check on him." Hopefully I'd laid it on thick enough that Maple would see the wisdom of trusting that Cat could take care of himself and choose not to risk her friend's life.

Maple looked away from Wiley's jacket and gasped, a huge smile on her face. "You would do that for Cat?" She threw her arms around me in a tight hug. "You're the best."

I gingerly patted her shoulder. "Well, if I do it, it'll be for you, not Cat."

She smiled against my shoulder. "Oh, Imogen, you softie. I know deep down you love that little guy."

"Eh." Iggy and I exchanged doubtful looks.

Maple pulled back and held my hands. "Please be careful."

Part of me softened. "Of course I will." I squeezed her hands.

"Because you'll be in animal form and you might scare him."

My face fell. "Gee. Thanks for the concern."

Her face lit up. "Oh, I have an idea." She unwound the black woolen scarf she wore from around her neck and wrapped it around mine. "This way he'll smell my scent on you and trust you."

Misaki cleared her throat. "We need to hurry if this is happening."

"You know I love you." Maple hugged me again. "But he's just our little baby."

She slid an arm around Wiley's waist and they both pouted at me, genuinely distraught for their little Frankenstein's monster of a pet.

"Okay." I shrugged, resigned. "I guess I'm doing this."

"I'm coming, too." Sam stepped forward. "Let'sss go assss sssnakesss. We can ssslither through the cracksss."

I lifted my brows and grinned. "Thanks, Sam. That's a good idea."

"Wait." The chatter stopped as Hank walked up to me. "This is dangerous. You shouldn't be risking your life, but if you are, I'm coming, too."

My stomach fluttered and I bit my lip as I looked up into his rain-streaked face. "Thanks. I could use a sidekick." I hoped that wasn't too much teasing, too soon. We were just getting our groove back.

A smile tugged at the corner of his mouth. "You can *think* I'm the sidekick if it makes you feel better about being *my* sidekick."

I grinned back. "*Right*." I put my hand out. "Team snakes on three. One—" I looked at Sam and Hank. "Come on, guys, hands in."

Rhonda put her hands on Sam's slim shoulders. "Don't feel pressured to do anything you don't want to."

I dropped my arm to my side. "Oh, come on. Really?"

Rhonda snickered.

I handed Iggy over to Maple. As she took him she leaned close to be heard over the raging wind, her eyes serious. "If he won't come to you, try calling him 'kitty Cat, piggle wiggle.' He always runs right over when Wiley or I call him that. But you have to sing it. Like—"

She opened her mouth, but I just shook my head. "Nope. I can't with that."

Iggy opened his eyes wide in mock innocence. "Oh, come on, Imogen. Let's sing." He bounced his head side to side with his little tune. "*Kitty Cat, piggle wiggle*." He stopped and scrunched up his face. "Ew. Even as a joke it just tastes bad in the mouth."

I grinned and moved next to Sam and Hank. "All right, team snakes. Let's do this."

I closed my eyes and exhaled, preparing to suck in magical energy with my inhale.

"Thing is—"

I peeled an eye open.

Hank slid a hand under his hood and rubbed the back of his neck. "I don't actually know the spell."

I lifted my brows. That's right, I'd forgotten. I licked my lips, trying to remember how Horace had taught me. "Well... hm... it's just like any other spell, really, you just have to visualize what you want to be. You know, like what it feels like to have no arms or legs, to scent with your tongue. And—then you're a snake." I shrugged.

"O-kay." Hank nodded, a crease between his brows. "I can try that."

I closed my eyes again, took a deep breath and sensed the immense power of the hurricane building around us. In a flurry of magical wind, I opened my eyes and found myself looking up at all my friends, who towered above me. I lifted my head and wiggled my tongue around in the air. I could smell-taste Sam to my right. I looked over and found a green snake my size looking back at me. The ground vibrated below me, medium shakes when my friends took a step closer, a giant shake when a bolt of lightning struck the ground.

I coiled up in fear. After the thunder that followed, I lifted my head and looked around, tasting the air with the long, forked tongue that slid out from my mouth. Where was snake Hank?

I scented him and uncoiled further, lifting my head

higher to see. My eyes widened when I spotted him, still standing tall above me. He looked at his hands, the whites showing around his pupils and his mouth open, aghast. I nodded, bobbing my little snake head. Yeah, I'd had some issues when Horace first taught me, too. Still, Hank's was a pretty spectacular fail. Instead of fingers, ten wriggling snakes sprouted from his palms.

Maple shrieked and jumped back.

The ground rumbled with her footstep. "Hey!" Little snakes down here. But my protest only came out as a hiss.

Maple's face turned down toward Sam and me. "Oh. Sorry, you two." She looked up. "Everyone watch your step."

She sounded so loud, even with all the noise from the wind and rain and thunder.

My friends and the guards gathered closer and looked down at us, though everyone gave Hank and his snake fingers a wide berth.

Jun crouched lower and looked between Sam and me. His face loomed huge above us. "Remarkable."

My tongue snaked out, and Sam and I looked at each other. We needed to get going if we had any chance of finding Cat. The storm was picking up and the light fading. I looked up at Hank. He closed his eyes, a magical wind whipped around him, and this time a second snake head sprouted on his shoulder, as large as his real head.

I would've screamed if I could have, but Maple did it for me. Wiley grunted and stumbled back.

Yann blinked. "Oh my."

The snake head hissed and bared its fangs, sending out a spray of venom. Everyone scattered.

Hank rolled his eyes and squared his jaw. He reached up a hand and clamped the snake's mouth shut. "I just haven't practiced it. I just need another try, I'll get it." His voice came out tight. He tried again, and again, but ended up with scales all over his body, a snake tail, and finally managed to shrink himself down to snake size but in human form.

"This could work." He gave me a half-hearted shrug. "I could squeeze through the rocks."

I frowned.

He started toward the avalanche, but his tiny legs sank in the mud and he fell face-first into a puddle the size of his entire body. Francis reached down and plucked him up by his pack, then righted him. Hank's face darkened behind all the mud. "It'll work. I'll get it."

I slithered over and gave him a nuzzle with my scaly head. I wanted to tell him that we were just going to check on Cat, make sure he was all right, and we'd be back in minutes. That it was all right if he hadn't mastered the spell yet, I'd be okay with Sam. But I couldn't speak, so I tried for an encouraging smile.

He lifted a thick brow, so I wasn't sure that expression translated on my snake face, but it was time to go, either way. I nodded at Sam and we slithered off toward the avalanche.

Maple knelt down beside tiny Hank. "They'll be okay."

Sam and I slithered across the muddy path, quick and fluid, straight toward the enormous rocks that blocked our path. My stomach tightened as we neared. Despite all my misgivings, I hoped we'd find Cat... and that he'd be okay.

22

SLITHERIN'

I t took Sam and me some time to make our way through the tangle of rocks. Rain dripped down through the labyrinth of cracks, but the boulders mostly shielded us from the wind and lightning. Still, as I slid over and under and turned around when I hit dead ends, I hoped that no more lightning would strike and send boulders falling down on us. Call me crazy, but I didn't feel like being crushed to death in snake form.

By the time we made our way through, the storm and the deepening dusk left us only dim light to see by.

We spun back into human form and searched all around. The rain continued to pound down, obscuring any tracks. I cupped my hands to my mouth. "Cat!" I turned. "Cat!" I listened for a response of any kind, but heard nothing over the howling wind and rush of rain. I sighed and rolled my eyes, then cupped my hands again. "Kitty Cat Piggle Wiggle?" Nothing.

"Imogen." Sam ran up and tapped my shoulder. I followed him down the path and around a hill. "Look." He pointed down the mountainside.

I squinted in the blue, dim light. I thought I could spot a figure making its way down. I blinked. "That must be Kai."

Sam nodded. "Yesss. But look in hisss pack."

I shook my head. "I can't see that far."

"Ussse a magnifying ssspell."

Oh. Duh. I had my magic back. I kept forgetting. I frowned. I'd never tried this spell before, but I imagined looking through binoculars with spotlights on them and pulled magic to me. I opened my eyes and jumped. A bush loomed before me, close and sort of blurry. "Uh. What am I looking at?"

Sam gently took my head in his slender, cold hands and turned my head slightly to the left. "Do you sssee him?"

I squinted and the world came into focus. "Yeah." Wow, it'd worked. Kai bounded down the path, glancing back every few steps as though he were being pursued. Weird. Sam had mentioned his pack, so I looked closer. It seemed fuller than it had before and something stuck out of the top. It looked like a stick or a piece of dark rope or— I gasped. Cat's arm protruded from the pack, limp and bouncing with each step. I'd know that weird little monkey paw anywhere.

"He's got Cat." I watched as Kai neared a fork in the path.

"Maybe that meansss Cat'sss sssafe?" Sam said, beside me.

I wasn't so sure. From our vantage at the peak of the mountain I could see that the left path of the fork wound around the base of the mountain and led into the forest, back toward the town. The right path went straight into the forest below, deeper into the heart of the island. When Kai reached the fork, he cast one last look back, then dashed down the right path—away from the village. I gasped again, pulled magic to me, and reverted back to my normal eyesight. The transition was jarring and my stomach twisted with nausea. I pressed a hand to my middle and gulped. "Sam. He isn't heading back like he said he was."

Sam's milky blue eyes widened behind his thick glasses. "What isss he doing?"

I looked the way Kai had gone, but he'd already disappeared into the trees that grew up the base of the mountain. I shook my head. "I don't know, but I don't have a good feeling about it. I think he's up to something."

Sam gasped. "Sssomething bad?"

"Yeah, Sam." I set my jaw. "Something bad."

I glanced back at the avalanche. "We should tell the others, but I'm afraid we'll lose him if we don't go after him now." I shook my head.

Sam shrugged. "We could follow asss animalsss and track hisss ssscent."

I frowned. "Won't we lose it in all this rain?"

My friend shook his head. "No."

"Oh. Well. Okay, then." I shrugged. He was the snake, after all; I'd trust his judgment.

We flew back into snake form and made our way through the rock pile. It was faster going this time, as we were able to scent the path we'd taken through and retrace our steps— well, slithers. When we reached the other side and returned to human form, our friends and the guards rushed around us.

"Did you find him?" Maple grimaced. "Is he okay?"

Wiley held her close and waited breathlessly for an answer.

I took a deep breath. "Kai has him."

"Oh good." Ben nodded.

I shook my head at the young guard. "Maybe not. Cat seemed unconscious."

Maple gasped.

"He was hurt?" Jun asked.

I bit my lip. "Kai headed deeper into the forest instead of taking the path back to town."

Jun and Misaki looked at each other, eyes wide.

"Where could he be going?"

I glanced at Maple. She looked ill with worry.

Misaki shook her head. "The only thing down that path is the ruins of the old magic rock mining town. No one goes there."

I drew myself up taller.

"Sam and I are going to follow him."

Hank's brows pinched together. "Wait for me to figure this sssssspell out. I'll go with you."

A forked tongue slithered out from between his lips and I couldn't help but crack a smile. "You're still trying?"

"This whole time." Iggy shuddered. "I've seen some things I can never unsee."

I addressed the group. "Try to find a way through and follow us."

Jun nodded and looked toward the slope above the path. "The lightning seems to have stopped. We might be able to go over and around, but it'll take some time." A muscle in his jaw jumped. "Especially in the dark."

My eyes darted past him to the setting sun, barely visible through the clouds. I nodded. "Be safe."

Maple squeezed my hands. "You, too." She hugged Sam.

Hank stalked up, threw his big arms around me, and pulled me tight against him. He didn't let go. Even though I couldn't breathe, I'd never felt more relieved. "I know everything's not settled between us, but... we'll get there." He leaned back and took my cheeks in his hands. He searched my face. "Don't do anything reckless."

I scrunched up my nose. "Like breaking into prison? Or running down the side of a volcano? Or—"

He lifted a thick brow. "Yes. Like those." He leaned his forehead against mine. "Imogen. I love you."

My stomach fluttered and happiness coursed through me. He was right. We still had a lot of explaining to do, but it felt so good to hear him say those words.

"I love you, too."

The rain poured over us, but I didn't care. Hank and I would be okay.

A light touch on the end of my nose startled my eyes open. Hank's forked tongue disappeared into his mouth as I wiped my nose and grinned. "That tickled."

A deep pink blushed over his cheeks and throat. "Sorry. I don't have this down yet."

I gave him one last smile, then turned with Sam toward the rock pile. "We'll see you guys soon. Hurry."

With that, Sam and I changed and slithered our way back through the rocks. On the other side, we paused.

"I think I should change into something faster so we can catch up with him." Kai had already disappeared into the tree line far below. I lifted a finger. "And I refuse to use the speed spell."

Sam nodded his agreement. "Bearsss are fassst."

I lifted my brows. That was a pretty good idea.

Minutes later, I barreled down the mountain as a giant bear with shaggy auburn fur. Sam could have ridden me in human form, but it would've slowed us down, so I carried him gingerly between my jaws in snake form.

I galloped toward the tree line, my bear nose wiggling this way and that, smelling the pungent trail of an unshowered Kai, his pack full of sweet-smelling kusuri, and of course, Cat's ferret-like scent.

I grinned inwardly as I pictured us. Just a bear/human hybrid carrying a snake/human in its mouth, running down a mountain during a hurricane. *Nothing to see here, folks.*

I pushed on, my clawed paws splashing in the muddy puddles, eager to find Kai and discover what he was up to.

23

DOWN THE RABBIT HOLE

S am and I followed Kai until a clearing came into view ahead. I paused in bear form at the edge of the tree line, Sam still hanging as a snake from my mouth. Kai continued on in front of us, Cat's hand still dangling from his pack. A broken wooden ramp sloped down into a large hole in the rocky side of a mountain. A rusty mining cart perched on the ramp above the opening.

Kai jogged through the sideways rain and paused at the entrance, which was lit by torches burning on either side. Two tall, burly men dressed in head-to-toe gold stood guard beside the hole in the rock, their wands held at the ready. I squinted. Kai exchanged a few words with the one the left. The guard nodded and stepped aside and Kai disappeared into the hole. We had to follow him, but how would we get past the guards?

I frowned as Sam, still in snake form, wriggled a little in my mouth. Kinda gross. I lowered my shaggy bear head and set him down as gently as I could. The little green snake that was Sam whirled in a twist of magic back to man form. I closed my eyes, pulled from the torrential rain, and opened them again. I wiggled my human fingers in front of my face and arched my back. It felt good to be me again.

"Ssshould we sssneak in?" Sam lifted his brows.

I nodded. "Misaki mentioned this path led to an old mining town—this must be one of the mines." I shuddered as I imagined entering the cold, spider-infested hole. I felt pretty certain there would be spiders.

"Okay." Sam pushed his glasses up his nose. "I'll be a sssnake again. What will you be?"

I shrugged. "I'll follow suit. Snakes it is, you trendsetter."

Sam flushed pink.

I squeezed his shoulder. "I'm glad you're here with me. This would be a lot scarier on my own."

He dipped his chin and his glasses slid down his nose, but I caught a big smile on his face. "Me, too."

We magically transformed into snakes and slithered the long way around, sticking to the trees as long as possible. Night had come quickly in the forest, the deep shadows of dusk melting together and eating up all the light.

I'd been grateful for my keen bear sense of smell—I'd have felt blind otherwise. Now, the darkness provided us extra cover as Sam slithered out of the trees ahead of me. As the guards looked out into the night, we skirted along the edge of the mountain and slid into the old mining shaft behind them. I let go of the breath I'd been holding once we made it past the entrance.

The tunnel went on, deep into the mountain for a ways. I could feel a rhythmic shaking of the ground coming from below us. What could be happening here?

We kept close to the cold, rough walls, which were studded with flaming torches every twenty feet or so. The old mining cart track had been covered with a velvety golden carpet that led straight back and then down, deep into the bowels of the mountain. What was this place?

I stuck out my forked tongue and tasted the air. Smoke from the torches filled the low-ceilinged tunnel, but under that came another scent, a frightening one—the metallic taste of blood. The orange firelight bounced off the walls and ceiling and sparkled off the black and purple crystals embedded here and there in the walls. I started as a drop of water fell from the ceiling and landed in a puddle beside me. Tiny heart racing, I wiggled faster and caught up with Sam. The deeper in we went, the colder it grew.

After descending quite a ways, the tunnel leveled out and Sam and I slithered around a corner. A giant expanse opened before us. The ceiling of the cave loomed high above; the light from the wall torches and bowls of fire scattered about didn't even reach its height. A cacophony of voices, pounding drums, and guttural animal howls assaulted me, setting my bones rattling. A huge crowd of strange people milled about, some dressed in fine silk and glittering jewelry, while others scuttled about in rags with shifty eyes. Men passed coins back and forth, waiters walked about carrying trays of sparkling drinks, and scantily clad women danced with magical flames. Sam and I exchanged looks. Whatever I'd expected, it wasn't this.

"Hisss." Sam jerked his green head to the right and I followed his gaze. Kai, escorted by a guard dressed in gold, dipped through a doorway cut from the rough stone. I nodded at my snake friend and we slithered on, sticking to the wall of the cave. We skirted the party floor and slipped into the doorway Kai had entered. A heavy gold velvet curtain hung over the entrance and slid over my scales as I moved under it.

Beyond the curtain, the entryway continued as a short

tunnel, and then a bigger stone room opened beyond. Several men, including Kai, stood around an imposing wooden desk. And behind the desk sat Ryuu Tanaka, the rich councilman. My breath caught and I turned to Sam. Without a word, we melted into the shadows of the tunnel and listened.

Ryuu Tanaka steepled his fingers together, his elbows resting on the polished desk. "Did you get it?"

Kai nodded and swung his pack off his back.

"Gently." Ryuu Tanaka half rose from his seat. He settled down when Kai lifted Cat out and set the limp little creature on the desk.

24

RYUU TANAKA

O h, this was definitely not good. I watched carefully and spotted Cat's furry little chest rise, then fall. I let out a breath of relief. He was alive.

Ryuu Tanaka's eyes widened and he lifted an unsteady hand. Slowly, he settled his fingers on Cat's black fur and stroked his side. "You did as I instructed?"

Kai nodded, his back to Sam and me. "Yeah. It worked like you said. The kusuri was like catnip to it. It just went all lazy like this and I grabbed it when the others weren't looking. The storm was perfect cover. I just called down some lightning and caused an avalanche that separated me from them." He gulped. "Then I did like you said and gave it a tranquilizer to keep it knocked out. Just in case."

My breath caught. Sea snakes! Kai had kidnapped Cat for Ryuu Tanaka and caused that lightning storm. But why? I shook my head. There weren't any good possibilities.

The older man practically purred at Cat's lifeless body. "You will be my crowning glory."

Okay, weirdo.

Ryuu Tanaka looked up, a wild gleam to his black eyes. "Well done."

Kai looked down and grunted.

Ryuu's eyes narrowed. "What?"

"Thing is." Kai rubbed the back of his thick neck. "I think Misaki's starting to suspect me."

Ryuu Tanaka grew still. "I thought we agreed you were to deal with her. The lightning didn't work?"

"No. I missed." Kai's words came out in a rush. "I tried before, though, too. I got this kid, Reo, to plant attrahunt in Misaki's pack. I figured it'd lure a monster to her and bam, she's dead, no one suspects a thing. The forest's crawling with monsters."

I froze. Kai was the one who told Reo to plant the herb?

Ryuu Tanaka leaned back. "Why did you involve this Reo person?"

"I figured, hey, in case someone sees something, they see Reo, not me, right? Plus I thought the kid would do anything for me, to fit in. I thought he might be a good recruit for you, too."

Ryuu narrowed his eyes. "Do not ever presume to know my business."

Kai froze. "Yes, sir."

"Proceed."

Kai cleared his throat. "It turned out the pack wasn't Misaki's. She was snooping in the foreign prince's, and when the monster attacked—" He shook his head. "It accidentally killed one of the guards. One of my friends. And— and it was Reo's brother. So then Reo felt guilty and I did everything I could to change his mind, but he wanted to fess up for it, which would've thrown suspicion on me, and—"

Ryuu cut him off. "What did you do?"

My heart thrummed in my chest. Kai had tried to kill

Misaki, not Hank. And he'd been trying to shut Reo up—*that's* why he'd been spending so much time with him, not because he was consoling the poor kid.

"It's fine." Kai lifted his hands. "I'm pretty sure everybody bought it. I stabbed Reo with his own sword, made it look like a suicide. Everybody had seen how messed up he was from his brother, I'm sure they bought it." Kai hunched his shoulders as he waited for the other man's verdict.

I inched back. Kai had killed in cold blood—twice. I glanced at Sam, who stared back at me with huge eyes.

The councilman glared at Kai. "You've made a mess of it all." He narrowed his dark eyes further. "If you're so certain everyone 'bought it,' then why do you believe Misaki suspects you?"

"Er." Kai hung his head and scratched the back of his neck. "She, uh, she figured out something was up when she saw the sword you gave me. I told her I'd been working security shifts for you, like you told me to if anyone ever asked questions." He looked up and his voice came out choked. "I'm going to be kicked out of the guard."

Ryuu Tanaka shrugged. "Who cares? You're making five times your salary being a monsterman with me."

I frowned. Monsterman? That was a profession?

"Besides, here you have fame, glory. In the guard you're just another nameless grain of rice in the bowl."

"What will I tell them? When I don't make it back to town right away?" Kai lifted his thick palms.

Ryuu sniffed. "You'll say your path was blocked by another avalanche or fallen trees or something, and you had to stay out in the forest for a couple days till the storm let up."

Kai jerked his chin at Cat, who lay limp on the desktop. "What about it?"

Ryuu's mouth stretched wide into a cruel grin as he stared down at Maple and Wiley's beloved pet. "Say you saw it run off into the forest." He lifted a brow. "It's a wild animal, after all. It escaped."

I glared at the man. Maple and Wiley would never buy it. I frowned. Then again, it wouldn't matter, because everyone else probably would. I gritted my tiny snake teeth. We had to get Cat out of here.

Kai cleared his throat. When he spoke, his voice cracked. "The-there's one more thing."

Ryuu's face darkened. "What?"

Danger hung in that word.

Kai cleared his throat again. "We— I— Misaki needs to be killed."

Ryuu Tanaka lifted a brow. "I already planned on it. But why?"

Kai shifted on his feet. Ryuu's guards, dressed in gold, stayed perfectly still. "She's uh, she's relentless about finding Captain Kenta."

Ryuu Tanaka nodded. "Yes. That's why I ordered you to take care of her, which you failed at, miserably. But she wanted this little expedition. Perhaps, when she finds nothing, she'll give up and stop being a problem to us."

Kai rubbed his buzzed head. "She did find something, though."

The older man leaned back in his chair and let out a sigh. "I'm growing impatient. Spit it out."

"That night Kenta caught me, I—I took his necklace." Kai's voice grew darker, full of malice. "He loved that stupid thing, paraded it around like, 'ooh, my family's so wealthy and powerful.' How powerful are you now?"

Ryuu Tanaka leaned forward and passed a hand across

his mouth. "You idiot. You not only kept it, but Misaki found it?"

Kai tipped his head to the side and grew contrite again. "Well, Jun found it, but—" He paused. "I made something up real quick, but when she thinks about it, she'll have more questions for me. She won't drop it, I know her."

Ryuu scoffed. "Unbelievable." He shook his head and his lip curled back. "We'll deal with Misaki later. We can probably just blame her death on the foreigners."

I sucked in a little breath. *Hey!*

Ryuu pointed a long finger at Kai. "You're lucky you're my top monsterman."

Was that like a furry fetish thing?

Kai straightened. "Thank you, sir."

If it was, it was apparently a compliment.

Ryuu shook his head. "Don't thank me yet." He leaned forward and the flickering orange light from the torches lit up his eyes with fiery intensity. "Be as brutal as you need, but you'd better make me win tonight." His hand closed into a fist atop his desk. "I keep you on because you're my best trainer. But let me down and I'll find I don't need you around anymore."

He stared at Kai, who held very still. Only the sounds of the burning torches and the dull roar from the crowd outside filled the cool, damp air.

"Understand?" Ryuu's lip curled back into a snarl.

Kai bowed deeply, his forehead almost touching the desk. "I won't let you down, sir."

Ryuu gestured at Cat, then jerked his chin in dismissal. "Prep your monsters. We're starting the fights soon."

Kai grabbed the little guy by an ankle and lowered him back into his pack. He slung the bag over his shoulder and spun on his heel. Sam and I pressed tighter to the wall, hiding in the shadow of the low-ceilinged entryway. Kai took a step toward the door but paused when Ryuu Tanaka spoke again. "That Captain Kenta has been a thorn in my side. Make him pay for it."

I gasped. They still had Captain Kenta?

A ghoulish grin spread across Kai's face. "Yes, sir." He stalked toward the exit, purpose in his step. As he neared, I realized too late that though I'd pulled my upper snake body tight to the wall, I didn't have a good sense of how long I was. My tail trailed out into Kai's path, a fact I realized only a split second before his foot came down hard on my tail. The bottoms of his boots were made of soft leather, otherwise it would've been worse, but still, he was a big guy and the weight of him sent shooting pains throughout my body.

I cried out, a hiss that turned into a yelp as the pain broke my concentration—and my transformation spell! I looked up into Kai's wide-eyed face. His mouth hung open, aghast, his foot still planted heavily on my ankles.

"The foreigner!" Ryuu Tanaka hissed.

I gasped.

"There's another one." Kai pointed at Sam, hunkered against the wall.

"Run, Sam!" Or slither, but whatever.

Sam, the little green snake, made for the exit, moving as fast as lightning. Kai raised his wand, but I grabbed his leg and yanked as hard as I could, which tripped him flat on his back.

"Catch him!" Ryuu Tanaka ordered.

I closed my eyes and pulled power from the roar of the crowd outside, magic to defend myself and Sam. "Ow!" My breath caught and I opened my eyes to find one of the gold-clad guards holding a blow gun aimed right at me. I patted the stinging part of my neck and found a feathered dart in it. "Again? Really?"

My connection to the magic died as I tugged the dart from my neck. It undoubtedly contained the antimagic serum Misaki had hit us with a few days ago. I rolled over and whimpered when I spotted Sam. Three red-feathered darts stuck out from his green scales. The poor little guy looked woozy, slithering in aimless swerving lines.

I gritted my teeth and scurried past the splayed-out Kai. I gently lifted Sam into my lap and carefully pulled out the darts. I stroked his head with my thumb. "It'll be all right, Sam."

Kai shoved to his feet, his face purple with fury. He stalked toward me, and I cradled Sam to my chest, hunkering over him to protect him. Kai's shadow loomed over me and I tensed for a blow. "Where are the others?"

I peeled an eye open, my mind working fast. "They're nearby—and they're bringing even more people, backup." I glared up at the beefy guard.

Kai turned away from me, and he and Ryuu Tanaka exchanged looks.

The older man's face glowed with a sick glee. "They're alone."

Kai sneered, and my stomach sank.

The older man leaned forward. "Shifters, hm? I quite think our audience would enjoy seeing them as bait."

Kai grunted and grinned cruelly at Sam and me. Then he frowned. "But how will the audience know they're shifters—that one just looks like a dumb snake."

"Take them to the stables and get them ready." Ryuu waved a hand, dismissing us. "After you dump them in the pen, we'll hit them with the antidote."

Kai chuckled.

Ryuu Tanaka bit his lip as he looked me over. I willed myself not to shrink back. I lifted my chin and he grinned wider.

"I'll enjoy watching you try to squirm and slither your way out." He glanced at Kai. "Now, go."

The burly guard grabbed me by the collar of my standard-issue ninja shirt and dragged me to my feet. He snatched Sam away and clutched the little snake in his beefy fist.

"Hey! Be careful with him. Don't squeeze so hard."

Kai shook me, then snarled as he dragged me toward the raucous party in the big cave. "Trust me—that's the least of your worries right now."

25

CAPTAIN KENTA

Kai dropped Sam into my hands without warning and shoved me into the giant, barred cage. I stumbled forward, fumbling to keep hold of my snake friend. My feet clanged on the metal grate floor. *BANG!* I hunched up my shoulders and whirled around as Kai slammed the door shut with his wand. *CLICK*. The lock turned, trapping us inside.

He moved off down the line of cages. I held my shivering snake friend close to my chest and edged back toward the stone wall behind me. Bars formed the other three walls of the cage, with more grating above. I let out a shaky breath, the moisture forming mist in the chilly space.

I nearly dropped Sam, my hands shook so badly. I hugged him closer and looked around, every nerve on edge from the monstrous shapes and noises and smells that surrounded us. The cages around us, there had to be at least fifty of them, held monsters of all shapes and sizes.

An enormous black spider with a woman's face and long black hair scuttled around the cage across from us. She fished her legs through the bars and pawed at a dog-sized toad in the cage beside her. The toad cowered, as far from her as it could get. The tips of the spider's spiny legs just barely brushed its shoulder. The little green creature squeezed its eyes shut and let out a continuous whine. A torch on the wall above it illuminated the horrifying scene and the spiderweb of scars, some red and fresh, others old and crusted, on the poor toad's wet skin. When the spider woman failed to catch him, she let out a piercing wail. I frowned—how could she have? Her beautiful, pale face didn't even move. Then I realized—the woman's face was a decoy, a sort of hat it wore above its true face. Dozens of black eyes, like fish eggs, shone in the dim light and its wide mouth split open to wail again.

The hairs rose on the back of my neck.

ROOOAARRR.

I spun. In the cage to my right, a lion with wings lay hog-tied on its back. Its tawny wings beat helplessly against the hard floor, which sent feathers flying. A metal brace held its mouth open while a greasy man with long hair and pale skin held up his wand and used magic to file the creature's teeth to razor-sharp points. I staggered back, and had almost put my back to the cave wall, when I glanced over my shoulder and recoiled.

"Ugh!" I staggered back to the middle of the cage, the grating ringing under my feet. An enormous metal chain with two shackles at the ends hung bolted to the stone wall. Dark red stains surrounded it.

My chest heaved as I spun around, my senses completely overwhelmed. I choked and covered my mouth to keep from being sick when I spotted another man whipping a giant bear that moaned with every lash. Its ribs showed through its brown, matted fur. They must have been starving it.

"Oh, Sam." I held my trembling friend close. "I think we're in trouble this time." Suddenly I remembered that Kai still had Cat in his pack. I rushed forward and slid my head through the bars at the front of the cage. I looked down a long aisle of shrieking monsters and cruel men beating and teasing the beasts. Kai stopped, pulled the limp little guy out of his pack by the ankle, and tossed Cat unceremoniously into a cage. He held his wand up and the door slammed shut.

Chest heaving, I backed away. "Maybe Hank and everyone will get through that avalanche and find us."

Sam blinked up at me. It was hard to tell with his snake face, but he didn't seem convinced. Yeah, I wasn't either. Even if they did find a way through and managed to find this hidden tunnel before the storm broke, then what? This place was packed with armed guards and vicious monsters. I let out a shaky breath. Sam and Cat and I were on our own.

"Hello."

A hoarse, raspy voice startled me and I whirled to the left. A man who looked to be in his early thirties sat in what amounted to a large birdcage hung from the ceiling of the larger pen. He hugged his knees to his chest as an alligator with two heads crawled below him. One head appeared to be asleep, eyes closed, but the other held its triangular mouth open to the sky, right below the man, ready to snap.

The man bowed his head. Sam and I exchanged surprised looks (I assumed, it was hard to tell on a snake), then turned to the man and bowed back. As I took in his raggedy black ninja clothes, realization dawned on me. "Captain Kenta?"

The man sat up straighter, a bit of life coming into his sunken eyes. "You know me?" He had a heavy accent, but still, I was amazed I could understand him.

I nodded. "I've heard of you. You speak English?"

He dipped his pale chin. Bags hung under his eyes and his gray cheeks looked sunken. "I come from a wealthy family. They insisted on a thorough education."

I lifted my brows. Thank goodness, because without that or the magical translation spell, we wouldn't have been able to communicate.

"Where are you from?"

I opened my mouth to answer "St. Louis," but these days, Bijou Mer felt more like home. "The Water Kingdom. My name's Imogen. I came here with others. Misaki and Jun and —" I frowned. "Kai, and the other guards were escorting us to gather kusuri and to look for you."

The man's chest heaved and his face darkened. "And Kai betrayed you?"

I tipped my head side to side. "Yeah. We followed him here and he found us out."

"We?"

I held Sam up. He'd wrapped himself around my wrist. "This is Sam. He's a shifter."

Kenta's eyes widened. "Pleasure to meet you, Sam."

I let out a shaky breath and jumped a little as the winged lion behind me roared again. "What is this?" I used my free hand to gesture around us.

Kenta pressed his pale, chapped lips together. "From what I overhear, it is a monster convention. A huge fighting event organized by Ryuu Tanaka."

I looked around me, my breathing coming in little pants. They planned to fight these monsters? "Why?"

Kenta gave a small shake of his head. "I had no idea this went on, on our island, till those traps started turning up empty. Apparently Ryuu Tanaka recruited Kai to steal monsters for him, to train and fight them. I suspected something when Kai started buying fancy new clothes and showing up for his shifts late and tired. He acted differently too, more confrontational and cocky." Kenta looked down. "I followed him, at night, and found him stealing a monster from a trap. I confronted him, and would've stopped him too, but some of Ryuu Tanaka's goons who were there to transport the monster overpowered me." Kenta scoffed and looked up and away. "He taunted me. Kai loved that he had me caged." He shook his head. "We'd never been close, but I thought the bond of being guards, the honor we shared, meant something to him." His throat bobbed. "He bragged to me that night that he'd been working for Ryuu Tanaka for months, stealing monsters and breeding and training them." He curled his lip back. "By training I mean he tortures them, starves and beats the poor things. They keep bait in their cages, just out of reach." He smirked wryly and gestured at himself, hanging over the two-headed alligator. "To drive them crazy and make them more aggressive."

I shook my head. "This is horrible. Why do all this?"

Kenta shrugged. "They bet on it, *big* bets, so there's lots of money to be made." He sneered. "Ryuu Tanaka's brought several councilmen through on a tour of the stables, as he calls these cages, so I suspect it's a way to network and gain influence, a sort of social club, too."

I shook my head. "That's messed up."

"Kai said he's paid huge bonuses if his monsters win. I think he feels important in this world. He has money, power, prestige." Kenta dragged his hands down his face. "He told me he hated me from the day we met, because I come from a rich family." He pressed his lips tight together and looked away. "As much as I hate him for this, I can't help but feel I should have tried harder to connect with him."

The alligator below Kenta hissed, and Sam wrapped tighter around my wrist.

I stood still. I wanted to collapse, but really couldn't bring myself to touch that stained, stinking floor below me. My breath came in short gasps. "What are they going to do with us?"

Kenta leveled me a hard look. His sharp cheekbones protruded from his gray skin. "My guess is, we'll be fed to the monsters."

I had suspected that was coming, but still, it sent a shiver of fear through me to hear it said out loud. We had no magic, though Ryuu had said something about giving it back to us once we were in the pen. I thought he assumed I was a shifter too, and that the audience would enjoy seeing Sam and me change. I gritted my teeth. We'd be novelties for these people's cruel enjoyment.

I shook my head. There was a chance, a small chance, that we might be able to fight a monster off with magic, but then what? Shrieks and roars and cries filled the air, a horrifying cacophony. There were many, many monsters confined here, more than we could handle. Sooner or later, they'd take us down.

My ears pricked as the roar outside the cave quieted.

A muffled voice boomed, "Five minutes to showtime."

26

DRAGON SOUND

K ai and a few of Ryuu Tanaka's gold-clad guards came for us. The guards yanked me out of the cage. I fumbled to keep ahold of Sam, and he helped by wrapping himself tightly around my wrist. Kai used his wand to stun the alligator next door and dragged Captain Kenta from his cage.

They marched us past the rows of monsters, some snarling and vicious, others cowering and terrified. I felt as though I was in shock, barely able to process what I was seeing, much less form a plan to save myself and my friends.

We rounded a corner and the deafening cries of the creatures were replaced with the roar from the jeering crowd. The guards, one on each side of me, practically dragged me down a long stone tunnel. My legs seemed to have stopped working, and gave out from under me every few feet.

We stepped out of the shadow of the tunnel and passed under an iron portcullis into a large, round pit carved from the dark gray stone of the cave. I slipped and the guards caught and righted me. The ground was wet and slick, as though it'd been hosed off. I looked up.

Spectators leaned over a half wall to watch us. People were packed into every available space along the circular arena, with more looking on from behind. The room seemed to spin around me. I could barely think, the crowd roared so loud. Their voices echoed off the rough roof of the cave and the tall walls of the pit.

Kai shoved Captain Kenta forward and sent him stumbling into a hard fall on his knees. The crowd cheered and Kai's face split into a cruel grin. He punched a beefy fist into the air and turned back toward the tunnel they'd marched us down. My guards walked me forward and released me, then followed Kai. After they'd reentered the tunnel, the iron portcullis dropped into place behind them with a heavy bang. We were trapped in the arena.

I took a few shaky steps to Kenta, grabbed his cold hand in mine, and helped him to his feet. I got a better look at him in the bright lights of the pit. Torches lined the circular wall every few feet and spotlights shone down on us from above.

Kenta stood a few inches taller than me and might have been handsome if he hadn't been starved and dehydrated. I could see why Jun might feel jealous, but from my talk with Misaki, I didn't think he needed to be. My stomach twisted. Not that any of that mattered now. I'd probably never see them or any of my friends again.

I wished Iggy were with me. He'd make some terribly timed joke that would somehow make me smile in spite of the pit in my stomach that made me want to hurl. I gulped. I was grateful Iggy was somewhere undoubtedly safer than here, though.

I spun in a slow circle, willing myself to take it in, to

form some sort of plan. Several more arched doorways opened into the arena, each blocked by a heavy metal gate.

"Give a big welcome to the bait for tonight's first match!" The faceless announcer's voice bounced off the walls, as though it came from every direction. The audience broke into applause and Kenta and I exchanged grim looks.

I frowned. "Wait—I can understand him."

Kenta nodded. "He's put a translation spell on himself— for the different dialects spoken on the island."

I shook my head. There were so many more people in the Badlands than I'd even imagined.

Something whizzed by my face and I jumped back, my feet slipping on the wet stone. I caught my balance and looked at the half-eaten apple that rolled around the ground. I frowned up at the crowd, squinting against the bright lights. Oh come on, I was bait, wasn't that enough torment? Did they have to throw fruit at my head on top of it? I narrowed my eyes and tried to find the culprit among the jeering crowd above.

Women and men munched on snacks or passed money around or shouted down at us in a language I didn't understand. I sighed. That was probably for the best; I doubted they were shouting encouragement. I raised a hand to block the blinding spotlights.

"And now," the announcer boomed again. "Let's welcome our first fighters!"

The crowd broke into applause and three monsters came up to three separate gated entrances. They lurked, mostly hidden in the shadows.

"First up, we have Furio the dragon!"

The gate directly across from me lifted and a gold-and-green-scaled dragon clawed its way into the light. A thin woman with one long, black braid over her shoulder led the dragon forward by a thick chain around its neck.

"Furio is led by monsterwoman Tish Miyagi, sponsored by sake magnate Riko Akita!"

The crowd cheered again at the announcer's words and the slight woman bowed and waved at the crowd. The dragon threw its head back and roared, a stream of flame shooting from its mouth. The crowd gasped, then laughed and applauded, apparently thrilled with the display.

I shook my head and backed up. Great, a fire-breathing dragon, easy peasy. But as I watched it, I spotted a scar over its left eye, which was white and cloudy. He'd been blinded. And a ring of scales was missed from the area around its neck where the chain rubbed, revealing red, scabbed skin below. I gulped. As much as I didn't want to pity the fearsome creature that was about to try to eat me, I couldn't help myself. Absentmindedly, I stroked my thumb over Sam's smooth scales as he wrapped tighter around my wrist.

The next gate lifted and the announcer's voice cut over the din of the crowd. "Next, we have the one-eyed spider Spineripper, trained by monsterman Kaito Endo and sponsored by moneylender Hinata Takahashi." The crowd clapped and cheered as an enormous black spider, nearly as big as the dragon, scuttled out of the shadows. One large, eerily human blue eyeball blinked at us from the center of its round body. Its long legs hugged close around it, knees bent high above its trainer's head. But this creature was just another victim. Great, bloody gashes crisscrossed its hairy black body, and one of its eight limbs trailed limply behind it, broken. *Poor thing.* I frowned at myself. Was I turning into Maple?

The third and final gate lifted. Out marched a four-limbed creature with a tree sprouting out of its back.

Twisted, wooden branches formed its limbs, and a humanoid, noseless face looked out at us. Its branch-like ribs showed through the bark on its sides and black scorch marks marred its body all over, places where the creature had been burned. I gritted my teeth. What kind of sickos could torture animals? I shook my head. Apparently the same kind of sickos who could throw people into pits to be eaten alive by them.

"And lastly, we have the tree creature, Shish, led by Asahi Abe and sponsored by developer Yuuto Endo." The crowd cheered again.

The trainers left their beasts, who remained stock still, at the entrance to the tunnels. The two men and woman shook hands with each other, and then moved to each other's beasts.

I frowned. What were they doing?

The woman aimed her wand at the tree creature and light flashed from the end, again and again, though nothing appeared to be happening.

"They're examining each other's monsters."

A familiar deep voice cut through the din and made me spin around. I shielded my eyes with one hand and peered up into the crowd. Ryuu Tanaka sat on a gold throne right at the edge of the ring, directly behind me. Two beautiful young women who could've been his granddaughter's age sat beside him, stroking his arms.

"Why?" One batted her dark lashes.

The women leaned closer as Ryuu Tanaka explained. I rolled my eyes—I was sure he was just eating this up.

"They're checking for hexes or illegal potions."

One woman's eyes widened. "Do people cheat?"

Ryuu Tanaka shrugged. "It's happened before. But I run a clean monster fight."

I scoffed. *Clean,* my barnacles. There was nothing *clean* about this whole disgusting business of torturing and murdering for sport.

One of the women pointed right at me. "Why do they put those people in there?"

Ryuu Tanaka caught me looking. My first instinct was to turn away, but I forced myself to stand still and meet his gaze, even though my legs trembled under me.

His lips curled back. "They're there as bait, to get the monsters good and aggressive and ready for the kill before they turn on each other."

Well, I might just throw up now.

"Monstermen and woman, do you approve of each other's competitors?"

The announcer's voice boomed and I spun around to watch the creatures again. The two men and woman returned to their own monsters and nodded their agreement.

"Excellent! Then the fight will commence as soon as you have taken your places."

The trainers bowed to each other, then the crowd, and finally to... me? I frowned, then realized they'd bowed to Ryuu Tanaka, who sat directly behind me. They retreated back into the tunnels and the gates slammed shut behind them.

I inched closer to Captain Kenta, who stood doubled over with his hands on his knees. The man could barely stand. "What do we do?"

He looked up at me and shook his head.

"Come on, we have to at least try to fight back, right?"

He licked his dry, chapped lips. "I can barely stand, Imogen, much less fight off three monsters."

I looked up at the three creatures in the ring with us.

They all stared right at me and Kenta. Long lines of saliva dripped from the dragon's jaws, and the spider's pupil narrowed to a tiny pinprick.

"Are you ready for one of the most thrilling, savage shows in the world?" The announcer's voice echoed around the pit and the crowd went wild.

"Come on, Kenta," I growled. "We can't just let them make a spectacle out of us. We have to fight back."

He looked up at me and gritted his teeth. His nostrils flared with his breath and finally he gave a sharp nod. "You're right." He straightened up and I slid an arm around his shoulders to steady him.

Behind me, Ryuu Tanaka's voice cut through the crowd. "Return their magic to them. We want this to be entertaining." The crowd shouted and laughed and more fruit and trash flew through the air into the ring.

Ow. I pressed a hand to my neck. Something must've hit me. I patted at my throat, and instead of a piece of debris, I found a feathered dart in my neck. One stuck out of Sam's scales and another from Kenta's back, as well. A shimmering net spread over the top of the pit and suddenly my sense of magic returned. Those darts must've held the antidote.

I took a quick breath, pulled in magic from the frenetic, bloodthirsty energy of the crowd, and spun. I fired a summoning spell right at Ryuu Tanaka's head to drag him down into this pit with us. But a flash of light glinted off the shimmering net and fizzled out with a small sizzle of black smoke. I frowned as Ryuu Tanaka sneered.

"It's a shield." Kenta glanced up. "Nothing's getting in or out."

"Great." I let out a shaky breath and turned back to face the creatures. "What do we do?"

Kenta's breath came in pants. "I've been a guard for years

now, and I'm familiar with these monsters." He gulped. "I'm not strong enough to do much, but you and your friend might be."

Sam uncoiled from my wrist and in a whirl of magic spun back to human form. I wrapped my arms around him in a tight hug and he leaned his head on my shoulder. I grabbed his thin arms. "Be brave, Sam. We can do this."

Tears welled in his milky eyes but he nodded.

The announcer's voice boomed. "Trainers, are you ready?"

The crowd cheered and the trainers raised their wands from behind the grates.

Oh goddess, it was happening. I lifted my palms, as ready as I'd ever be.

"Trainers!" the announcer called out in his gleeful tone. "Release your beasts!"

27

THE SHOWDOWN

F lashes of light flared in the darkness of the tunnels as the trainers cast their spells. The thick chain dropped from the dragon's neck, the one-eyed spider stretched out its cramped legs, and the tree creature's branches rattled and waved on its back, as though a wind blew through them.

Sam, Captain Kenta, and I retreated as the monsters shook their heads and tested their freedom by taking a few tentative steps toward us. I looked around at the arena. The walls that trapped us had to be at least twenty feet high and made of smooth-cut stone. There was no way I was scaling them, much less Kenta, as weakened as he was.

I looked over at Sam, and then back up at the cheering crowd around us. Men and women clapped their hands and joined in some chant they all apparently knew. The shimmering forcefield blurred their faces. If it weren't for that, I'd have told Sam to shift into a snake and then I'd have tried to toss him out and see if he could find his way to safety out of the tunnels. I shook my head. It was no good, we were all trapped.

As I looked around, I took note of the torches burning in their wall brackets. They were mounted high on the wall, but we could summon them with magic. I'd keep that in mind.

The dragon tossed its massive head, then threw it back and bellowed to the ceiling, sending up a stream of flame. The crowd gasped and applauded, while Sam shrank against my left side. The one-eyed spider pulled a pretty sweet move and climbed up the wall. It scuttled toward us, staying just below the forcefield. Meanwhile the tree creature bounded away from the dragon, the branches and vines on its back snaking and writhing.

I tensed my body, palms raised, and glanced at Kenta to my right. He pressed one hand to his stomach, his face a shade of pale green. Sweat beaded on his forehead despite the cold in the stone pit.

He swung his gaze to me, and despite the pallor of his face, his dark eyes burned with intensity. "I'm captain of the guard and I know these creatures well. I may not have much strength left, but you two do."

My breath quickened as the spider scuttled closer and the tree creature appeared to notice us for the first time. The plants on its back grew absolutely still as it stared at us.

Kenta gasped in a breath and continued, though his voice came out strained. "The tree creature—it's afraid of fire."

Sam whimpered as the thing advanced on us, stalking forward like a lion tracking its prey. I racked my brain. Did I know a fire spell? If only Iggy were here. Maybe we could get the dragon to turn on the tree thing? My breath came in pants. I glanced around and remembered the torches on the wall. We could use them. Then I spotted the spider. It was more than halfway toward us, creeping forward with those spindly black legs.

I jerked my chin at it. "What about the spider?"

Kenta, nearly doubled over, darted his eyes toward it as it advanced on him from the right. "It doesn't have great vision and it has a soft underbelly. If we can distract it, maybe one of us can come up from below and strike."

I pressed my lips tight together. That would work if the thing came down from the wall. And even if it did, then one of us had to crawl underneath a giant spider and burn it with a torch—while still under it.

The dragon roared again, and the hairs on my neck and arms stood on end. It thrashed its head and paced the edge of the arena, coming toward us from the left. "What about it?" I jerked my chin toward the scaled creature.

Kenta braced his pale hands against his thighs. "You have to hit it between its scales. Normally that's just between its toes, but the chain's rubbed its neck raw and exposed skin there."

My stomach twisted as the dragon passed a torch and it lit up the bloody, scabbed extent of the damage from the chain. The crowd grew louder and my forehead and underarms grew wet with a cold sweat. The creatures closed in on us.

Kenta grunted and stiffly stood tall. I had to admire his determination. He must've been starved and dehydrated from days of confinement. I gulped as I took in the advancing tree creature and the scorch marks on its bark. How much more had these animals endured? I bit my lip. But it was us or them, right? Now was not the time to feel pity.

Captain Kenta gritted his teeth. "All right. I say we split up. It's Sam, right? You go for the dragon, can you do that?

Just get its attention. Imogen, you and I will lure the tree creature toward the dragon, and we'll get them to turn on each other."

"Uh-huh," I answered absentmindedly. I could barely focus. The chanting and cheering from the crowd pounded into my brain, fear set my nerves on edge as I looked from one enormous monster to the next, and as I steeled myself to kill them or be killed, I couldn't help noticing the protruding ribs, bloody gashes, and blistered burns. I definitely felt like murdering someone. It was just Ryuu Tanaka and all the sickos who found this entertaining, not the creatures.

"Then we'll take on the spider. We'll need to lure it off the wall if it doesn't come down on its own. I'll pretend to be injured, which won't be hard." Kenta gave a humorless chuckle.

My eyes darted from creature to creature. "Uh-huh."

"I usually use a wand, but think I can still manage to focus some magic, though it'll be limited. How about you two?"

I think Sam answered but I didn't hear it. The tree creature had stopped again a mere fifteen feet away. It lowered its head and stared right at me with its weirdly human face, the leaves of its branches quivering. My heart pounded in my chest and I could actually hear my heartbeat in my head.

My hands trembled as I lifted my palms. The spider crept, slowly but steadily, looming just over Kenta's shoulder. Its broken leg dangled down the side of the wall. The dragon roared and scraped its scabbed neck against the side of the arena. It stood near enough to torch Sam and me with its fire.

The sound of my own heartbeat and the panting of my breaths drowned out the raucous crowd. They could probably sense the creatures were about to strike and it drove the spectators to a frenzy. They stood, screaming and pounding the half wall that bordered the pit, but it sounded muffled to me, as though I were underwater.

"Imogen?"

I looked over, blinking. Kenta frowned at me. "I said, are you ready?"

I nodded, but turned away to face the crouched tree monster. Ready for what? What was the plan again? Were we really going to kill these beasts?

"One. Two." Kenta counted, though his voice sounded faraway.

I made a decision. I just hoped it worked. I held my breath and closed my eyes.

"Three!"

I opened my eyes, sucked in a huge breath of air, and magically pulled from the monsters with all my might. Their energy rushed into me, a flood of power, wild and inhuman. It knocked me backwards and I fell hard, banging the back of my head against the stone floor. I lay flat, the breath knocked out of me, black spots dancing before my eyes. I blinked to clear my blurry vision, and Sam's and Kenta's faces suddenly hovered over me.

"Imogen. Are you all right?" Sam knelt closer and took my hand.

My limbs shook violently and my teeth chattered. I finally managed to suck in a gasping breath, my chest heaving up off the hard ground.

"D-did. I-it. W-w-work?" My teeth clattered together and I shivered uncontrollably. It was too much energy all at once.

Kenta sat heavily down beside me and grinned. "Yeah. It worked. I don't know how, but you took them all down."

I shuddered, and my head jerked to the side. I pressed my eyes shut tight, struggling to get control of my body. "Th-they're n-not de-dead. I di-didn't w-want t-t-to hurt th-them."

Sam squeezed my shaking hand tight and smiled, tears in his eyes. "I didn't either. The poor thingssss."

Despite the throbbing in the back of my head and the frenetic energy that ricocheted through my body, I felt warm with pride. I'd managed to both save us and not hurt the monsters. But something seemed odd.

I blinked, and with Sam's and Kenta's help, propped myself up on my elbows. I looked around. The three monsters lay sprawled on the ground, unmoving except for the rise and fall of their breathing. Then it hit me—the silence.

I looked up through the glimmering forcefield. The spectators sat or stood, as still as the unconscious monsters, their mouths agape. I turned my head, though it sent a burning pain through my neck, and looked behind me at Ryuu Tanaka. His eyes blazed with steely anger. *Ha!* Bonus —I'd totally ruined the "show." *Suck it, Tanaka.*

I grinned, though my teeth still chattered, and it seemed to break the spell. The crowd erupted with "boos," and groups of men fought over money, with punches thrown. Ryuu Tanaka stood, his lips curled back in a snarl. "How?" he bellowed.

I grinned wider and Kenta lifted a thick brow. "I'm wondering the same thing, you know?"

I shrugged. I knew I looked smug, but didn't really care at the moment. "Guess you guys have never met a swallow."

As the crowd raged around us and the gates lifted for the trainers to collect their defeated monsters, Sam and Kenta grabbed my arms and helped me to my feet. My legs trembled under me and I couldn't stand on my own, but I beamed. "I had a real *Indiana Jones* moment back there, huh?"

Sam blinked at me, puzzled, and Kenta frowned.

"You kn-know." My teeth chattered, still. "You were laying out this whole plan, l-like the guy with the s-sword in the marketplace, and I was just like, *bam*!" I made little gun hands. "You know, with the p-pistol?"

They shook their heads.

"Like I'll j-just pull from the monsters, like Indie with his gun and—"

Kenta patted my shoulder. "You should save your strength." He whispered behind my back to Sam. "I think she's delirious."

Sam giggled.

I gasped and looked from one to the other. "W-well, if this is w-what I g-get for sav-saving you, then I—"

The announcer's voice interrupted me. "What a stunning upset, no one saw that coming! The bait takes down the monsters? It's an event to go down in history, and you were here to witness it, folks."

The crowd booed back.

"But don't worry, our gracious host Ryuu Tanaka has more in store for you next as he unleashes the vilest, most vicious creatures in his stables!"

My stomach twisted and my legs buckled under me. Sam and Kenta dipped to help bring me back upright. Another fight? With even more terrifying monsters? I gulped. "Uh-oh, Dr. Jones."

Kenta looked Sam up and down. "I didn't know you were a doctor."

28

CAT FIGHT

F or several minutes, the ring remained empty aside from Sam, Kenta, and me. The angry, disappointed crowd milled about above. Sam and Kenta still supported me, an arm under each of mine.

I blew out a breath and set my jaw. "Okay, I'm feeling better." I looked at Sam on my left, and Kenta on my right. "When they bring out the next monsters, I think I'll be able to pull from at least one or two." I turned to my right. "Kenta, maybe you can give us the lowdown on the monsters' weaknesses and you guys can work some magic, too?"

As Kenta opened his mouth to reply, a gust of air tickled the back of my neck and a sharp sting burned on my forehead. I frowned and turned to look at Sam. A feathered dart stuck out from the side of his neck. I grimaced. "Sam, you've been hit."

He looked up and his pale eyes widened behind his thick glasses.

I frowned. "What?"

"Imogen, you've got sssomething on your—" Sam pointed to his own forehead.

My shoulders slumped. "I have a dart sticking out of my head, don't I?"

He nodded.

Great.

Suddenly, the last of the magic I'd pulled from the monsters stopped ricocheting around my body, and a warm sense of calm flushed through me. Briefly.

"Oh no." I grabbed the feathered dart, yanked it from my head, and tossed it to the stone ground. Kenta and Sam removed theirs from their necks and dropped them. "We don't have magic anymore." I looked up to Ryuu Tanaka where he sat on his throne at the top of the wall, the beautiful women fawning all over him. His lips curled into a cruel smile and he flashed his eyes at me. At the sound of a shout nearby, Ryuu frowned and turned from me to look down the aisle of seats.

Kai pushed his way through, his face red and the veins of his thick neck popping. He stepped on feet and shoved past angry spectators until he stood beside Ryuu Tanaka. I strained to make out Kai's words.

"I know, but I told the guard I had to hear the order from your lips. I haven't trained it." Kai's eyes blazed.

Ryuu Tanaka lifted a brow. "I don't care. Put it in the ring."

"It could be dangerous."

Ryuu's face reddened and he gripped the arms of his throne. "Good. This crowd needs a show. I won't allow those idiots to ruin my big event." His eyes flashed to me, Sam, and Kenta.

I stood up straighter and lifted my chin. *Ha!* I felt proud to be one of those idiots.

Kai's eyes shifted to me, then back to his boss. "But—it's like their pet or something. What if it won't attack them?"

Ryuu Tanaka's face darkened. "Make sure it does."

"But—"

The older man cut him off. "Use the potion."

Kai whitened. "It's banned."

Ryuu bared his teeth. "He's not going up against anyone's monster, just these losers. No one will care."

A cruel grin spread over Kai's face, then he bowed. "Yes, sir." He straightened and shoved his way down the aisle as spectators cried out and hissed at him.

Kenta shook his head and grinned as he watched Kai trip over a woman's long dress. "Oh Kai, always popular."

Sam giggled.

I looked between them. Since when did Sam giggle?

I cleared my throat when they continued to grin at each other. "So. We have no magic, and it sounds like they're throwing Cat in here after doping him with 'the potion,' whatever that is." I nodded as my stomach twisted tight with icy fear. "Not looking good, guys."

Kenta's smile dropped from his face. He shot me a side-eyed glance. "Do you have any ideas?"

I swallowed, my throat tight, and looked at Kenta. "Not a single one." I shrugged. "But Cat knows me and Sam—maybe he won't attack."

The space between Kenta's brows creased. "Why are you smiling?"

"Oh." I let out a high-pitched giggle. "It's just a fear smile." I waved a hand. "It's this thing I do when I'm afraid I'm going to be murdered."

Kenta's frown deepened as he looked from me to Sam and back to me. "Does that—happen often?"

Sam's eyes widened and I shrugged at him, then turned back to Kenta. "Uh, you know, a few times, yeah."

The announcer's voice cut through the din of the crowd. "And now, a special surprise from your illustrious host, Ryuu Tanaka. A mystical creature you've only *dreamed* of seeing in the ring—"

The crowd "oohed" and quieted down. Men and women leaned over the half wall to get a better view of the arena.

"A beast so rare and so fearsome, many said it could never be captured."

I could practically feel hundreds of breaths being held. The air buzzed with tension as the crowd hung on every word. I frowned. All this for Cat? *Our* Cat? I still figured the council had made a mistake when identifying Cat as this terrifying monster. I mean, creepy and unsettling, yes, but worse than a dragon or that giant spider? There was no way.

"I present to you..." The announcer drew out the dramatic pause. The audience leaned forward in their seats. "A neko!"

The crowd erupted into screams and whistles and applause. Men leapt to their feet and gathered in frantic circles, passing coins and I assumed taking bets. I leaned over to Kenta. "What does 'neko' mean?"

Kenta leaned in, his eyes glued to the gate ahead of us. "It means cat."

My jaw dropped. "You've got to be kidding me."

He glanced at me. "No. Why?"

I scoffed. "Bec— Why would— He looks nothing like a cat!"

The portcullis lifted over one of the tunnels and Kai marched in. He walked, chest puffed out and chin high, to the center of the arena.

He dragged Cat behind him by a heavy chain. The little

guy staggered right and left, and his globular pug eyes rolled back in his head. Kai glanced our way, but ignored Sam and me. He only had eyes for Kenta. Kai sneered and pulled out Kenta's necklace from under his shirt, then swung it back and forth, taunting the captain.

I glanced over. Kenta had turned even paler, the shadows under his eyes growing more prominent.

I glared at the burly idiot in the middle of the arena. I wanted to punch him in the face, and it wasn't even my necklace.

"Cat doesssn't look ssso good." Sam wrung his thin hands together at his chest.

"Must be from the potion Ryuu ordered Kai to give him." I frowned as Kai dropped the chain, then jogged backwards. He kept his wand aimed at Cat, who staggered in circles, shaking his head.

Captain Kenta set his sharp jaw. "Ryuu Tanaka said the potion would ensure your Cat would attack us."

I lifted a finger. "Well, he's not *my* Cat, first of all. Let's make it clear that I would never keep *that* as a pet." I lifted my palms. "Not that I have anything against Cat. He's, you know, great in his own way."

The gate slammed into place behind Kai. From behind the safety of the undoubtedly enchanted iron, Kai's wand flashed and the chain dropped from Cat's neck. The little guy stood still, his back to us. Sam and I exchanged puzzled looks.

"Cat?"

Still, he didn't move. The crowd quieted. All right. This was eerie, but eerie was sort of the norm for Cat. I gulped, then eased forward, Sam and Kenta following a few steps behind. Cat's black wings trembled at his sides and his tail and head hung limp. I shot Sam a worried look, then eased forward another step. "H-hey there, buddy."

Cat didn't answer. I shook myself. *Of course he didn't answer, he doesn't speak!*

I eased a little closer and stretched a hand out. I tried for my babiest of baby talk voices. "Hey der, wittle guy, it's me, Auntie Imogen, and we're going to make sure nobody hurts you or—"

Cat whirled to face me and I lurched back. "Ah!"

He hissed, specks of saliva flying from his sharp-toothed Cheshire grin, and he spread his wings wide, shaking them at me. I stumbled backwards into Sam and Kenta.

"This is my worst nightmare!" I shook my head. "Oh, Iggy, we always knew he was terrifying."

Sam turned to me and squeezed my shoulder. "Imogen. Iggy isssn't here."

He and Kenta exchanged pitying looks. *Really?*

"It was rhetorical, like I was—" I shook my head. "No, never mind. We need to focus."

The crowd's jeers and taunts grew louder.

Cat crouched, his bulging eyes staring hard, then bounded straight at me, his claws digging ruts in the hard stone ground. I gasped and we scattered. The crowd went wild. I looked back—the little guy was gaining on me. Maybe it was worse to run? I spun around to face him. "Hey wittle—"

Cat slammed into my chest.

"Oof!"

He was heavier than he looked. I toppled back and the side of my head slammed into the stone again, with Cat snarling on top of me. I shoved my arms up against his warm, furry body and struggled, muscles burning, to keep his gnashing mouth from my face. His back legs kicked mine as I fought to get my legs up and under him.

"Errr." I gritted my teeth and willed my arms to stop shaking as I pushed into him. Sam appeared above me. He gripped Cat's tail in his hands, and pulled, his face red with the effort.

Kenta sprinted over and yanked on Cat's legs. But Cat sank his claws into the stone above my shoulders and pulled his body closer to mine.

"Hey. Buddy." I grunted. I turned my head away from his rotten fish breath and tried, hard, not to vomit. "It's." I groaned. "Me." My arms couldn't hold him off much longer and then those razor-sharp shark teeth would close around my face.

His shiny pug eyes loomed closer and I pressed my cheek harder into the wet stone below me. I strained with everything I had to push him away but he was stronger. His hot, panting breath blew my bangs across my forehead with every gust.

A stillness came over me. This was it. I was going to die, my face eaten off by my best friend's dangerous pet. This was exactly like that Oprah episode I'd seen where the pet chimp ripped that woman's face off. I gulped. This *literally* was my worst nightmare.

29

FINAL ROUND

My chest heaved and I waited for the death blow —or bite. It didn't come, and Cat seemed to relax a little. I no longer had to try so hard to push him away, and my arms stopped trembling. I peeled an eye open. Cat still reached for me, but his claws had retracted, and he made grabby hands.

I frowned and looked past him toward Sam and Kenta. Sam's jaw dropped in bewilderment and Cat's tail slipped from his hands, wagging from side to side. My last bit of strength drained away and Cat fell heavy on my chest. He wrapped his monkey hands up in my hair and nuzzled against my chest. He made a steady chatter of odd grunts, squeals, and dolphin clicks.

"How?" Kenta stood over me, blinking down.

I frowned. Yeah, how did this happen? Cat's bat nostrils flared and then he buried his face against my shoulder. "Oh." The realization hit me and I grinned at Sam. "Maple's scarf!" I turned to Kenta. "I smell like his mom."

Kenta froze and his eyes darted from me to Sam. "You know his mom?"

I grinned as Cat nuzzled into my shoulder. I hated to admit it, but it felt kind of cute. "Not his actual monster mom, but my friends Maple and Wiley adopted him and—" I froze and held my breath as I suddenly noticed the deep silence in the arena.

I looked up. The crowd looked down on us from the other side of the shimmering barrier, faces purple and contorted with anger. Ryuu Tanaka rose slowly from his seat, his nostrils flaring with each quick breath.

My grin widened. "I think they're upset they're not getting a show."

Sam gasped. "They're bringing in more monssstersss."

He pointed with a trembling hand and I followed his gaze to the gated tunnels on the other side of the arena. Cat lifted his head and sniffed the air. His bat ears swiveled from side to side as four trainers marched up to the gate with monsters in tow, lurking in the shadows of the tunnels.

"So many twists and turns tonight!" The announcer's voice boomed through the cave, and the crowd answered with boos.

Warm pride flooded my chest at having denied these cruel dummies their spectacle of innocent people and beasts murdering each other. Sam shrank closer to my side as the gates rose.

Deep weariness swamped me. How long could we hold out? I'd seen how many monsters they had in the "stables." They'd keep coming till we were dead.

I looked down at Cat in my arms. He snuffled against the scarf wrapped around my neck, where Maple's scent must have been strongest. The vague outlines of an idea began to form in my head. I looked to Kenta. "Is it true that Cat has the power of mind control?"

Kenta looked down at me and nodded. His pale skin

hung from his sharp cheekbones and dark bags shadowed his eyes. I doubted he could hold out much longer.

I let out a shaky breath as the gates clanked into place and the trainers stepped forward into the torchlight with their creatures in tow. After the first four left the tunnel, four more followed.

Great. I shook my head as I stared down the semicircle of thrashing, shrieking, drooling creatures before us. "Eight versus three—sounds fair."

I shook my head as I watched a sweaty trainer guide in a white horse with a black mane and the head of a duck. It trotted around tossing its weirdly luxurious mane and quacking happily as a crab the size of a car strained against its chain toward it, snapping its claws. Another bait animal, I guessed. The trainers left their monsters and scrambled back to the tunnels. A pale blob that seemed to be made of magical, teeming maggots writhed as the gates slammed shut, closing off the tunnels. The trainers cast spells at the announcer's cue, and the chains dropped from the monsters' necks. Chaos broke out.

My voice came out pinched. "What are we going to do?"

The giant crab scuttled sideways toward us while all around the arena, the monsters spread out, moving closer and closer to us. The crowd shouted and chanted and egged the monsters on. The white horse with the ridiculous duck head frolicked around the arena, bucking its hind legs and tossing its beak into the air. Poor oblivious, stupid creature.

As the crab and its snapping claws scuttled nearer, I grabbed Sam's and Kenta's arms and dragged them to the right. "Run!"

CLACK! The crab's red claw clamped down on the air where my head had been just a moment ago.

Cat clung to my neck as I ran with Sam on my left and

Kenta on my right. We skirted the round wall with the giant crab on our heels and a frog either on fire or made of fire looming ahead. I skidded into a sharp left turn, jostling shoulders with Sam and Kenta as they did the same. I sprinted toward the center of the arena, my heart pounding in my chest. The maggoty blob flashed past, chasing the duck-headed horse. I risked a glance back. A monkey with spiders for hands leapt onto the back of the giant crab. Spiders flowed up its arms and onto the crab.

My stomach turned. "Ew, they're on the crab's eye stems and—oh no, they're on its eyes." My stomach cramped and I pressed my hands to it. I doubled over—I was going to be sick.

Sam frantically tapped my shoulder and I looked up. The fire frog leapt closer and we sprinted on again, skirting the wall toward the gates. Another inkling of an idea popped into my head.

"Cat." The little guy looked up and blinked his black, bulging eyes at me. I stuffed down the thoughts of how stupid an idea this was, that of course he couldn't understand me, and tried anyway—it was our only hope. "Cat—can you understand me?"

Cat blinked.

That might have been a yes. I dove right and slammed my back against the wall, letting the blob of maggots streak by, chittering as it scrambled after the duck-headed horse. I pumped my arms harder and sprinted along the wall, leading Kenta and Sam toward the gated tunnels. "Buddy—if you can understand me, I need you to use your mind control powers and make the people lift the gates."

My eyes darted up. I doubted Cat's powers would work through the antimagic forcefield above, but the gates didn't seem enchanted in the same way. I skidded to a stop in front of the first gate. A tall guy with stringy hair and a face tattoo lurked in the shadows. He had his hands cupped to his mouth and was shouting at his monster. He froze when I slid into view followed by Kenta and Sam.

I held Cat toward him, my arms shaking with the little guy's surprising heft. "Okay, Cat. Do your thing." I dearly hoped I wasn't just being a crazy person talking to an animal and expecting it to understand.

The guy hissed something in a language I didn't understand and scrambled back a couple steps. I glanced back as the fire frog hopped toward us. "Anytime, Cat." I bit my lip and shifted to lift Cat higher. Yeah, this had definitely been a mistake—and probably my last.

Cat threw his head back so he looked at me upside down and his mouth split into a wide Cheshire grin of sharp, pointy teeth.

Disturbing.

He closed one globular eye, then dropped his face back toward the trainer on the other side of the gate. I frowned. Had he just winked at me? My back heated up and I glanced back as the fire frog leapt closer, just ten feet away.

"*Now* would be good, Cat!"

The little creature's furry body vibrated in my hands and I suddenly became aware of a low humming noise. I pulled Cat closer and peered around the side of his face. His mouth stretched wide—he was making the noise! And his eyes— lights and flashes floated across the normally vacant black orbs. I leaned closer—and closer, trying to make out what was in them. A hand on my shoulder made me jump, and I whirled on Kenta.

He jumped back. "I didn't mean to startle you, but I think you were being drawn into his trance."

I frowned at Cat, then at the man behind the gate. He

lifted his wand, his face vacant and mouth slack. A flash of light blared at the end of his wand and the gate rose in front of us. Some cries went up from the crowd.

I gasped. "You did it, Cat!"

The little guy tipped his head back to look at me again. And he winked! Come to think of it, how had I never realized how beautiful and sweet and angelic this magnificent creature was with all his—

"Ow!" I turned to Sam. He still held his hand up. "You slapped me!"

"Sssorry." Tears welled in his eyes. "It'sss jussst he wasss hypnotizing you, and—" He spun and whimpered.

I followed his gaze to a sizzling puddle. It was all that remained of the fire frog. The teeming gray blob of maggots loomed over the remains, a frog leg hanging from its mouth. Was it even really a mouth if it was just a shape the bunch of magical maggots formed?

Strong hands grabbed my shoulders, and Kenta spun me to face the blob as it launched at us like a dust devil.

"Ahh!" I screamed and shoved Cat toward it. The little guy continued to hum, the sound reverberating through his ribs where I held him. The maggots froze and dropped to the ground, just a bunch of underdeveloped insects crawling around without a unified shape or purpose. I let out a shaky sigh, and Sam, Kenta, and I exchanged relieved looks. The feeling didn't last.

Ryuu Tanaka rose from his seat and pointed at us through the forcefield. "Take them down!"

His gold-clad guards leaned over the half wall from every possible angle and pointed their wands at us. I hunched my shoulders up and squeezed my eyes shut, bracing for the spell that would end me. Angry shouts rang out and I peeled an eye open.

"Then lift the forcefield!" Ryuu Tanaka's face had turned a shade of purple I didn't think was possible for a human. The torchlight illuminated the specks of saliva that flew from his mouth.

"Come on!" I jerked my head toward the tunnel, and we made a run for it. I glanced back as we sprinted into the shadows, leaving the arena behind. The shimmering force-field disappeared and flashes of light ricocheted off the tunnel near the entrance, but none reached us. We'd made it—for now. The duck-headed horse and the now-blinded crab scurried into the tunnel behind us, followed by the surviving monsters.

My heart pounded in my ears and I hugged Cat tight to my chest, making sure not to look at him. "What—now?"

We rounded the corner and the smells of the stable hit me—the iron of blood mixed with the stench of feces and rot and fear. I crinkled my nose and pushed forward. Sam's hands bounced where he held them in front of his shoulders and I caught Kenta's notice, and smiled. The howls and shrieks of the monsters behind us mingled with those still left in their cages. I held Cat out as we passed trainer after trainer, and he stopped them in their tracks before they could finish drawing their wands.

"There's a way out from here!" Kenta skidded to a stop and pointed to the right. "It's a service entrance so they can bring the monsters in without having to use the main one. It's this way."

I glanced at Sam. He paled, though two bright red spots glowed on his cheeks. His thin chest heaved as he looked around at the scarred, moaning creatures around him. He blinked his milky blue eyes. "We're jussst going to leave them all like thisss?"

A muscle jumped in Kenta's jaw and voices echoed from

the tunnel up ahead. "Of course not. We'll come back—with backup."

Sam looked to me. "But—but what if they hurt them all before we can?"

I bit my lip and looked from Sam to the suffering creatures to the tunnel behind me—the voices and shouts grew louder. Ryuu Tanaka and his guards would be on us any moment and I wasn't sure how powerful Cat was—we needed to go, now. But still I hesitated.

I didn't like the idea of leaving all these creatures behind either, and who knew how many of these people would escape and go unidentified before we returned? The monsters, and the evil people who saw this as sport, deserved justice—though in different ways. I looked around. There had to be a dozen trainers down here, all standing stock-still under Cat's trance.

I hugged Cat closer. "Okay, buddy, I feel like I'm really pushing my luck here in terms of what you must be capable of understanding but—it's worth a try." I gasped as the first guards poured into the stables. "Okay, Cat, make the trainers unlock the cages and let the monsters out."

Kenta's eyes widened. "You sure that's a good idea?"

I nodded. "Not at all."

Cat vibrated harder and the trainers dropped their knives and whips and lifted their wands to the cage doors. Loud clicks sounded throughout the stables. The rushing golden guards skidded to a stop as cage doors swung open all around us. A herd of monsters burst out.

Dragons stretched their leathery wings and took flight, the cave's ceiling barely tall enough to accommodate them. A giant wolf with a scorpion tail bounded toward the exit and sent the golden guards scattering. A stampede of monsters followed, and chaos descended upon the stables.

We scrambled into the narrow space between two cages and huddled up.

"Now what?" Kenta's chest heaved and he looked left and right, panicked.

"You know." I rolled a hand. "The monsters are free now, and they return to the wild." I shrugged.

He shook his head. "I meant for us!"

"Right."

Sam looked like he was about to cry. "People who hurt poor animalsss make me ssso mad." He sniffed. "They ssshould have to be in cagesss and sssee if they like it."

Kenta and I exchanged looks.

"That's a pretty good idea, Sam." Kenta lifted a brow and Sam blushed a deep red. Look who was getting all bashful.

I nodded. "If Cat can round them all up, we can lock them in and make sure they answer for what they've done."

Kenta nodded. "After that we'll still have to go get backup... I just hope these criminals won't find a way out in the meantime."

"Ooh!" I lifted my brows. "We can hit them with those darts that take away magic...." I scrunched up my nose. "That'd take a while though."

"We'll just have Cat make them do it to themselves." Kenta lifted his palms and I nodded my agreement.

"Perfect." I tipped my head from side to side. "It's just, we're kinda verging into creepy territory with Cat and his mind control powers, so let's make sure we don't take it too far." I winked. "We don't want a Jessica Jones Kilgrave situation."

Kenta and Sam looked at each other and my snake friend shrugged. "I don't know."

Ugh. I really needed just one human friend to fully appreciate how clever I was with my little zingers.

The cage behind me rattled and I lurched back. The giant monkey with spider hands threw another guard against it, then another, and then the spiders flooded from its hand and spread out, engulfing guards and monsters alike.

I took a deep breath and blew it out. "All right, Cat, work your magic, you terrifying little cutie."

Cat chattered back in response and I forced myself to step out of our hiding spot and into the melee. Holding Cat in front of me and keeping one eye closed, I led our little group into the heart of the monster versus guard battle royale.

At first my stomach turned with unease. Holding Maple and Wiley's tiny, chattering fur baby out in front of me at first felt a lot like using a friend's beloved kitty as a shield. But as monster after monster fell into his trance and calmly walked and flew and slithered out of the cave, the feeling faded.

Guards, women in silks, and men with pockets full of money and illegal contraband walked themselves into cages and jabbed themselves in the thighs with the potion-filled darts, depriving themselves of magic. It took some time to round everyone up, but it went faster when Cat began to make people forcibly grab others and drag them to the cages. He'd come up with that idea all on his own, which I found particularly terrifying. We'd just thrown Ryuu Tanaka into a cage slick with maggot slime when Kenta pushed Kai in behind him.

"Hold on a moment."

The spelled Kai froze.

"I want my necklace back." Kenta held out his hand while the dazed Kai pulled it from his neck. He dropped the jade fish necklace into Kenta's waiting hand and then locked himself into the cage before snapping his wand and injecting himself with the potion. Cat chittered, and Kai and Ryuu Tanaka turned to face each other, their eyes glazed. They reached out and punched each other in the crotches, then doubled over groaning.

"Cat!" I gasped at the little creature in my arms. "So not necessary."

Kenta turned away, and I winked at Cat and whispered, "But pretty funny." Cat nuzzled against me.

Kenta let out a sigh of relief. "That's the last of them."

I bit my lip. "I hope we got them all."

Cat stopped humming and sniffed the air, his bat nostrils flaring. I frowned. "What is it, little guy?"

His giant eyes grew bigger and he scrambled up my shoulder and perched on top of my head. I turned to see what had gotten him so excited, just as voices sounded from down the tunnel that led to the main cave.

30

REUNITED

"Where is everyone?"

"We'll find them."

I grinned. I'd know those voices anywhere.

A moment later, Maple and Hank rounded the corner. Hank held one hand palm up at the ready, while Iggy in his lantern dangled from the other.

"Guys!" I rose on my toes and waved.

Their faces swiveled toward us as Wiley, Rhonda, Francis, and everyone else piled into the stables behind them. Maple gasped and pressed her hands to her mouth while Hank stopped dead.

His shoulders dropped. "You're alive." His eyes shone and his chest heaved. "Thank the goddess."

"Psh." Iggy scoffed. "I leave you alone for a few hours and you've already replaced me with *that*."

I rolled my eyes upward to where Cat perched on my head.

"Ow."

He clutched bunches of my hair in his monkey hands.

Iggy sniffed. "Your loss."

Hank strode toward me, a determined look on his face. Real determined. My heart fluttered and I glanced around uncertainly as Cat abandoned ship and scampered over to Maple and Wiley. Was Hank going to stop? He never slowed, just walked right into me and gathered me up in his arms.

He buried his face in my neck and held me tight. Tears trickled down my cheeks as I slid my arms around his waist and squeezed him back. His chest heaved against me, warm and broad, and his heartbeat thrummed away in my ear.

A smile stretched across my face as I realized that even on an island forgotten by the world, a million miles away from the place where I lived, in a cave dungeon, Hank was all it took to make me feel like I was home. I grinned wider and nuzzled my face into his chest. Man, I was corny when I was happy.

I peeled an eye open and glanced over at Iggy. He dangled from Hank's hand against my side. "You know I could never replace you."

He blinked slowly. "Obviously."

"At least not in a couple hours—it would take me at least a day or two."

He narrowed his eyes. "Witch, you wish."

I chuckled and Iggy's face softened. "I'm glad monsters didn't eat your head."

"I know, Iggy." I smiled at my little flame, tears in my eyes. "Me, too."

"Kenta!"

I leaned back and looked around Hank's shoulder. Misaki shoved her wand in her wide waistband and sprinted past the cages crammed with Ryuu Tanaka, Kai, and hundreds of their fellow criminals. Kenta froze, his eyes wide with surprise as Misaki skidded to a stop right in front of him.

He bowed. "Misaki."

She waited for him to straighten, then threw her arms around him, pinning his arms to his sides. "You're alive!"

I grinned up at Hank, and though he looked pale and still shaken, his lips pulled to the side and he flashed me that handsome grin of his. We pulled apart reluctantly as the rest of our friends and the guard rushed over. Sam and I took turns hugging everyone, and Yann wrapped Sam and me up together in a giant bear hug and hefted us up off our feet.

Hank handed Iggy over to me and I looked at my little friend.

"So does this mean you're camp Cat now?"

I plastered on a huge grin. "Absolutely."

Maple beamed at Cat in her arms, and Wiley bent over to scratch under his chin.

I lifted Iggy close to my face until his heat warmed my cheek and hissed, "But I find him more terrifying than ever."

Iggy's eyes widened and he nodded. "So all these people are under his spell?"

I nodded. "Pretty much."

He grimaced. "For how long?"

I shrugged.

Iggy shook his head. "Horrifying."

"Hm?"

Iggy and I spun to look at Maple, who nuzzled her face against Cat's.

I shrugged, and Iggy blurted, "Nothing!"

Maple frowned, but I turned to Hank before she could question me further about her scary pet. "How'd you get around the rocks?"

Hank grinned. "I figured out the transformation spell."

I gave his arm a little punch. "Look at you!"

He chuckled.

Wiley lifted his brows. "He turned into a giant bear and carried all of us on his back."

"That's what I turned into!" I turned to Hank, wide-eyed. "But all of them?"

He nodded, a smile playing at the corner of his mouth. "I was a big bear." He tipped his head side to side. "And I ate some of that kusuri herb—it gave me a little surge of strength."

Rhonda appeared at my side and slid her arm through mine. "Oh, girl, you two are gonna have some fun." She winked.

I frowned at Hank, and he looked as confused as I did. "Because we can both turn into bears?"

She winked again. "Have you ever heard of furries?"

I pressed my lips tight together. "Yeah, nope."

Her eyes lit up. "Okay, so you're basically living their dream, it's like when—"

I held up a hand. "No, I know what they are. I just meant, nope, we're not having this conversation."

"Oh." Rhonda nodded. "Got it. We'll save this for a private conversation." She winked and patted my arm, then moved off to join Francis in chatting with Captain Kenta, Sam, Misaki, and Jun. Jun stood with his chin dipped as Kenta accepted a swig of water from Misaki's canteen.

I sighed. "Our friends are so weird."

Hank slid an arm around my shoulders and hugged me tight to his side. "Yes."

Warm happiness flooded my chest.

"I was pretty proud of myself when I finally figured that spell out." Hank grinned down at me, though his eyes looked glassy in the torchlight. "Figured we'd sweep in here and save you two." He lifted a thick brow as he looked around at all the caged monster fighters. "You're welcome, by the way."

"Ha!" I hugged him tighter.

"Yep." He nodded. "Clearly couldn't have done it without me." His smile faded as he took in the bloodstains, shackles, and grated floors. "Another brush with death, and I was right there, by your side," he finished flatly.

I swallowed my throat tight. "Hey." He looked down at me, his blue eyes wide and vulnerable. "For the record, I'd like to think I won't have any more brushes with death, but this is me we're talking about."

His lips quirked to the side.

"So if and *when* I do, I *want* you there by my side." I let out a shaky breath. "I need you to be." I shrugged and fought to hold back the tears welling in my eyes. "I just kind of need you, period."

Iggy sighed loudly. "I am *right* here."

I rolled my eyes and threw my arms around Hank. "I didn't mean it like that."

Hank hugged me tight against him, cupping one huge hand around my head. He slowly rubbed his fingers through my hair, massaging my scalp, and I melted into his warmth. "I mean, that's not the *only* way I meant it."

"*Right* here!" Iggy dangled from my hand behind Hank's back.

The prince chuckled and the deep sound vibrated through my cheek resting against his chest.

"I'm grateful to see you safe."

I turned my head. Jun bowed deeply to Captain Kenta and then reached out and shook his hand. Kenta grinned back at him. Jun looked from Misaki, who stood beside

Kenta, back to the captain. A muscle jumped in his jaw. "You're a very lucky man." He pressed his lips in a tight line as Kenta's brows drew together in confusion. "Misaki took charge and wouldn't take no for an answer. If it weren't for her dedication and bravery, we never would've found you." Jun dipped his head again with a tight-lipped smile and then turned and moved slowly away.

I bit my lip. Poor guy, he had it bad for Misaki. She frowned and looked between Jun and Kenta.

Hank's deep voice sounded in my ear. "You know, I'm impressed you—"

"I'm sorry, can you hold on just a second?" I lifted a finger and grinned up at him. "I'm eavesdropping." I jerked my head towards Misaki.

"Oh." Hank lifted his brows and watched Misaki watching Jun. "She's into him, right?"

"Right?" I grinned, delighted Hank was up to speed. "But maybe she's into Kenta?"

"Shh, I'm watching."

I gaped and Hank winked at me.

Misaki took a big breath and ran after Jun, her top knot bobbing. I bit my lip. She tapped his shoulder and he turned to face her. They stood between two rows of cages. The criminals locked inside watched them, blank faced. Maybe not the ideal romantic setting, but I held my breath, hopeful for them.

"Do you—do you think I have feelings for Captain Kenta?" Misaki spoke in a rush.

"Oh." Jun scratched the back of his neck and looked down. He towered above her. "I thought that might be part of why you wanted to find him so badly?" He held up his long hands. "Not that that had to be a reason, but I just got that feeling that—it might be."

Her chest rose and fell as she stared up at him. "I wanted to find him because I admire him. He's a great captain and a good friend." She stepped closer, closing the gap between them. "And *only* for those reasons."

A smile played at the corner of Jun's mouth, and he moved closer to her. "Oh."

They stared at each other. She leaned in. "In fact, I have feelings for someone else."

"Oh." Jun's face fell and he dipped his chin. "Well, I— You know, I wish you the best of luck with that and—" He half turned from her.

"It's you, you dummy." She grabbed him by the front of his shirt and pulled. He turned, his face lit up with delight, and dipped down to kiss her.

"Awww." I nuzzled into Hank's chest, happy for Misaki and Jun.

"Voyeur," Iggy quipped from behind Hank's back.

The prisoners in the cages put their hands together and clapped in unison, the oddly rhythmic applause echoing throughout the cave.

Hank frowned down at me. "Why are they clapping?"

"You know, they're happy for—" I frowned. "The people who locked them up," I finished flatly.

I glanced around Hank to where Wiley stood with his arm around Maple. She held Cat like a baby. Just a happy little family. Cat clapped his monkey hands together and lights danced in his eyes.

"Ew. He's making them, isn't he?"

I pulled Iggy around to face me and nodded. "Yep." My nostrils flared in distaste.

Misaki and Jun leaned away from each other, a blush on their cheeks as the applause thundered through the cave.

My little flame shook his head at Cat. "I can't with that one."

Galloping hooves echoed from the tunnel that led to the main cave, and my friends and I spun toward the sound. My heart froze in my chest—were there more coming?

The duck-headed white horse trotted into view. It threw its head back and quacked.

I shook my head. "Get out of here!" The thing trotted closer and I widened my eyes at Maple. "We set it free earlier, and the dopey thing is back?" I scoffed.

Maple pressed her lips tight together and narrowed her eyes, as though she were about to give me bad news.

I lowered my brows. "What? What is it?"

She sucked in a breath over her teeth. "That, Imogen, is a unicorn."

My face fell. "No." I shook my head. "No way. Unicorns are pure, innocent, majestic creatures, and that—" The duck-horse thing ran into a wall, and its hind legs buckled. "I mean, look at it. Besides—uni, one, corn—that must mean horn, right?"

Hank cleared his throat and looked down at me. "Actually, it comes from the latin *cornu*, which can mean horn, but in this instance means *bill*, as in a duck's bill."

The corners of my mouth drooped. "No." I shook my head. I'd had too many shocks today; this couldn't be one of them. "But all birds have one bill, that doesn't even make sense."

Hank shrugged, and Maple mouthed, "Sorry."

I shook my head. Just when I'd thought the worst was over.

31

STEAMY

We knelt in the meeting room at the front of the guesthouse Misaki's grandma owned. The council sat at the long, low table before us. Ryuu Tanaka and a few members who'd been present at the monster fight were notably absent.

"And so, after we rejoined Captain Kenta and the others and had a—" Misaki paused. She stood before the council and a deep blush spread across her cheeks. I grinned—it looked cute on her. She cleared her throat. "A happy reunion, we spent another sleepless night in the cave, and left at first light to return here ahead of the storm."

A sheet of rain crashed against the windows behind us, and Maple and I jumped and looked back. We'd *just* made it, too. Hank and I had transformed into bears and carried the party up the last leg of the mountain as the winds thrashed the forest and rain showered down. I sniffed—no lightning though, that'd been all Kai.

Misaki continued. "And so we hope to return to the old mining caves as soon as the storm lets up with large contingent of the guard to arrest Ryuu Tanaka and Kai and all others involved in the monster fights." Her throat bobbed. "And to recover the bodies of Reo and Sora." She knelt back down and bowed her head. "That is all, thank you, council."

Jiji, Misaki's grandma, sat at the far left end of the table and petted her big white cat as it lounged beside her. She sniffed. "I say we just leave them there to rot."

The center councilwoman lifted her thin brows. "Jiji!"

Misaki's grandma shrugged and continued to scratch the cat's head. "Not the bodies, of course. Ryuu Tanaka and the other lowlifes."

The councilwoman in the center frowned and adjusted her silk dress sleeves. She took a deep breath and blew it out before lifting her head to address my friends and me, along with Misaki and the guards. "We owe you all a great thanks for helping to expose this shameful behavior and to bring justice to those responsible." She nodded to herself, then looked past the guards kneeling in front of us to my friends and me in the back. "It is the least we can do to accept you newcomers as full citizens of Kusuri."

I turned to my left and grinned at Hank, who knelt beside me. Jiji had fed us all a meal of hot, hearty ramen and tea as soon as we'd arrived. Hank's face now had more color to it.

He slid his hand into mine and squeezed it. "I guess we get to stay." He grinned.

The councilwoman continued. "And we shall certainly see that justice is done to those who committed these horrendous crimes. Are you sure they were locked up securely?"

Captain Kenta's eyes danced. "They've been injected with the antimagic potion, locked into cages, and are surrounded by a raging typhoon and a forest teeming with angry monsters." He grinned. "They're not going anywhere."

The councilwoman's mouth stretched into a thin smile and she dipped her chin to hide it. She looked up, once again composed. "Very good. Then as soon as the storm relents, we shall set out. In the meantime, I hope you will all get some well-deserved rest. Oh!" She lifted a finger. "And I must commend you on retrieving the kusuri herb our town is named for. You have saved many more lives with the potions we can make from it." The councilors bowed their heads and I leaned my forehead to the woven mat floor in response.

The special meeting broke up, and the guards and councilors hurried back to their homes before the storm got too bad to go out in. Jun squeezed Misaki's hand before dipping his tall frame through the curtained doorway and out onto the porch. Jiji saw her guests off with the white cat perched on her shoulder, and Misaki came over to me.

"My grandmother says you can all stay here."

"Oh." I looked from Hank to Maple.

Hank's brows pulled together. "We don't want to impose."

Maple shook her head.

"You're not. This place used to get lots of visitors before the monsters came, but now we just have a bunch of empty rooms upstairs. So you're welcome to them."

Maple bowed. "Thank you so much." When she straightened up, she turned to me. "I love bowing—it's fun."

I grinned. "Super fun."

Misaki nodded. "Plus, besides everything else, my grandma's overjoyed that Ryuu Tanaka and his cronies are off the council. She thinks maybe now we'll get some more forward-thinking members who are more accepting of change."

I lifted a brow. "Change like us coming to your town, change?"

"Exactly." Misaki grinned. "Come on—I'll show you to your rooms."

"I want to help." Her little sister Fumi skipped around the corner and led us to the wooden staircase in the main room. Upstairs, we peeled off to our own rooms, but Hank paused in the long, narrow hallway and squeezed my hand.

"Meet me in the bathhouse in five?"

I grinned. "Sure." As he turned away to go to his room though, my face fell. We'd made up, that was for sure, but we still needed to talk.

A FEW MINUTES LATER, I padded down the long wooden hall in fabric slippers and a thick, woven cotton robe. I'd tucked Iggy in for the night with a pile of his new favorite wood, cedar. The rain tapped away at the roof above as I navigated the staircase down to the main floor and entered the back rooms through a sliding paper door.

"At the end of the hall, to the left." I repeated Misaki's instructions for finding the bathroom. I half expected to run into my friends, but I didn't see anyone until I slid open another paper door and found Hank waiting for me.

I stepped into the steamy room and slid the door closed behind me. I lifted my nose and took a deep breath. The hot steam smelled like rosemary and something floral. I stepped out of my slippers and moved in bare feet across the chilly clay-tiled floor.

"It's cold."

Hank looked up at me and smiled, handsome stubble across his strong jaw. He sat in a beige robe identical to mine at the edge of a rectangular pool. His feet hung in the steamy water and red flower petals floated across the misty surface. I plunked down beside him, my legs aching, and slid my feet into the water. Pins and needles tingled my feet and calves, but as the heat melted into them, my muscles relaxed.

I closed my eyes and sighed. "This is heaven." I opened my eyes as Hank gently handed me an earthenware mug. "What is it?"

"Green tea."

I peered down at the light green liquid. While I appreciated the gesture, I wasn't sure I was in the mood for something so bitter.

"With milk and sugar."

I grinned at him. "You know me so well."

We smiled at each other a moment longer, until a thought flashed through my mind. Unless he thought he *didn't* know me. I'd kept so much from him. My smile faltered and I looked away toward the wall of greenery in front of us.

Hank had slid the paper wall open to the lush garden behind the guesthouse. A constant sheet of rain poured down, a calming and steady rush of water. The wind shook the bushes and tall, slender bamboo stalks outside, making being inside the warm bathhouse all that much cozier.

I sighed. "Hank, I—"

"You didn't trust me enough to tell me about Horace."

I looked up.

Hank stared down at the green mug cupped in his hands. "That's what hurt the most."

I licked my lips. "I'm sorry. I lied to you—for a while."

My throat tightened. "I hated it. I really did. And I wanted to tell you, it was eating me up."

"Why didn't you?" He looked up, into my eyes.

I shrugged and fought back tears. "I should've been honest. I wanted to be. I wanted it to feel like we were just Hank and Imogen, two ordinary people. But your duties, your dad, your betrothal to Shaday." I let out a sigh. "You being the prince." I shook my head, searching for the words. "I didn't want it to, but it created some distance between us."

His big hand slipped around my wrist. He ran his thumb over the back of my hand. "That's a big part of why I'm upset —with myself."

I found his eyes and frowned, confused.

"You may not know this about me, but I'm not the best at relying on people." His eyes lifted to mine, a smile playing at the corner of his mouth.

I grinned, though my eyes welled with tears. "You don't say?"

"My only friend I ever had was Colin—and he was paid by my parents and fifteen years older than me." Hank licked his lips. "I'm not used to having friends or people I can trust. But you see the real me, Imogen, not the prince." His throat bobbed. "I got so upset because I felt like you not telling me — it was you treating me like the *prince* version of myself." He shrugged. "But what did I expect? I say I want you to see Hank, not Prince Harry, I tell Maple not to curtsy to me, as though I'm a regular guy, and then I turn right around and say I have to go through with the wedding to Shaday and put my duties and public opinion before our relationship. I ask you to go to boring luncheons and have dinner with my detestable father, all precisely *because* I'm the prince." He shook his head. "I've been deeply unfair to you."

I nudged his shoulder with mine. "Maybe. But it was

worth it, to me. I didn't want you to have to choose between me and your crown and family."

A tear trickled down Hank's cheek and my heart ached. I reached up and wiped it, my fingertips brushing against the rough, dark stubble of his beard.

His throat bobbed. "I was also worried—" He shook his head, then started again. "I was worried that you weren't thinking for yourself, that Horace was just this con man, pulling one over on you, exploiting your kind heart." His nostrils flared. "There I was, thinking it mattered that I follow my father's laws, my father's wishes, even though so much about them, and him, struck me as wrong. I've been complacent with a man who did despicable things. And *he*, more than Horace, more than anyone, was the con man, and me his blind follower!" His nostrils flared. "I'm sorry, Imogen. I'm so sorry for everything, and the way I've reacted."

I found his hand and squeezed it. "You didn't know what he'd done—and as soon as you did, you made the right choice and stood up to him." I frowned when Hank hung his head. "I *hope* you think it was the right choice?"

He looked up, his gaze locked on mine, eyes intense. He squeezed my hand, hard. "You are always the right choice, and I will always choose you."

Tingles rushed up my spine. He slid his big hand behind my neck and leaned in to kiss me. I pulled back and lifted a finger. "Wait. I'm sorry, too."

Hank blinked, looking a little dazed.

I gulped. "And thank you for seeing that Horace is not just this evil guy through and through."

Hank nodded. "He's your brother. And I understand that, in his own bizarre way, he was working toward the greater good. He exposed the truth of these massive crimes, and for that I am grateful." He sighed. "I get that he's... he's more complicated than I gave him credit for." He lifted his brows. "It doesn't mean I like him, but I get it."

I nodded. "I know. And I appreciate that. I don't know if I can trust him either, honestly. He's..." I shrugged. "Enigmatic. But you—I can trust you, and I should've remembered that. You are the most honest, admirable man I've ever met, and I never want to keep anything from you ever again." I sniffed. "We're a team and I know you'll be there for me." I lifted a finger. "But if I mess up, and I will, you can't stop talking to me. That was awful."

Hank dipped his chin. "I'm sorry. I'm not used to having friends or people I can rely on, so when I felt like you betrayed me, I did what I always used to do and pulled back." He looked up. "And I think I was having trouble forgiving myself. For putting you through that almost-wedding to Shaday and making you feel like you had to run away." He scoffed. "To *here*, of all places. And we ended up here anyway."

I scooted closer to him. "It's not *so* bad." I grinned at the flower petal bathwater.

He slid an arm around my shoulders and hugged me tight to his side. "Are we okay?"

I nodded. "Yeah. If you are?"

He leaned his cheek against the top of my head. "Yes."

"I think we were just in a hard situation." The rain poured down outside and my eyelids drooped. The tension eased out of my blistered feet and aching calves. "But the next time we're in one, I'm going to talk to you. And tell you how I feel. And I'm not going to run away."

Hank hugged me tighter. "And I'll talk to you too. I'll tell you how I feel and I won't pull away—I'll stay right beside you. And if I know something's bothering you, I'll be there for you until you're ready to tell me about it." He passed his mug to his left hand and held his right one out. "Deal?"

I grinned and took his hand in mine. "Deal."

We shook. Then we stared out at the falling rain for a while, enjoying the sound and the cozy warmth of the bathhouse.

"I love you, Imogen."

I smiled, and tears welled in my eyes. It might have been the exhaustion or the relief, but at least some of it was gleeful happiness. "I love you too, Hank."

"I know this is a crazy situation. I wish I knew what was happening in the kingdoms. I'm worried about Amelia and your brother and the BA."

My heart sunk. "And Maple's family."

Hank nodded, his head still leaning against mine. "But somehow, as long as you're with me and *we're* okay, none of that seems quite so daunting."

I looked up at him. "I'm glad you're feeling more friendly toward Horace."

Hank made a face. "Friendly might be pushing it."

I held up a finger. "He healed you, remember?"

Hank squeezed his eyes shut tight. "True."

"Because once this storm lets up I intend to find him. He has portal mirrors—a way back."

Hank nodded, his eyes faraway. "That's a good point." He looked at me. "I'll help you."

I smiled.

"But in the meantime, maybe it won't be so bad here." He grinned. "Maybe this is our chance to be just two ordinary people. Hank and Imogen, without all the royal pressure."

I took a sip of my sweet and earthy green tea latte and let out a happy sigh. "You know, it's raining outside and we have no ladies' luncheons to attend or royal dinners to suffer through. It's just you and me and a lot of free time." I leaned back and Hank lifted his head to look at me. I gave him an exaggerated wink. "You thinking what I'm thinking?"

He blinked his bleary eyes, but gave me his best rakish look. "You want to go up to my room, curl up on the floor mattress, and—" He leaned close and breathed the next words against my ear. "Sleep. Hard."

I chuckled, then groaned. "Yes. A thousand times, yes."

Hank helped me to my feet, we stepped into our spa slippers, and then shuffled back upstairs, hand in hand. We collapsed onto the floor futon and snuggled together, still wearing our soft robes under the thick cotton sheets and warm wool blanket. The rain tapped away at the roof tiles.

I yawned and snuggled into Hank's chest. "You know." I closed my eyes, unable to keep them open any longer. "I think it's been about three days, a prison break, a quest, and a monster fight since we last got any real sleep." I sniffed. "Hank?"

A low, slow snore was the only the response.

<<<<>>>>

Did you enjoy Due East, Beasts & Campfire Feasts?

You can make a huge difference by letting others know what you thought.

Please leave a review on Amazon

It's the best way to help indie authors, like me, by helping other readers discover the book.

Sign up for the Erin Johnson Writes newsletter and stay up-to-date

at

www.ErinJohnsonWrites.com

As a thank you for signing up, you'll receive
Imogen's Spellbook
a free book of illustrated recipes featured in
The Spells & Caramels Series.

A NOTE FROM THE AUTHOR

I've always dreamed of being a published author, and to realize that dream, and have people like you actually read my book (now my 7th one!)—I can't tell you how much it means to me. So, truly, thank you.

If you enjoyed the story, and you'd like to help me as an author, please leave me a review on Amazon. It doesn't matter how long or short, a review is the very best way you can help me stay in business and keep writing. Plus, you'll help other readers discover Imogen and her adventures.

Thanks so much,
Erin

ABOUT THE AUTHOR

A native of Tempe, Arizona, Erin spends her time crafting mysterious, magical, romance-filled stories that'll hopefully make you laugh. This is her sixth book.

In between, she's traveling, napping with her dogs, eating with her friends and family, and teaching Pilates (to allow her to eat more).

Erin loves to hear from readers! You can contact her here:
erin@erinjohnsonwrites.com

facebook.com/EJohnsonWrites

twitter.com/EJohnsonWrites